Magnitude

Victor Jimenez

Zeppelin Publishing, LLC

To my high school chemistry teacher,

Mr. Robert Thanski,

Who long ago ignited my love of science.

Acknowledgements

There are many people I would like to thank for constant support and help. First, my dear wife whose encouragement and help has let me pursue my goal of writing. Secondly, my daughter, a fine artist whose work graces the cover of this book. Thirdly, the writing group I belong to, White Gold Wielders, an amazing set of writers instrumental in my development. And finally and certainly not least, Richard Dansky, who believed in me. Thank you, one and all.

Foreword

One of the great pleasures you get from being a cranky old writer is watching someone new to writing blossom and grow. Everybody's first steps are awkward, everyone's first stories are clunky and unrefined. With only a vanishingly few exceptions, nobody nails it right off the bat.

What a great joy it is, then, to work with someone who says they want to be a writer and who then works at it and grows visibly before your eyes. From story to story, project to project, draft to draft, I've watched Victor metamorphose from an enthusiastic fledgling into a writer of uncommon skill. For all that he protests that he's just an engineer (which is nonsense - he's one of the smartest and most talented polymaths I've ever met) and that he's just, in his words, a "serial assembler of words", he's steadily and resolutely honed his craft to the point where you, dear reader, get to experience it in all its glory.

To be fair, Magnitude is not Victor's first attempt at a novel. His early tries were earnest and had interesting ideas at their cores, but to no one's surprise they lacked the polish and craft that come with experience. I read them, I commented on them, I sent them back. And Victor read the comments, and tried again, and did better each time,

And then along came Magnitude. I read it pretty much in one sitting and when I was done, I said, "Yup, this works."

Was it perfect? Of course not. It needed work and polish and iteration, like any book. But for the first time, Victor had harnessed his talent in a way that made for an engaging read. I made my notes and passed them along, and so did many other people, and Victor worked his alchemy on those notes and the manuscript to come up with what you've got in your hands today.

What is it, you might ask? We'll, it's a fun, fast, exciting read. It's a technothriller with a sci-fi bent. It's got the ambition of big-scale science fiction novels with the action of a spy thriller, and it marries the two seamlessly. It starts with a big question but dives into small, human concerns and tackles both equally well. It shows of Victor's immense knowledge but in a way that's inviting rather than off-putting, a lure to learn more rather than a barrier to keep readers out.

So, dear reader, strap in. You're about to get in on the ground floor of something fantastic - a new writer announcing his voice, filled with wisdom and experience and knowledge and wicked sense of fun. You're going to get to say "I was there from the beginning", for this is most assuredly the beginning of what's going to be a fantastic literary journey. And you get to experience the thrill ride that is Magnitude, where the stars literally look down on you and the action doesn't stop, and you're going to have an absolutely fantastic time. So, to sum up: This is a heck of a book. Victor is a heck of a writer. And he's just getting started.

Enjoy!

-Richard Dansky, author of Firefly Rain

Contents

Prologue

N ight crept in after the longest day. Twinkling stars formed familiar patterns in the dome of the sky. Just after midnight, a new star appeared on the horizon below Pisces.

It was easily a magnitude 2 star, one warranting further investigation, to discern its properties and see if it would brighten even more. David's phone started to receive message after message in the twilight. It buzzed uselessly on the counter.

If he had looked at his phone, he would have heard of the continuing wonders over Greenwich. There, another star rose, burning in the darkness and looking very much like the first star. A theory of satellite flares being mistakenly observed was quickly dismissed when yet another new magnitude 2 star started glowing at the skyline.

The phone didn't stop vibrating for the next two hours as star after star began shining just above the horizon, hoisted into the sky by Earth's rotation and joining its brethren, forming a new asterism momentarily unnamed by humans.

Astronomers weren't the only ones who noticed the constellation. Everyone who looked up saw the 137 lights forming an asymmetric outline of a giant set of eyes, human eyes, staring down from the heavens. Night owls roused the sleeping populace and news cameras trained on stars informing the world. Billions stayed up to see the glowing pinpoints for themselves as night fell in their locale. A sort of quiet panic gripped the globe under the spectral eyes, now the focus of innumerable conversations. The populace demanded some sort of answer to allay their fears before the encroaching night.

Orders for all telescopes were sent out, email, text, phone calls, every possible way, to be trained on the new stars as they rose into sight for those locales. Every instrument of humankind was pointed at The Eyes and they were analyzed and determined to be identical in every respect human technology could devise. They were beyond the Oort cloud, but no further than 150 light years away where there was a known gas cloud that didn't occlude one of the new stars.

As night approached again, observatories geared up for a second night of observations. Sure enough, astronomers in Europe gathered around their instruments, to study the latest lights in the firmament. But something unexpected happened.

No sooner had the last new star risen above the horizon at Greenwich than all the lights of the newest constellation went out, simultaneously, emulating an impossible switch of cosmic proportions being thrown. Astonished, astronomers scrambled, looking for any trace of the stars, thankful that all their instruments were still looking at where the lights had been.

Well, almost all the instruments.

One

The Date

The right front wheel of the library cart wobbled forcing David to slow down. He wanted to escape as soon as possible. His last duty of the day was to get the carefully stacked tapes with his recordings from the radio telescope off to a group of fellow astronomers studying interstellar hydrogen. For all the good that would do. He relaxed when he reached his office and saw nobody was there.

At his desk, he affixed the identifying '648' sticker on each reel and numbered them. There were no mailing materials for him to pack them in. He had planned to get them over the weekend. A sharp exhale. Something else to do on his trip. Labelling complete, he furtively peeked out his door. He kept his head down as he guided the cart down the hall again, this time quicker. The wheel squeaked.

"David. David!" The dean's high heels rapidly staccatoed on the tile. David ground to a halt, exit in sight. "Did you finish installing the USB hardware? You said you would have it done last week." Her accusing words came out in rapid succession.

"Yes, ma'am. It's all working and I tested it." He patted his pants front pocket, the shape of the memory stick an indicator of success.

"Took you long enough. Don't know what good those are." She nodded her head at the tapes. "We need to talk. Soon." She walked away shaking her head. Not quite out of earshot, David heard, "Unbelievable."

David's shoulders slumped. He pushed the door open with the cart.

The dry heat of the mid-afternoon Arizona summer always felt like a blast furnace when he came out of the building's air conditioner. He shielded his eyes with one hand, pushing the laden cart toward his minivan.

Over the last few days, he spent a lot of time sitting in the equipment shack, staring blankly at the instruments. Occasionally, his hand hovered over the switches on the receiver, or the knobs of the oscilloscope, even the buttons on the now redundant tape drive. Not actually touching any of them. Normally, he enjoyed his duties at the radio telescope he ran at the university. It was his dream job, working there, having the opportunity to look at the stars in their eternal dance across the firmament while his equipment listened to the music of the atoms.

He pulled out his cellphone. Plenty of time before the post office closed. Shouldn't be a problem getting everything mailed. It pained him that such an advanced endeavor was stored on such primitive media. But next week, now that he finally figured out how to install the USB equipment, a thumb drive in an envelope should do the trick. Astronomy tended to produce too much data to send over the internet.

He wanted to believe his pet project of scanning the heavens for radio signals was worthwhile, but truthfully, David knew it was over when the ghostly image of a pair of human eyes appeared in the heavens a few nights ago. A shudder went through him at the recollection of the night. Everyone now knew that humanity was not alone in the Universe and was being watched. He concentrated on loading the reels into the cargo well of his minivan.

Never underestimate the bandwidth of a minivan hurtling down a highway, he thought, getting ready to leave work.

He stared at the dun-colored hills in the distance across the campus. His trip to the office supply store was really inexcusable. This wasn't some new task. He had been doing it every few days for almost a year. Why did he wait this time? Now it was another item in the litany of screwups. Sighing to himself, he understood the wrath of the dean since he was possibly the only astronomer on Earth who didn't point his telescope at the new stars. He climbed into the driver's seat and started off.

First things first. Buy packing materials, hit the Post Office, then finally, head home to the apartment for another lonely evening.

Wonderful.

Driving past the solar park, he stopped at the highway intersection traffic light. At the green arrow, he placed his foot on the gas pedal.

Movement out of the corner of his eye caused him to slam on the brakes. A white cement truck barreled through the space just in front of him, barely missing him.

A stream of expletives came out of David's mouth. He cursed the seeming indifference of people ever since... He trailed off, stopping just short of naming the nighttime incident. Checking on the waiting cars, he accelerated and turned onto the highway.

At the strip mall he parked in the shade of a palo verde tree, hoping to keep the minivan a little cooler in the late afternoon desert sun. It would be a long time before the relief of night came.

He hurried into the store, coming out with a package of flattened cardboard boxes and a roll of bubble wrap under his arms. David was grateful people weren't panic buying this stuff. The strangest of things were no longer readily available. Looking across the parking lot, he saw a woman and a man standing by his vehicle in the shade. Coming closer, he saw the man swing a baton at the woman. The woman grabbed the man's arm but he managed to swing the end of the baton around and tapped her. Down she went.

"Hey!" David shouted, dropping his purchases and racing toward them. The man jumped into an idling car and peeled out of the parking lot. David bent down and took her arm, helped her stand. "Are you OK?"

The woman reached out and put the other hand against his van. David let go of her arm. She said, "I'm fine. I'm OK. Who are you?"

"I'm David. That's is my van. What happened?"

The woman snatched her hand from the van, tried to straighten her disheveled flannel shirt. "Sorry. I was going to the coffee shop when a car pulled up and that guy came out. He ran over to your van and tried to break in."

David stared incredulously at her. "And you tried to stop him?"

"Well, I couldn't just let him do that." She shrugged and looked at him. Her long, black hair cascaded with her motion, offsetting her grey-green eyes.

"Lady, that's, that's dangerous! People have been acting super crazy ever since... well."

"I know." She offered a sheepish smile. "My name is Katerina, by the way." She wiped her hand on her blue jeans and extended it.

He shook her hand. It felt strong and warm in his grip. "Well, Katerina, I'm very happy to see you're OK."

David suddenly remembered why he was there. "My boxes!" Letting go of her hand, he ran back to where he had dropped his supplies. Katerina followed and helped him pick the fallen goods.

"Thanks a lot. You really didn't have to do that. You've done enough already," he said apologetically.

Katerina picked up the last piece of cardboard. "Hey, random acts of kindness are important. Especially now, with everything else going on."

"That's so true." He couldn't help but smile at her when she helped him load the van. She had tucked her shirt in, accentuating her curves.

"Well, David, good luck with your boxes."

David bit his lower lip. "Didn't you say you were going to the coffee shop? Can I buy you a coffee or something? To say thanks?"

Katerina looked at him and smiled back, her tan showing off her perfect pearly white teeth.

"I'd like that."

***

David brought their cups to a table by the window. "I really can't thank you enough. People have been so weird these last few days." He took a sip of his coffee.

Katerina blew on her black coffee before bringing it close to her generous lips. "It's been a little discouraging seeing how people are reacting."

"I know. I almost didn't make it here, in fact."

She arched an eyebrow. "Oh?"

"Yeah, a cement truck ran a light and almost creamed me." He motioned a swipe with his free hand. "Swoosh. Never even slowed down." He rested his free hand on the table in front of him.

"My goodness!" She touched his forearm. "You have to be careful! Things are different at the moment. I sure hope it's temporary. I remember when I first moved out here. People went out of their way to help each other." Katerina took an experimental sip of the hot coffee. It must have been fine as she took a larger swallow.

"I know what you mean. I moved out here for my job a few years ago and I can see differences too." David tried not to stare.

"What do you do?" The sunlight sparkled in her eyes.

"I work at the university, on the radio telescope."

"Wow! That's fascinating! I came out here to work on my pottery. But I have a secret." She leaned in conspiratorially. "I moved out here to better see the night sky." And she laughed, a sweet, musical laugh. He joined her.

"That's awesome! Did you get to go out much and stargaze?"

"I do! I really enjoy it. I go out on my porch and sit in my rocker looking up." A shadow passed across her face and she carefully looked down at her cup and lowered her voice. "That is, I use to enjoy it. Until four nights ago. I thought the stars were, I don't know, permanent. I felt so small, exposed. I wanted to hide."

David knew exactly what she meant. He reached out and put his hand on hers.

"Hey, it's alright. Things are going to work out. Nobody is knocking on our door."

"I hope so, David. It's a different, new world all of a sudden." She didn't move her hand out of his.

David gave her hand a squeeze and offered a smile. Katerina gazed back, right into his eyes.

He cleared his throat and asked, "You wouldn't like to go to dinner with me sometime, would you?"

Katerina's face lit up, rewarding David with her perfect smile. "That'd be wonderful!"

***

David got to his apartment on the cusp of evening. He dropped off the tapes and shipping materials just inside his front door after he fumbled with the lock. Katerina was easy to talk to and shared many of his interests so he found himself opening up to her. The rest of the afternoon slipped by.

First thing in the morning, he would pack the tapes and run to the post office. But now he hurried to keep the dinner plans with Katerina. Thoughts of a date later in the week went out the window when she cheerfully suggested that she was free tonight.

Sullivan's, the local steakhouse, was fancy-casual. So, nice, but not formal. He was relieved when Katerina was enthusiastic about the place. It was modestly priced, something he could afford on his salary.

After showering the salt and dirt off, he stared at his closet. Regretfully, it was rather empty, the pile of laundry a testament to the recent celestial appearance. Something else he meant to do over the weekend. He realized that he had been wearing the nicest clean set of pants he had. Mostly clean. A brief shrug convinced him that it didn't matter and he pulled the khaki pants on again. He picked out a nice white button-down shirt to go with his black sports coat but no tie.

Dressed in record time, he went out his door and turned to lock it. His neighbor Pete, dressed in work clothes and florescent vest was just getting home as David finished twisting his key.

"Whoa, looking good, Dave. Going somewhere special?"

David grinned as he locked the door. "Got a date tonight. We're meeting at Sullivan's."

"Fancy! I guess things are finally serious. Say hi to Ellen for me." Pete unlocked his door.

David hemmed at the remark. "Naw, Pete. Why would it be Ellen? It's someone I just met."

Pete, halfway in his door, stopped and turned to gaze at him with a puzzled look. He put his hardhat inside and ran his hand through his salt and pepper locks. "Really? That's... different. You're usually kinda slow to warm up to people."

David felt his face grow hot before he stammered out, "Well, we hit it off really well."

"Huh. I guess everyone is entitled to act a little weird now. You still coming to game night tomorrow? Ellen made it a point of telling everyone that it's still on, regardless. I think she picked up a new board game and really wanted to play it, especially with you."

"I'll think about it. Hey, I gotta go. I don't want to be late." He pointed at a nonexistent watch on his wrist.

"See you later. Hope it goes well." Pete waved goodbye.

Dave went down the stairs to his minivan and left. Sullivan's was a fair distance away through rush hour traffic.

***

Despite the heavy traffic, he arrived a bit early to a crowded parking lot.

He scratched his head before remembering the news stories of the widespread run on the food stores and problems with supplies. Maybe people were eating out in response?

He wondered how late these people would be out. The radio talk show he was listening had been full of callers expressing fear of the dark sky and wondering if the aliens were about to land. David didn't blame them. He hadn't felt like looking at the stars either and it was his job. He gave a slight shrug and went in.

Going up to the host, he asked for a table for two and was promptly informed of a wait. It was suggested to him that the bar was open.

Not quite believing that he had an actual date with someone out of his league, he decided it was a good idea to acquire a little liquid courage to ease the tension he felt. Not too much, however. Maybe later, after she didn't show.

He picked a stool where he could still see the entrance and kept an eye out for Katerina and ordered a rum and coke. Sipping it while he waited, the nervousness started to mount. Thankfully, it wasn't a long wait. When he spotted her, he waved to her from his seat. Katerina's face lit in recognition and she crossed over to him.

Giving him a quick embrace, she asked, "What are you drinking?"

"Rum and coke. Can I get you something?"

She pulled out the tall chair next to him. "Sure! How about a mojito? It's one of my favorites?"

She was wearing a short, light blue dress with little white flowers that was tight around the right places. The sight of her tanned legs and cowboy boots made his heart skip a beat. "You look great. How are you feeling? Rescue anymore cars?"

Katerina giggled. "Thanks, you look nice, too. Nope, just rescued one today. I'm feeling fine and getting better. Did you mail your tapes?" A smile that lit up the room graced her face.

David thought himself lucky.

"Eh, no, I just dumped them at home, got ready and came here." He gestured around the room with some embarrassment. "I'm sorry that this place is so crowded. We'll have to wait for a table."

Katerina looked around the room. "It's not usually like this? I don't normally come here."

"Not on a Wednesday." The bartender pushed a tall glass over to them. "Oh, here's your drink. Cheers!" said David, passing her the libation.

"Cheers!" She clinked glasses with him and drank half in one long swallow. He stared at Katerina. A look of dismay came over her. "I was thirsty! I swear I don't normally drink like that." She paused and looked down, hiding her eyes. "OK, I'm a bit nervous."

"Ha, it's alright. I'm nervous, too. Everyone has been acting a little different." He took a deep breath, and drank half his glass in a show of support.

"So, how have you been holding up? I mean, ever since, you know..." Katerina lowered her voice.

"Since the Eyes appeared? That's what everyone is calling them, right? 'The Eyes'?" He performed air quotes.

"Yeah, the Eyes."

"Well, this is going to sound weird, but part of me felt vindicated. When I was small, I would stay up late, looking at the stars out my window. They looked like tiny diamonds on velvet to me. I always thought they were the most important thing."

"Oh really?"

David took another sip of his drink. "Yeah. In high school, I found out you can listen to them on a radio. So I became a radio astronomer because I thought it would be cool. The music of the stars." He gave a little shrug. "I had an experiment going at the time the Eyes showed up. I was surveying the sky at 1420 MHz. It's called scanning the hydrogen line. It's a radio band where nature is just quiet. People have suggested that if there were aliens, they might try to communicate there, since any signal there wouldn't be natural. It's my little private research. Looking for aliens. Oh boy."

"So you pointed your equipment at the Eyes?"

A cough shook him and he took another sip. "No, I didn't. I was too ..." David paused, searching for a word. "Distracted. I got caught up in the excitement and, well, fear. Mostly fear. I felt bad the next day." Now it was his turn to look down at the floor.

She held her hand over her mouth. "Oh no!"

David gave a small shrug. "It's no big deal. I have rinky dink equipment, compared to the big boys. I'm sure all the major observatories were pointed at them. Probably all the minor ones too. I really wouldn't have been able to add much to the data anyway."

Katerina tilted her head. She looked so beautiful. "What were you looking at? Is that the right term, for a radio telescope?"

"Yeah, it's all light. I was pointed at a patch of sky around Arcturus."

"Arcturus?"

"I'll show you when we leave. It's really bright. Fourth brightest star actually."

"Wow! I didn't know the name."

"There are all sorts of old names for the visible stars. Some say that the oldest stories we have are about the stars."

A slight smile played across her lips. "I find that romantic, that those old stories are still around."

David smiled back at her.

"Table for David, party of two," announced the host.

Standing up and offering his arm, David asked, "Shall we?"

Katerina stood and slipped her hand around his arm. "Let's."

***

David thought dinner was successful. Katerina laughed at his attempts at humor and they shared a few meaningful gazes into each other's eyes. The food was good despite the substitutions. They talked a long time about all sorts of things, much to the dismay of the staff. When they left, he pointed out Arcturus, halfway to setting on the horizon. He walked her to her vehicle. He wondered how to end the evening but she resolved it for him. She kissed him goodnight there in the parking lot under the stars. And it wasn't just a peck on the cheek either. He talked with her through the window of her pickup truck. They made plans to see each other over the weekend. After exchanging numbers, she made him promise that he would call her when he got home.

The lot was now deserted compared to earlier. The restaurant had steadily emptied as the time grew later. People just didn't want to face the night sky yet and he understood it. There was hardly any traffic compared to earlier. He felt buoyed by the start of a new romance and it removed some of the ill effects of the last few days. Those events had started him down a depressing path, like so many other people, and he retreated from the world. But now he found himself signing along with the radio, an old Sinatra standard about going to the Moon. Off key, of course, which made his smile grow.

Pulling into his apartment complex, he noticed a large number of police cars and firetrucks. Red and blue flashing lights fractured the night into colored shards. Alarmingly, they all seemed to be clustered around his unit.

His customary parking lot was blocked by the emergency vehicles so he circled around and found an empty spot some distance away. Walking between the parked cars toward his apartment, he saw his way was blocked. There were firefighters and police cordoned off from a crowd of onlookers by yellow tape. The firefighters were stowing equipment and the police seemed to be talking to his neighbors. Confused, he looked around, trying to find an explanation.

He saw his friend, Pete, from across the hall, talking to a policeman on the other side of the tape. "Pete!" he called out. After some hand waving and pointing by Pete, the officer came over and lifted the tape for David to pass before returning to his notebook. David crossed over to his friend quickly, who was leaning against a bicycle rack, rubbing his graying temples.

"Dave. Wow, what an evening. I was about to call you." Pete sounded tired. He was still dressed in his work clothes, sans vest and hardhat.

David looked around, trying to absorb what he was seeing. "I don't understand."

"I was calling my Mom before changing and making dinner. You know, I hadn't talked to her since before the Eyes. The nursing home switchboard has been swamped. I finally got through and was on hold when I heard a loud crash. I looked out my window and saw your door swinging open. I knew something was up. I called 911 right away."

Concern filled his voice. "Are you OK? What happened?"

"I'm fine, buddy. Nothing happened to me. But something happened to your place ." Pete looked toward David's apartment. David followed his gaze.

A fire inspector was descending the staircase. Both of them watched while he walked over to a police officer. A quick discussion ensured and the policeman pointed at them. The inspector nodded and came over to Pete. "Sir, your quick action probably saved this whole building."

"Did you come from my apartment? What happened?" David pointed back to the stairs.

"You're the tenant? Yes? I'm afraid your apartment was destroyed, sir. Overall, I'd say you got real lucky you weren't there. The fire spread quickly. It looked like it started right by the entrance. Judging by the damage, the intensity of the flames by the door meant you wouldn't have been able to get out that way. We're investigating the scene at the moment. You should make arrangements for tonight. You won't be allowed back in for a while."

A couple of firemen were walking past them carrying hoses. A young looking man said, "That was a nasty firebomb."

The inspector turned to glare at the talking man. The firefighter noticed and ducked his head. He hurried away.

David stared in disbelief and pointed at the fleeing man. "What did he say?"

The inspector held up his hands. "I have no further information at the moment. We will be in touch with you." The policeman approached the fire inspector. The two walked away and spoke in hushed tones.

David felt lightheaded. He leaned against the bicycle rack.

Pete reached out and steadied him. "Hey, you OK?"

"I'm fine, I'm fine." David had trouble focusing his eyes.

Pete snapped his fingers in front of David's face and studied his friend. "Dude, you're not looking so good. I'd let you crash on my couch but I don't think they're going to let me up there either." Pete thought for a moment. "Hey, let's ask Ellen if we can crash at her pad."

"Ellen? Why would she say yes?"

"You kidding me?" Pete studied David. "Fucking clueless," he said under his breath.

***

A solitary knock was all it took for Ellen to open the door. She greeted them dressed in shorts and tee-shirt with a faded white circle with a cutout of a man wearing a hat on it. A TV showed a rendered corridor with a hand holding a gun. One look at the pair and she invited them in.

From behind him, Pete pushed David in. "Thanks for letting us come over. I know it's really late. We appreciate it." Pete spoke over his friend's shoulder.

"I was so worried! I kept seeing all these firetrucks and police heading toward the back, by your unit." She closed the door to shut out the rumble of trucks going by. She pushed back the short, tight blonde curls hanging down over her eyes.

Pete maneuvered David into the living room, away from the door. "Yeah, Dave's apartment was gutted. I haven't been allowed back in mine."

"Wow! Has management contacted you guys?"

Pete shook his head. "Not yet. I figured that's something to do in the morning."

Seeing David blank expression, Ellen turned to Pete. "Is he okay?"

"I think he's a little shell shocked. His apartment was firebombed while he was out."

Ellen's mouth dropped open. "What?!"

"Somebody kicked open the door and threw a device in to start a fire."

She looked at David with big, soft brown eyes and rested her hand on his shoulder, "David? You're going to be fine, honey."

David blinked and looked around the apartment before settling his eyes on Ellen. "Hi Ellen. The fireman said it was deliberate."

"I heard." Ellen squeezed his shoulder.

"I think I'd like to sit down."

"Of course." She guided David to the kitchen table. There were papers and books covering the surface. Pulling out a chair, she gently got him to sit down in it. Pete followed and sat at the table opposite David. "Can I get you something? A beer?"

Pete raised his hand. "I'd like one too. You got anything to eat?"

Ellen returned with three cans of beer and a sleeve of crackers and passed them out before sitting at the head of the table.

Pete opened the saltines. He pointed at the cover of the nearest book. "Codebreaking and Cryptograms by Nola Kaye? A little light reading?" His hand wandered over to it.

Ellen snatched it out of his reach before putting it down next to David. "Security. It's part of my job, Pete. Drink your beer."

Pete popped the top of his beer and lifted it in salute toward Ellen. "Thanks." He took a long drink from it and munched one of the crackers.

David's unopened beer sat in front of him.

Ellen reached out and held David's outstretched hand. "Hey, it's alright. You can stay here however long it takes. It's not a problem."

David replied automatically. "That's really nice of you."

Ellen blushed. "Don't mention it. I'm very glad you weren't there. That could have been bad. Where were you?"

Pete interrupted, "Oh, this is going to be good!" and settled back in his chair, taking another long sip. Ellen's eyes shot daggers at him.

"I went on a date." David stared at his beer, unsure about what to do with it.

"A date? With who?"

"Katerina. She's very nice. And pretty."

Ellen removed her hand from his. "Really?"

"I just met her today. At the office supply store parking lot. I went to get stuff to mail my tapes." David decided to reach for the beer, after all.

"My, haven't you had an exciting day." Ellen's lips were pressed together in a straight line.

David inspected the can, as though puzzled by the pop top. "It has been eventful. I just want things to calm down. Too much has happened in these last few days. All this excitement is bad for me."

"Well, did you like the 'excitement' earlier in the evening?"

He twisted his head to look directly at Ellen, his eyes focusing on her. "Hey, we just talked a lot. We seemed to get along well."

"Let me guess, she laughed at all your jokes. Did you show her some stars after she said she was interested in them? Did you exchange numbers? How did you even meet? I bet you rescued her or something."

David's ears burned. "Well, sort of. Someone was trying to break into my car and she stopped him. The other guy took a swing at her."

"And you fell for it?" Ellen folded her arms. "What's so funny Pete?"

"Nothing, nothing at all." Pete took another sip, hiding his mouth behind the can.

Ellen peppered David with questions. "You didn't stop to think it was a scam? Wasn't it awfully convenient, to be there to stop a break in? Didn't you stop to think she might be after something?"

David was taken aback. "Well, the joke's on her. I literally have nothing anymore." He managed to sound angry and hurt at the same time.

Ellen's face softened and she rubbed her hand across her forehead before brushing back her blond curls. She took his hand again. "Oh, David, I'm sorry."

David looked at Ellen and squeezed her hand, "It's OK, I'm sorry too. I'm a bit of an idiot sometimes."

"Aww, the two lovebirds are making up. It's the start of something beautiful."

Ellen and David both blushed and said at the same time, "Shut up, Pete!"

Just then, David's phone rang. David's face fell.

"Aw crap, I said I'd call her when I got home."

Ellen let out a breath and took her hand back. She shook her head negatively ever so slightly while looking at David.

David held the phone to his ear and automatically answered, "Hello? Who is this?"

"Hey silly!" Katerina's happy voice filled his ear. "Who else would it be? Did you forget to call me when you got home?"

"I'm so sorry. Something came up when I got home." David's voice was strained.

There was a slight pause. "What? What happened? You don't sound right."

"Somebody firebombed my apartment." Equal parts of unbelief and stress colored his voice.

"Oh no! Are you okay?"

"Yeah, I'm fine. I lost everything though, at least that's what the firemen said. Well, almost everything." He put his hand on his pant's pocket, feeling the memory stick there.

The voice over the phone had a bit of tremolo. "I'm about to cry for you."

"You're so sweet. I can't believe how nice you are. I guess the next few days are going to be busy for me. We'll have to postpone our next date." A pang of regret came over him. Of course it was too good to last. He breathed a heavy sigh, the weight of everything that had happened to him today pressing down on his mind. "I'll have to talk to the apartment managers, see what's left of my stuff, go by the post office..."

"Go by the post office? Are you still worried about the tapes? Didn't they just get destroyed?"

"Well, I guess the tapes were destroyed. But I still have all the data on a flash drive with me." He absently patted his pants pocket.

Silence was the response, silence that stretched out so long that David finally said, "Hello?"

The voice was steel. "David, I want you to get into your car right away and drive to the address I'm texting you. You're in danger."

Two

Hot Pursuit

D avid looked at the phone at arm's length before bringing it back to his ear. "What?"

Katerina's voice was calm and clear over the phone. "Someone didn't want what you had getting out. They tried to break into your car to take it and barring that, they firebombed your apartment to destroy it. In fact, they probably were the ones who tried to run you over with the cement truck."

"Are you kidding me? What do I have? Or rather, had?" David voice was tinged with suspicion.

"The tapes, David. They wanted the tapes. They were willing to kill you for them. And, apparently, they don't care about anyone else, either."

"What is your new friend saying to you?" Ellen was loud enough to ensure she was heard.

"Right now, they think they got to the only copy. What do you think is going to happen when they figure out you have another copy?" said Katerina.

David was very confused. "Copy? Of what? I wasn't pointed at the Eyes. Not even close. What could I possibly have?"

Ellen held her hand out. "What is going on? Let me talk to her." Dave waved her off.

Katerina was all business, emotionless on the phone. "I don't know what you have. But how long is it going to take for them to come looking for the USB stick? Especially since you just told them you have it?"

"I didn't...I'll just hand it to them."

"I don't think that's going to work. They don't seem interested in the soft option. Please, I've been on the line too long. Hurry and come to the address." The call dropped.

David just stared at the phone.

"What did she say that's got you so spooked? I wouldn't blindly believe her. I don't think she's who she said she is." Ellen eyebrows were drawn together in a scowl.

"I don't know what to believe at the moment."

David's phone buzzed at the incoming text.

Pete put his beer down and studied him. "Buddy, what's going on?"

"I'm not sure what's going on. Katerina seems to think that I have something very valuable."

"Valuable? Like worth a lot of money?" Pete eyes narrowed.

David shook his head.

"Show's what she knows. You have nothing left," said Ellen.

"She said that they would kill me for it. Tried to kill me. I'm supposed to hurry."

Ellen's hand came down on the table, shaking the cans. "That sounds like bullshit. What exactly do you have?"

David dug in his pocket and pulled out the thumb drive. "This," he said, holding it up.

"What's on it?" Ellen was momentarily puzzled.

"The data I collected while the Eyes were up."

"Oh shit!" Ellen lifted her hand to her mouth and abruptly dropped it. "Wait a minute, didn't you tell us you weren't even pointed at them?"

David shook his head. "I wasn't."

"What could..."

"What are you going to do now?" interrupted Pete. "Do you believe her?"

David looked at a point on the ceiling. "I'm starting to. All sorts of weird things happened to me today."

Ellen crossed her arms and stared at him. "Including rescuing a random, good-looking woman who wanted to have dinner with you?"

David blushed. He forced himself to look at her. "Yeah, even that." He thought for a moment. "I'm going to meet her. Maybe I should make a copy of the data?"

Ellen stood at the end of the table and leaned toward him. "If what you have is so dangerous, why on Earth would you want another copy? You should just get rid of it, fast. Or do you want people to hunt you down? Besides, how do you know she's won't kill you when you show up, like the people she's warning you about? Don't blame us when your body ends up in a ditch somewhere."

"Ellen has a point. We're going with you, Dave."

"What? No way. I'm not interested in going to see his new girlfriend. It's probably a trick to get him to come down for a *visit*. I'm not his chaperone," said Ellen.

"You just said he might end up in a ditch. Where did she say to meet her?"

David looked at the text message. He could feel the temperature rising in his cheeks. "It's at a motel on the East end of town."

"Ha!" Ellen smirked at him.

David sighed. "Look, you guys don't have to come."

"Man, listen to me. People's apartments don't get broken into and firebombed for no reason. And you just said all sorts of weird things happened to you today. I'm going with you and that's final."

David stared at his friend. He wrestled with gratitude and embarrassment. "Fine. And thanks Pete. What about you, Ellen?"

"Oh, alright!" Ellen threw up her hands, clearly exasperated. "I've changed my mind. I'm going with you, to make sure you behave."

***

It was just before midnight when they left. A third-quarter moon had risen in the east and gave the asphalt a dim glow. David was surprised at the number of cars out now, considering people's previous reluctance to be in the open. He soon saw why. Cars drifted between the lanes ahead of him. He slowed down because he wasn't sure of their intentions. Soon, several cars accumulated behind him, also showing erratic behavior judging from the way their headlights moved in the rear view.

David gripped the steering wheel tight. His knuckles paled from the effort. "Why aren't the police doing anything about this?"

Pete observed the weaving cars through the passenger windshield. "At least it's calming down. It was really bad last night."

"What were you doing out?" Ellen sat in the middle bench.

"Same thing all these other idiots are doing. Trying to get home."

Ellen smacked Pete's near shoulder. "What were you thinking? What if you got hit or hurt? You should have stayed put."

Pete shrugged. "I had to come home at some point. The police haven't been out these last few nights. They probably figure they have something better to do." He glanced out the window again. "Besides, we're out and about right now."

David concentrated on the road in front of him. "Well, we all better get back to normal and quick. Else, there's not going to be anything left for the aliens to visit."

"Fat chance of it settling down." Ellen leaned forward against her seatbelt, in the gap between the two front seats.

"I'm sure things will calm down and return to normal soon. They have to," David said without pulling his attention from the road.

Ellen arched her eyebrow. "Why? Because people have some sense and behave rationally?"

"Yes. Most people do."

"What planet have you been on? And, may I point out, we're going in the middle of the night to see someone who claims she's protecting you from unknown assassins." Sarcasm dripped from Ellen's voice and formed puddles.

"Well, strange things have been happening all around."

"We could go to the police," Pete said quietly.

David considered that before looking around. "The police aren't bothering to enforce basic traffic stuff. It took a firebomb to get them to come out to my place. I don't think they're going to take my word on it that someone is out to kill me. Over a USB stick, of all things. Now, can you guys please be quiet? I'm trying to drive."

Silence descended over the interior of the minivan. Ellen sat back and fidgeted in the middle bench. Pete looked out the passenger window. David's thoughts raced.

A few minutes went by. Ellen finally broke the quiet. "This is crazy. I'm sure she just wanted you to come by yourself."

David's exasperation caused him to speak through clenched teeth. "Well, she's going to have to live with disappointment when we all show up."

"Do you know what you're going to say to her? I'm just curious." Ellen just wouldn't stop.

"Dammit, I'm trying to drive!"

Ellen tone changed right away. "Hey, sorry, I just think you should be prepared for her to be upset with you."

Struggling to regain control of himself, he said, "Please, I'm upset already. Too many things are happening."

"Fine. Pete, can you turn on the radio? Maybe some music will help?"

David knew that Ellen was trying to calm him. All he could think of was regretting having them come along. Breathing slow deliberate breaths calmed him. "Go ahead, Pete."

Pete looked at David and sighed. He punched the button to turn the radio on. It was tuned to an oldies station. The words, "What's the frequency, Kenneth" came out of the speakers.

***

They arrived at the motel and parked at the far end of the lot. Another car pulled in while they walked to the open breezeway.

Pete stepped up on the sidewalk along the doors ahead of David and Ellen. He jerked his thumb over his shoulder toward the rooms. "What room is she in?"

David examined the room numbers and started walking to the right. "I think it's down this way."

"She better be worth it." Ellen mumbled under her breath.

David felt it would be best to ignore the remark. He reached the door number in the text message and knocked. Long seconds passed.

"She doesn't seem all that eager." Ellen looked at him with her arms crossed.

Grimacing, David knocked again. He heard Katerina's muffled voice. "Who is it?"

"It's me, David."

A dull thump and the sound of something being dragged was heard through the door. A few seconds passed. "Come in!"

Puzzled, the trio looked at each other.

David shrugged and turned the knob. Just beyond where the door swung, a bed and an armchair blocked the way. Katerina was in the back of the room, past the other bed. Only the right half of her body was exposed, the rest in the bathroom. She was wearing fatigues and had a towel over her exposed hand. A fairly large grey plastic case was closed at her feet.

The first words out of her were, "You brought company?"

"They're my friends. They were worried. Guys, this is Katerina."

She shook her head and let out a sigh. "Well, now they're involved."

"Who the hell do you think you are, lady?" Ellen was furious. "Where do you get off frightening him and telling him that his life is in danger?"

Katerina moved out of the bathroom and with her other hand, waved them in. "Please, come in and close the door."

"What's with the fatigues?" Ellen asked. "Shouldn't you be wearing something more *comfortable*?"

David flinched.

Ellen was right behind him, trying to peek over his shoulder to get a better look at her. Katerina stayed by the bathroom.

"Ellen, please don't yell," said Pete. He had his hands up, trying to calm Ellen down. "Let's listen to what she has to say."

"Close the door. Now, please!" Katerina sounded a little more urgent.

"Pete, close the door," said David.

"Is this your girlfriend, David?" asked Katerina.

"What? No!"

Ellen turned red and fell silent, her eyes downcast. David turned to her. "I'm sorry, Ellen, but we aren't exactly an item."

In a quiet, almost cracking voice, Ellen said "Is she your new girlfriend?"

"For crying out loud, I just met her! I'm here because she was right. Something weird is going on."

"Now that we have that sorted out, can someone please close the door!" Katerina didn't quite yell but her tone was unmistakable.

"Right, sorry." Pete turned and finally closed the door.

Katerina again motioned to them indicating to go around the chair. The trio squeezed past the obstacle and got to the space between the beds when Katerina held her visible hand up from the end of the room to stop them. "First, I have to say that now all of you are in danger. Only David should have come."

Pete answered in calm tones. "Well, I'm sorry, but to Ellen's point, who are you? Why should we trust you either? You just said Dave's in danger. What if you're the danger?"

Katerina sighed and started, "I'm just trying..."

A loud crash interrupted her. The door flung open and slammed against the wall. Two men stood in the doorway with their guns drawn.

"Get down!" yelled Katerina.

David dove for the floor in front of the chair. He could see Pete hit the ground next to him. Ellen was out of his view. He prayed that she'd found cover. Behind the chair, two guns loudly barked. He looked up in time to see the towel slide off Katerina's hand revealing a gun with a thick barrel. She fired two quiet, quick shots as she ducked behind the bathroom doorway. Two dull thuds were heard in the ensuing silence and an acrid, metallic smell filled the room.

"Is everyone okay?" Katerina's strained voice came from inside the bathroom.

A round of acknowledgement from the trio as they sounded off was the response.

Katerina peeked around the doorway and bounded past them, to the now still bodies of the two intruders. She kicked away their guns. Turning to the group, she said, "Why should you trust me? Because I'm the one saving your lives, that's why!"

David got up and helped Pete get up.

"She's got a point," Pete said.

Ellen was still on the ground, hands over her ears, between the beds. David went over to her and offered a hand up. "No thanks. I think I'm going to wait here until the police come."

Katerina, who was walking back, paused, looked at her and shrugged. "Suit yourself. Personally, I don't think that's safe," and continued to the case in the back. "David? Could you give me a hand with this? Pete? Is that your name? Could you please move the chair to one side?"

"What about the dead bodies here?" Pete looked down at the invaders.

"Try not to step in the blood. You don't want to leave evidence. Their buddies will probably come looking for them soon. Or are you staying with the girl?"

"You really think they're coming? Before the police?" David tried not to stare at the corpses. His stomach roiled.

Katerina shrugged. "I don't know. But they probably don't want to leave any loose ends. And they know who you are."

David stood by Ellen, looking down at her. "Ellen, I really think you should reconsider."

"No, it's fine. Leave her. That way, I win." Katerina was bent over her case. She pulled a box with a cable attached to it and a black bag out. They each went into different jacket pockets. She then closed and latched the box.

"Fuck you, I'm going with you." Ellen got up. "What do we do about the bodies?"

"Nothing. Don't touch them, be cautious stepping around them, don't leave a footprint." Katerina sounded like a well-worn record.

Carefully, Pete moved the chair aside and David and Katerina carried the case out, trying not to step in the pooling blood. Pete and Ellen followed them out.

"Where are we going with this?" David puffed while he helped carry the surprisingly heavy case the long distance to the car.

"I hope you came in the minivan. It's the only thing with room for all of us." Katerina seemed to take the weight of the case in stride.

"Right." David led the way to the vehicle. Opening the liftgate, the two put the case in the back.

"Keep the gate open," Katerina said.

Katerina fished out the box in her pocket. She started walking around the car, pointing the end of the cable at the car. She stopped by the front passenger wheel well and bent down, her hand patting the inside of the fender. A moment later, she withdrew her hand. A small, black cylinder was in her palm.

"Is that what I think it is?" said Pete.

"Probably," she said.

"Here, give it to me."

Pete took it and went to another car and put the capsule on it.

Katerina continued her walk around the car. Satisfied, she tossed the device into the well, next to her case.

Pete and Ellen were already by the side doors.

David closed the gate. "Good thing they missed you. When they shot at us."

"They didn't miss. I was just better prepared," responded Katerina matter-of-factly. Her hand a fist, she beat against her chest. A strange hollow sound followed.

David tilted his head. Katerina then put her hand inside the fatigue jacket and poked two fingers out of some holes.

"Holy shit! Are you OK?"

"I'm much better than those two. I just have a couple of bruises. We need to get moving. Everyone, get in and turn off your phones. Put them in the bag." She handed Pete the black bag and turned to David.

Ellen frowned at the command. "That's not how it works. Just turning it off is enough. The phone would have to be compromised. Either put a chip in it or install something."

Katerina looked at David.

"Ellen, please, we need to get going."

"Fuck it. Fine, here." She turned the phone off and put it in the bag. Pete followed suit.

"Thanks." David briefly smiled at her before doing the same.

Katerina took the bag.

"I'm driving." She held out her hand.

David paused. A flood of doubt assailed him, about the data, about Katerina, about his involvement. He didn't know what to do.

Katerina saw him hesitate. "Don't you want to find out what's so important about your data?"

Deflating, he handed her the keys.

***

The stars wheeled overhead, not caring about those below. David sat silent in the passenger seat and stared straight out the windshield. The twinkling points reminded him of nights long ago and he wondered what he had gotten himself into. Katerina headed south and west, on empty back roads, across empty desert. The thought crossed his mind that if she wanted to get rid of them, it would be a while before anyone found their bodies. They stayed on the lonely back roads for what seemed like hours. A single, solitary car passed them going the other way. David wondered where all the traffic was.

"Something is wrong with your van."

The words startled David. The van had been silent since leaving the motel. The incident in the room seemed so long ago and, in the quiet, he had started to drift off.

"What do you mean?"

"The engine, there's something wrong with it," Katerina said. "I keep pressing the accelerator and it's not going faster. I think it's losing power."

"It's due for an oil change but it was fine."

"Well, it's not fine now. I don't suppose one of your friends is a mechanic?"

Dave shook his head in the dark before responding "No." He looked back at the two in the bench behind him. Pete and Ellen leaned against each other and were fast asleep.

Now that he was feeling more awake, a gnawing suspicion chased the thoughts in his head. He finally gave it a voice.

"What were you going to do? Were you also after the tapes?" David carefully watched Katerina in the green light of the dashboard.

A frown settled on her face. She finally answered "Yes."

"How? I would have mailed them in the morning, before going to work." He gazed intently at her. He couldn't be sure, but he thought Katerina's face grew red in the glow.

"I was going to invite myself over when you called. Before everything else that happened." Katerina stole a glance at him.

"Really? That was your plan?"

"Would you have said no?"

Now it was David's turn to blush. "I guess not," was all he could muster.

"Too bad this happened. It would have been fun."

The minivan was now alternatively racing and slowing. Another mile went by when it raced one last time and stalled. They coasted to a stop in the quiet night, somewhere by Joshua Tree. Under Katerina's insistence, the engine turned over several times without success.

"Well, that's that." She sounded resigned and pocketed the key.

"Now what do we do?"

"We sleep. Good night, David." Katerina leaned against her door. David couldn't believe she would just go to sleep. A minute passed and another. He was going to ask again what was the plan when he heard the sound of soft snoring. Looking at Katerina, he saw her eyes closed and her mouth slightly open. Even like this, he thought she looked pretty.

David leaned against his own, cold window. Shutting his eyes, he let exhaustion and the aftermath of too much adrenaline take over.

Three

Repairs

Day broke upon on the desert like a wave crashing into the beach, its light rolling across the scrub. Heat from the local star followed and poured into the minivan. The increasing brightness and temperature stirred the population of the car into awareness as they started to sweat.

"Wake up. David, wake up," A low voice and gentle shaking insisted, hastening the rousing process.

David's eyes opened a slit. The aches and pains of sleeping upright in the car along with memories of the previous night made themselves felt. He looked around and recognized Ellen's hand on his shoulder.

Worried, David said quietly, "Ellen, are you OK?"

"I'm fine. Do you know where we are? Why did we stop?" She spoke in hushed tones.

He stifled a yawn. "Something happened to the car. I think we're by Joshua Tree."

"Yes, we are." Katerina stretched in her seat. "I'll have to find someone to tow the car into town. I believe Indio is just down the highway. We'll get it fixed and keep going to LA."

"How far is Indio?" said David.

Katerina shrugged. "Fifteen, maybe twenty miles? Not sure and I don't dare turn on my phone to get a map. Too risky."

Ellen sounded skeptical. "Do you really think that?"

"Doesn't matter what I think. Are you willing to chance it? We'd be pretty helpless out here, by ourselves with no one else around."

Ellen's face became a frown when she heard this.

"I'm going to change and take the bulletproof vest off. Then, I'm going to start walking toward town. Hopefully, I'll find someone to give me a ride. Normally, there's cars on this stretch, so it shouldn't be a problem. I'll find us a tow truck to come get the rest of you, hopefully by afternoon. If we're lucky, we'll be on our way again by night."

"What do we do? You want one of us to go with you?" said David.

"No, I think it'll be harder to get a ride that way."

David looked past her to the highway outside her window.

"Are you sure about that? I don't think I've seen any car go by. Are you going to be safe?"

Katerina snorted. "I'll be fine." She took her camo jacket off, got out, and went to the back. David followed her with his eyes, turning in the seat to watch her. Opening the liftgate and the gray case, she stripped her shirt off. Immediately he whipped his head around, eyes straight forward.

"Oh, for crying out loud!" Ellen, who had watched her, too, now looked out her side window.

David's gaze wandered over to the rearview mirror. There he could see Katerina. An ugly bruise was on her chest, just above her bra. She looked up and saw him. She blew him a kiss and continued to work on her pants. David felt his face grow hot and looked away.

Another awkward minute or two passed before the gate was slammed shut. Katerina, dressed in blue jeans, tight black t-shirt and cowboy boots, opened the door and climbed in. She had a six pack of water bottles in her hand. Pulling two loose, she put the rest of them between the front chairs of the minivan.

"I might be gone for a while. This is all the water I have. Stay with the car. Do not open the case under any circumstances. And whatever you do, don't turn on your cell phones. I'll try to hurry."

"You want us to just wait here?" Ellen was incredulous.

"That's exactly what I want you to do. Don't do anything stupid and you'll be fine." Katerina got out and put the jacket back on. She put her spare water bottle into one of the pockets of the coat. She opened the other bottle, took a good swallow, and started walking west along the highway. David watched her shrink into the distance until she disappeared over a rise in the road.

"Bitch."

David rubbed his forehead.

Pete yawned and stretched. "Hey guys, what'd I miss?"

***

The morning ground on and the temperature continued to rise along with the sun. The three sat in the van with the windows and side doors open, hoping for a breeze.

Ellen lay on the middle seat. "How long until your girlfriend gets back?" She peeled herself off and sat up.

David rubbed against the seat cover as he shifted uncomfortably. "She's not my girlfriend. And you heard her too, when she said when she would try to get back."

Ellen pulled her stiff shirt away from her skin in an attempt to circulate some air. "Hmm. I wish I had known we were about to set off, trying to escape some killers. I would have worn something more appropriate. Not all of us have a change of clothes handy."

"What exactly do you figure is appropriate for running for your life?" The heat made David's head buzz.

"Well, not this ratty t-shirt, shorts and crappy sneakers, that's for sure. I would have packed a bag, like your girlfriend."

"She doesn't have a bag. She has a case that we're not supposed to even look at. And again, not my girlfriend."

Ellen bore holes in him. "But you wish she was, don't you?"

David sighed. "Look Ellen, I don't know what to think. She killed those two guys without any hesitation. That kind of worries me. You have to wonder who she's working for."

"You think she's a spy or something?" Pete piped up from the back seat where he lay.

"What else would she be?"

Pete sat up and leaned on the back of the middle seat. "Some kind of operative for a three-letter agency?"

"Maybe. She did tell me she was after the tapes too." David's clothes stuck to the seat as he turned around to look at Pete.

"You should try to stay on her good side. She could have just shot you and taken the tapes. She still might, to get the memory stick from you." Pete made a gun with his hand and had his thumb trigger back and forth.

David nodded. "She's definitely dangerous."

"Good God," interrupted Ellen. "Will you two stop fantasizing about her? And stop talking over me."

Quiet descended in the minivan. The silence from the desert was overwhelming. The sounds of an occasional speeding car came from their stretch of highway and quickly vanished.

Pete grabbed his water bottle. "I'm going out to that tree over there. Maybe it'll be easier to catch a breeze." He climbed out the desert side door.

Watching Pete walk away, David felt Ellen's eyes on him. He was about to go follow Pete when she started.

"Are you so fascinated by her that you can't see what's in front of you?"

David swallowed, the dryness of his throat producing an uncomfortable lump. At least, that's what he thought. He looked down at his bottle. "I'm sorry Ellen. I just didn't realize that you cared for me."

"How could you miss it? We've been having game nights every week for the past six months. I've talked to you every time and played every game that you ever showed interest in. I even went outside with you a couple of times to look at the stars. Did you see me doing that with anyone else?"

He knew she was looking right at him but he didn't dare make eye contact. "I'm not too bright about some things."

"You're fucking stupid about some things."

At that moment, he would have given anything to crawl away and hide in a hole somewhere. "I'm really sorry," was all he managed to croak out.

"I think you should go sit with Pete and see if you can get a breeze."

David grabbed his water bottle and leapt out of the car. There were several Cholla and barrel cacti to avoid along his way to the smooth, green barked tree that had Pete sitting against it. A stony rampart rose in the distance.

Pete looked up when he heard David scuffling toward him. "Hey buddy, from your expression, I take it you were talking to Ellen. Have you worked things out with her?"

David grimaced. "No. I'm an idiot." He sat down under the shade of the tree.

"Uh huh. What did you say to her?"

"I apologized to her."

"And?"

"And nothing. I just apologized for not noticing."

Pete shook his head. "You really are thick sometimes. Or maybe young? You're not that young. Do you honestly think you have a chance with Kat?"

"Her name is Katerina. And I don't know what to think."

Pete looked down at something he was tracing in the dirt. "You said it yourself. She was after the tapes, not you."

"She rescued me." Dave held up two fingers. "Twice, counting the car thing at the strip mall."

"Right. Do you even know what you're looking for in a woman? I mean, I know you've been working on your career, but I didn't think you wanted to be alone over the long run." Pete seemed to be talking to no one in particular, still drawing an outline in the dirt.

David didn't answer. He felt angry at Pete's line of questioning. "I guess I don't know."

"Well, you better figure it out. And the sooner, the better. That's what all these grey hairs have taught me." He paused in his doodling and looked up. "Here comes Ellen."

Ellen was slowly making her way through the scrub toward them. Her shirt was tied in the front, exposing her midriff. Getting closer, Dave could make out her eyes were red.

"Gentlemen," she said, standing under the shade, "I sincerely hope it's better out here. It's too damn stifling in the car." She took a swig of water.

Pete pointed to a spot on the ground with a flourish. "Join us. I'm not sure it's better. The breeze is hot but it beats being cooped up inside the mobile oven."

"Thank you." She sat down cross-legged in the shady area, completing the triangle. "So, what were you two discussing? Figure out what's so special about your data?"

Relief flooded David. This topic was a lot easier. "I've been wracking my brain. I was just mapping the sky, part of a survey of the whole thing. Well, as much as you can see from the Northern hemisphere. One of these days..." He looked off into the distance before focusing back on his friends. "I was around Arcturus when the Eyes showed up."

Pete leaned in. "Haven't you said that pretty much everybody pointed their scopes at them?"

David heart skipped a beat and he looked around. "All but mine," he managed to stammer out.

"What's so special about that star?" said Ellen.

Furrowing his brow, David thought out loud. "It's really bright. Kinda low in the sky."

"What do you mean low? I think you've shown it to me before. It seemed pretty high up when you pointed it out."

"Right. I mean that its declination is pretty low. Declination is like latitude. Which makes it close to the equator."

Ellen's index finger traced a circle in the air. "Equator? Like on Earth, but straight up, in the sky?"

"That's right."

"So what's down there?"

"Well, nothing. Not anymore. Oh crap!" David's eyes went wide with realization.

Ellen was paying close attention now. "What do you mean, oh crap?"

"I don't remember exactly, but I think that's where Arecibo is located. Was located."

Both Ellen and Pete were looking expectantly at David now.

Ellen beckoned with her hand. "Which is ..."

David held his forehead in his hand. "It got destroyed a while ago. It was a huge radio telescope. The cables snapped and dropped the receiver into the dish."

"Why would you send a message there?" said Pete.

"I have a good idea why. Over fifty years ago, it was used to send a message out to the stars. Nobody expected anything back. It was aimed at a cluster that was really far away. Would have taken tens of thousands of years to get something back."

"You think this is a reply to that?" said Ellen.

"It makes sense. You would know the one spot on the planet that could receive a message back."

Pete had a puzzled look on his face. "You mean, they beamed it back to that spot?"

"Oh no. But Arecibo points straight up. Pointed. Mostly. I bet Arcturus was right over it at the time. It couldn't help but to pick it up. "

Despite the heat, David shivered.

***

The sun tilted down and was well on its way to the western horizon. Shadows lengthened in the stillness.

"Where the hell is your girlfriend?" Ellen sounded tired.

He didn't even bother correcting her. He empathized with her. Exhaustion had worn him down too, even though all they had done was to sit under a tree. Too much thirst and hunger and heat and everything else had left everyone with no energy.

"I don't know where Katerina is. I'm hoping she made it into town alright." He didn't know if she was joking with him or not. He thought back to several hours ago when a moment of hope and turmoil had occurred.

He had been sitting in the shade of the tree. His stomach growled as food became a distant memory. Scanning the road, he had noticed a car that seemed to be travelling slower than usual, not that there had been that many cars going by today.

The car had pulled off the road and was moving slowly on the shoulder.

David stood up. He shambled toward the road.

Pete and Ellen also got up and followed him, forgetting caution.

The car had stopped behind the van.

David's heart leapt.

They frantically waved at the car, yelling, as they ran through the cacti.

The vehicle lurched back onto the highway and peeled out.

Arms dangling by their sides, they watched it hurtle down the highway, over the rise and disappear from view. A long, winding growl faded to the serene quiet of the desert.

"Well, shit." Ellen stared after the vanishing automobile.

After that, David's spirits sagged even further. The trio shuffled the distance to their shady refuge. They sat there and stared at the now empty road.

Pete sounded angry. "What the hell is wrong with people?"

"I know." Ellen scowled. "Nobody else has even stopped. People have been acting strange ever since the damn Eyes."

David sat in silence. He turned around to look off into the distance, away from the road. The awesome quiet was broken by the sound of another car speeding by.

Ellen spoke up, startling him. "How's your water, David? Pete, you okay? We still have one unopened bottle."

Pete lifted his bottle, showing a finger left of water.

David couldn't face his companions, the results of his decisions crushing down on him. He stared at the distant cliffs. "I'm sorry I didn't believe you, Ellen. You were right. I really regret dragging you two into this. I've put you both in danger."

"Hey man, we're your friends. Nobody knew what we were getting into. We didn't know her at all. Still don't." Pete spoke softly.

"She could have murdered you to get what you have. I couldn't just let that happen." Ellen voice was harsh.

David flinched. "But she didn't. I don't think that's in her playbook."

"Oh, playbook, really? Your girlfriend shot two guys without hesitation."

"They shot her first. She could have taken the drive from me at gunpoint then. She could have shot us all dead and we wouldn't have been able to do anything about it. Not in her playbook." David shook his head.

Ellen looked thoughtful. "I suppose you're right. And yet, here we are. In the middle of the desert, thirsty, running out of water." Her stomach grumbled. "And hungry." She stared at David, boring holes in him. David did his best to ignore her. He returned to scanning the cliffs in the distance.

Pete noticed Ellen's glare. "Hey guys, I'm going to go stretch my legs for a bit. I'll be back soon." He got up, pulled each of his arms across his chest in turn and headed to the road. Turning west on it, he walked toward the rise. David looked after him, feeling betrayed, feeling Ellen's eyes on him.

"I keep trying to figure out what I did wrong. Why don't you want to go out with me?"

David frown. "I did want to go out with you, when we first met." He drew figures in the sand.

"But?"

David's shoulders slumped as he turned to face her. "But I was intimidated by you. I liked just being friends with you. It was safe. I thought I'd just blow it if I tried for more. I didn't want things to change."

"That's a pretty shitty thing to do. Especially if you saw me trying." Ellen took the last sip of water in her bottle.

David looked into Ellen's eyes. "You said I was dumb. I'm worse than that. I'm a coward. I told myself that you really weren't interested. I didn't want to mess things up. It was easier to think that instead of admitting I wasn't brave enough to ask you out."

She returned his gaze. "Why are you admitting it now?"

"There's a real chance that we could die. You deserve to know. I do like you. You're smart and attractive. I really am sorry about the way I acted."

The silence stretched out. David started to get nervous while he carefully watched Ellen for any sign of what she was thinking. Ellen stared back at him until he began to squirm.

Finally, she stood up. "Apology accepted." She wandered down the road, after Pete.

***

The sky turned into a painter's fevered dream of mauve, gold and crimson. The rocks seemed to glow through the shadows that spread on the ground. The beauty around them was strangely at odds with the predicament the three found themselves in. But with the sun fleeing from the sky, the temperature started to drop. The little traffic that had been going by dwindled to nothing, in fear of the advancing night.

They all made their way back to the minivan. They had run out of water, after sharing the last bottle, passing it between them as close friends might pass a bottle of wine around.

In the cabin of the car, Ellen sat in the middle bench. She seemed to be in a better mood, despite the current hardships. David was glad. He leaned forward against the steering wheel, gazing out the windshield.

Pete sat in the passenger seat, leaning against the window. "Do you think something happened to Kat? It's pretty late."

"I hope not. All she said was that we were on our way to LA. Right, Ellen?"

Ellen was looking at the desert through the sliding door window. It was closed now against the chill. "Yeah, she said that this morning."

"What if she doesn't show up tonight? What are we going to do tomorrow? Wait here? Start walking ourselves?" said Pete.

Ellen turned around to face forward. "I don't think we should wait here. We're out of water. We should start walking. And we should do it at night, while it's cool."

"You want to wait until midnight and then head out? Make sure we give her enough time?" said David.

"That sounds like a good plan," said Ellen. "That'll give us enough time to get to town before the heat of the day. Maybe someone will give us a ride."

Having all agreed, they kept silent watch out the front windshield. Across the road, the Milky Way rose in the velvet dark.

About an hour later, flashing yellow lights played across the desert. A vehicle crested the rise in front of them. With relief, David watched it approach and cross over to their side of the road. A few moments later, they were all out of the minivan, waiting as the tow truck maneuvered in front of the stalled vehicle.

Katerina got out as soon as the truck stopped. She came over to them and gave David a quick hug

"I'm so sorry it took so long. People were rioting over *toilet paper*. I thought I was going to have to steal a car to come get you. I brought food and drinks. They're in the cab. It was almost impossible to get anyone to come out here. The whole town was in an uproar. Nobody wants to be out where they can see the night sky."

Ellen rested her hand on David's shoulder. "We're glad you're OK and got back to us in time."

Four

The Good Guys?

They delivered the minivan to the parking lot of a repair shop where it would be examined in the morning. Everyone walked in the cooling night with the smell of mesquite in the air to a nearby hotel.

"I am so sorry, folks. I have to be careful with money at the moment. We can only get one room," said Katerina as she led them down the hallway to their room.

Early in the morning, she roused everyone to get started as soon as the mechanic opened.

David woke to Katerina's smiling pretty face hovering just above his as she tousled his hair. "Wake up, sunshine!"

He saw Ellen at the foot of the other bed, staring, her jaw clenched, a tendon twitching in her neck.

Embarrassed, he made what he hoped was a contrite face at her and hastily put his hands up, to push Katerina away. He encountered a problem, a soft, warm, full problem. A nagging familiarity made him hesitate. Looking now at Katerina, he realized what he had encountered.

Katerina looked down with a puzzled looked on her face. She laughed. "Well, I did get a dinner first."

The laughter broke his paralysis. He dropped his hands and he wanted to crawl under the sheets and hide. "I am so sorry!"

The door to the room slammed behind Ellen.

They grabbed breakfast in the hotel lobby and made the short trek to the repair shop where the wait started.

They spent the morning in the customer area examining various old magazines and watching TV. About mid-morning, the mechanic entered the room holding some cables.

The black insulation was missing in patches and bright copper was underneath. "Well, I found your problem. It looks like some of the insulation came off. I'm guessing that they made contact with the engine or hood while you were driving. But I can't for the life of me figure out what caused it. Nothing seems to be rubbing on them."

"Is it expensive to fix?" Katerina wrinkled her brow.

"No, but we have to order the cables from the dealer. It's going to be another hour or so. You want me to order them?" He held the old wires up.

"Thank goodness. Yes, please."

The mechanic left to procure the replacements.

David was troubled by the exchange. He spoke to Katerina alone. "How are you paying for all this? I thought we couldn't use our ATM cards?"

"I have an emergency stash. It should be enough to get us someplace safe but I do have to watch it. I've gone through a good chunk of it already."

"Well, thank you. I promise to pay you back. You shouldn't have to fix my car."

"David, I sincerely doubt that your car had anything wrong before you came over. And don't worry about the money."

Early in the afternoon, the repairs were finished. They got on the interstate and, within a few hours, they encountered the famous LA traffic, made worse by the coming weekend.

Seeing all the traffic made David wonder just how much it had been affected by the celestial phenomena. The normalcy of downtown reminded him of the only other time he had been in LA, an astronomy conference down by the Santa Monica pier. His limited knowledge of the area let him realize they were close to his previous destination and he began to wonder if he would catch a glimpse of the Ferris wheel. But Katerina turned south just short of the pier and into the surface road traffic.

Soon, she was picking her way through the airport, turning east under a highway and south yet again. David watched an enormously long building go by out of his window.

"We're almost there," said Katerina.

Turning east on a major street, Katerina drove into a residential area. She performed a series of turns while looking in her mirror, before turning back out to the street she had left.

Katerina saw the puzzled look on David's face. "Can't be too careful. There are secrets to protect here."

Finally, she pulled into the parking lot of a drab, beige three story building.

Ellen looked doubtful when she saw the building. "This is your headquarters?"

"It seems like a good disguise," said Pete.

Katerina shook her head. "Not our headquarters. This is where we can take a look at the data on your drive. We have some climbing to do. It's on the third floor. David, grab the bag."

David grabbed the phone bag from between the front seat and trudged up the steps, behind Katerina. The others followed. The hallway needed a paint job and some airing out. There was a musty smell that grew worse the further in he went.

Stopping in front of a worn door, Katerina turned to them. "We're going to have to crowd together. There's not a lot of room inside."

David saw his own puzzlement echoed on the faces of Ellen and Pete.

Katerina grunted as she pushed on the door and went in.

David held the door open. He was somewhat surprised at the required strength and wondered what was it made of. It opened into a small room with another door opposite of the first. A small box was mounted on the wall next to it.

"Come on everyone. Make sure the door latches behind you." Katerina stood by the far door and motioned with her hand.

David didn't think that would be a problem, judging by the strength of the doorspring. He propped the door open with his body.

Ellen and Pete came into the anteroom.

David moved out of the way and the door slowly closed behind him with a solid thunk. A leak of light under the door was the only illumination.

In the relative darkness, a fluorescent light overhead flickered on. The box's front plate lit up with a sequence of numbers and a diminishing bar over them. Below the digits, an image of a keypad appeared. Katerina studied the numbers and tapped out a response. A series of bolts being thrown resounded from the door in front of them.

"In we go." Katerina strained as she pushed the door open.

Once inside, an antiseptic white-walled reception room greeted them. A solitary desk blocked an opening to what looked like a hallway. Behind them, the door automatically shut. The sound of metal sliding into place rang out. David felt very much trapped.

He looked around the office. "So, now what?"

Ellen stood behind Pete, peeking around him. She whispered something in his ear.

Pete's eyes darted about the room.

"There used to be a receptionist here. But we had budget cuts. I think there's a button on the desk..." Katerina never finished the sentence. A pale man with long, black hair in a ponytail and short, thick beard came from the left of the opening behind the desk with his hands in the pockets of a lab coat.

"You're late," he said. "And who the hell are these people?"

Katerina shrugged. "Things happened. It was unavoidable."

The man pointed back and forth between the two of them. "You and I have different ideas of unavoidable."

"That's why I work in the field. Folks, this is Dr. Benjamin Shtern. Doc, this is David, Pete and Ellen. David is the astronomer."

"How do you do? I'm glad to meet you." David offered his hand.

"Yes, quite." Shtern didn't bother to move his hand at all.

David felt embarrassment come over him and quickly withdrew his hand.

Katerina spoke through clenched teeth. "David has the information you want. On his USB drive."

"It's not my fault you screwed up your field work."

"There were others attempting to acquire it."

"So?" Shtern stared at Katerina.

Katerina's words were short and clipped. "It was a hostile attempt."

"Oh?" Shtern said, and then his face registered comprehension. "Oh! How hostile?"

"I left two of them face down in a motel room."

The now nervous Doctor's eyes widened. "Do you think it was them?"

"Who else would shoot first over this?" Katerina's reply was matter-of-fact.

"Were you followed?"

"I didn't see anything. Still, I don't think we have a lot of time. You know how they operate."

Dr. Shtern nodded. Turning to David, he beckoned with a hand. "Follow me."

David walked past the desk into the hallway. He was a bit surprised to find out that the wall facing the entryway was merely a screen, just something to block the view of the open bay past it. Plywood covered the walls with a metallic mesh stapled to it. The mesh also covered the ceiling. He had to step up onto the raised floor. A number of workbenches were scattered around the floor and several metal cabinets were against the walls. But the thing that drew his eyes was a large metal box, about the size of a shipping container. It looked like it was riveted together. A couple of beefy air conditioning units had ducts connected to the box. A thick cable ran to it.

Ellen and Pete followed David and were looking at each other.

"You and me are going into the vault." The doctor pointed to a workbench right by the door of the container. "Please leave your cell phone there."

"Ah, it's in the bag." David shook the bag at him.

"Even better. Leave it there." Dr. Shtern pointed again at the table. David put the bag on the table.

"It's your time to shine, sweetheart." Katerina had the sweetest smile.

David smiled back and went inside.

***

Inside the vault, one whole wall was taken up by racks of computers, leaving a narrow passage against the other side. Warm air came from those racks and the smell of sweat and new electronics reached David's nose. Looking at the equipment, David wondered who these people were.

"I'll need the drive," said the man identified as Dr. Shtern. He sat down at a small desk near the door of the chamber, a laptop computer on the cluttered surface with a network cable running to the machinery behind him.

David hesitated, suddenly not sure if he trusted them. A quick reflection and he came to the conclusion that getting rid of the drive would mean that no one would have a reason to try and kill him anymore. He reached into his pants pocket and pulled the USB stick out.

"How much data is on it?" said the man.

"About a terabyte."

"Where was it pointed?"

"Got a piece of paper? I'll write it down for you."

Nodding, Dr. Shtern slid a small notepad over to him. David wrote down the declination and right ascension of his research target.

"Was it moved at all?"

"No, in all the excitement over, well, you know, I just forgot. What are you going to do?"

"First, I'm going to get the data off the stick. Then I'm going look at the frequency spectrum to try to isolate any signal particularly at ten Hertz around the carrier." He stuck the thumbdrive into the port in the laptop and proceeded to move and click the mouse in response to something on the screen.

"Do you really think there's something on there?"

Shtern stared blankly at him before saying, "What do you know about the asterism?"

By rote, David spoke. "That is was 137 sources of light. Same magnitude, same spectra. They all appeared one by one over the Prime Meridian and winked out at the same time the next night after rising over it. I haven't heard anything else from the other astronomers."

"Do you know why it was that number?"

"Oh yes, I knew before. But the news made a big deal of it, too. It's the Fine Structure Constant."

"Yes, well, as you undoubtedly know, that's not quite right. There's a fractional part, too."

An involuntary shiver went through him.

"In fact," said Shtern," if you assume that a magnitude two star is a 'one', the fractional part works out to about something that would have a magnitude of 5.6. Barely visible to the human eye in dark skies, certainly not under city lights. Do you want to guess where the 138th star appeared? While everyone was distracted?"

In a flat tone, David managed to say "Right over Arecibo."

"Very good. I see you've been thinking about it. I hope I don't have to explain why we theorize there may have been a radio transmission?"

David shook his head.

"This is going to take a while, to copy all the data off. Do you want to wait here for me to give you your drive back or do you want to wait outside with your friends?" The doctor jerked his thumb over his shoulder toward the door.

Resigned to the importance and danger represented by what he had accidentally recorded, he said, "I guess I'll wait outside with them."

"No problem."

David pursed his lips. "Can I ask a question? Who are you people?"

The man gave him a smile. "That's classified."

***

The three other people stood in a knot between the vault and the false wall. They all turned to look at David when he came out. The corners of Ellen's mouth were down-turned. Pete had a careful neutral expression and Katerina was smiling. David was starting to think it really wasn't a smile. Katerina came right up to David, wrapped her arms around him and planted a kiss on his lips. David felt an electric thrill go through him as her warm, moist lips press against his. He pulled his head back, flustered by what happened.

"What was that for?"

Pete looked on amused.

Ellen clenched her jaw and turned red. She leaned in close to Pete and whispered in his ear. Pete nodded.

"You did a great thing, David!" Katerina unwrapped herself from him but kept one arm around his waist as they turned to face the others. "You would be a hero, if we were ever allowed to talk about this!"

"Yeah, Dr. Shtern told me. It's all classified."

Katerina's musical laughter seemed a little too carefree for everything that had happened. She kept her hand behind him, on his waist.

Ellen stepped closer to the couple. "So, you were going to tell us what the hell is going on, David?"

David could feel Katerina's hand tugging on the back of his pants. He became even more uncomfortable as Ellen took yet another step closer to them. Attempting to step out of Katerina's embrace, he was stopped by the presence of her hand hooked in his belt loop.

"Well, it sounds like we were mostly right, with what we guessed in the desert." He finally managed to wriggle away from the restraint, causing Katerina's arm to fall to her side. David let out a small sigh. "There was something directly over Arecibo, another light but barely visible. I happened to be aiming at it. The doctor said he's going to analyze the data. Data I accidentally recorded."

Ellen stopped her advance. She was still fuming. "And what about what you were telling us? Who are 'they'?" She stared right at Katerina.

Katerina's smile faded. "Yes, well, there are opposing forces. This bit is on a need to know basis. I'm going to tell you what I know, since your lives are in danger so I figure you need to know."

"Put in danger by you." Ellen angrily pointed at her.

To her credit, Katerina nodded in agreement. "You might be right. Of course, I believe that it was just a matter of time before they figured out you had the USB stick. Then they would have hunted you down to make sure you didn't have a copy."

David felt dismayed. He knew that he would have made a backup copy of the danger-ous data before sending it off. "How, how did they know to look for me? In fact, how did you know?"

Katerina smiled again. "Not surprising, after the Eyes disappeared, a clearinghouse of what all the observatories were looking at was set up. This was based, of course, on current reported information from various sources. Yours stuck out. It wasn't pointed anywhere close to where all the others were pointed, so people ignored you."

Sudden understanding dawned in David. "Until you had the report of another light source."

"By that point, your data had conveniently been removed." Katerina positively beamed.

Pete tried to follow the conversation. "What are you two talking about?"

David waved him off. "I was part of a larger effort, to map the sky in various frequencies. Other people knew. But, if you removed the data, how did the guys with the guns know?"

"We're actually not sure. They just seem to know everything. We think they have moles everywhere. And it wasn't exactly secure." Her lips became a straight line and her brow knitted. "Don't trust anyone. They could be anywhere. Your best bet is to fly under their radar. Be anonymous. As soon as you draw their attention, someone shows up with usually fatal consequences." The smile had vanished.

"What do you call them? I don't want to just keep calling them 'them'." David's right eye twitched.

Katerina focused on them, eyes narrowed. "We just know them as the adversary."

"Are you done trying to frighten us?" said Ellen. "We're not children. The only thing that is really scaring me right now is how hungry I am." She looked over at Pete who nodded.

A sigh escaped Katerina. "Fine, let me check on the good doctor and we'll go to dinner."

Katerina pulled the heavy vault door open and stepped inside, leaving the door partially open. David could just hear her voice, talking to Shtern.

Ellen sprinted to the door and slammed it shut, twisting the dial on it. "Pete! Push the bench over!"

Pete was already behind the bench, scraping it across the floor, pieces of equipment and tools clattering to the ground. He butted it up against the door.

David was astonished. "What are you doing?"

"Come on, man! Move it! We gotta get out of here!" Pete rushed past David and into the anteroom.

"Let's go, David. We have to get moving before they get out!" Already there was banging on the door of the box. Ellen grabbed the bag and David's arm and pulled him into the adjacent room.

In the reception area, Pete was studying the door.

David protested. "This is wrong! We can't just leave them there!"

"This is for your own good. They have the data. What else do they need? We have to get out. Did you figure it out, Pete?" Ellen dug through the bag and pulled her phone out.

Pete hit a large, red button next to the door that said "Emergency" on it. Alarms immediately sounded and the door issued a number of loud clanks.

"Run, David!" Ellen dropped the bag to use both hands to wrenched the door open. Turning the handle on the far door, she ran out of view. Pete was hot on her heels.

David looked over his shoulder. He could hear some yelling now. *Shit, they have what they came for!* and he went through the double doors, flying down the hallway, down the stairs at breakneck speed and out into the street.

There, he nearly ran into is two friends who were standing just outside of the door, looking down the street bathed in the late afternoon light. "Whoa!" he said. "What do we do now?"

"There's a bus coming. The bus stop is right over there," Pete pointed across the busy street. "We've got to hurry."

The traffic in front of them didn't share their sense of urgency.

"Shit, the corner is too far. We'll never make it." Ellen looked both ways. She grabbed David's hand. "Let's go. Now." A hard pull and they were half-way into the first lane.

"Wait!" died on David's lips. Cars sped past them as they stood on the dividing lines between the lanes. Horns blared and Pete joined them on their refuge. An opening in the procession of cars and they were off again, crossing the last couple of lanes. David's heart felt like it was going to burst from his chest.

"You can thank me later." Ellen pointed at the bus stop a few yards away on the sidewalk. The bus was already waiting there.

The three of them ran to the waiting vehicle. No sooner had they boarded than the driver closed the door and told them to sit. Paying the fare, they made their way down the aisle. David sat on the street side of the bus.

Looking across the road that they had just danced over, David saw Katerina emerge from the building. She was scanning the street. David slump down in his chair. *She looks pissed* he thought.

The bus made its way through traffic and turned south. David saw stores, restaurants, strip malls, all the assorted minutia of a modern neighborhood along the way. The bus came to stop at a number of places while passengers came on and got off.

"Where are we going, Ellen?"

"Don't know. Far enough that they can't find us."

The bus turned toward the ocean and went into a large parking lot. It pulled up to a fancy bus stop.

"All off for the pier," announced the bus driver.

"Is this where you turn around?" asked Ellen of the driver.

"It sure is, lady."

The three got off. Faint music called to them from past the stop. A broad concrete way, teeming with shops and restaurants stretched away from them, over the swelling sea. The smell of the ocean teased David's nose with its unfamiliarity. Interspersed with it were aromas of different cuisines.

Suddenly hungry, David turned to the other two and said, "I bet we can get something good to eat here."

***

The group wandered down the pier, looking at the different offerings. They finally settled in a bar that was upstairs over a restaurant. An octagonal room with picture windows for walls offered them a gorgeous view of the sunset. The hostess seated them at a table in time to watch the sun sink beneath the waves in a show of red and orange. The room burst into a round of applause at the spectacle. The sky deepened in color and the sea matched it.

David was quiet the whole time, staring at the table.

Ellen reached out and put her hand on his. "Hey, we're going to be fine. We got rid of the drive and them. Let's get a drink and some dinner. I've got points at a hotel chain. I bet it's enough to get us a room for the night."

David nodded. In the low light of the bar, he studied Ellen who sat across from him. He felt terrible at having dragged her into this mess. She looked so pretty in the low light. He thought about what they had talked about in the desert and how she had been right. Ellen locked eyes with him, before he looked away, guilt driving him.

Pete broke the awkward silence. "Boy, that was a fantastic sunset! Here comes the waitress. Did you see that there's a drink special here? I bet this place is good." He rubbed his hands together.

Picking up the menu, David did his best to bury his attention in it.

They ended up ordering a round of the special that came in a short but heavy commemorative glass that they got to keep. A little while later, the table received their seafood choices.

The alcohol started to take effect on David and, in spite of everything, he started to relax. The events of the last couple of days began to lose their immediacy and the balm of sharing a meal with good friends eased the burden that he felt.

Buoyed by the good feelings, he smiled at Ellen. And Ellen smiled back.

Pete had just finished an improbable tale of a landlocked mermaid. On cue, the two of them laughed while looking at each other.

Pete looked at the two of them. "Hmm, you think you can get a couple of rooms with your points, Ellen?"

"I think something can be arranged." Ellen sounded very happy. She paid for the meal.

"I'll pay you back Ellen." David felt terrible at not being able to pick up the check for her.

"Forget about it. Think of it as our first date. Besides, you don't have much of anything at this point. I should have grabbed your cell phone for you. Sorry."

David shook his head. "It's alright."

"Well, I'll pay you back. And for the other room too, once we get home," said Pete.

"You better! I ain't running a charity." She giggled.

They strolled back through the crowd of people out for a Friday night, under strings of incandescent lights. Their warm glow made everything look magical to David. Reaching the parking lot, they stood there facing the cars in their rows.

Ellen pulled out her phone. "I'm going to get us a ride."

The other two looked at her in alarm.

"Are you sure? Katerina warned us to turn off our phones," said David.

"Even if what she said was true, we'll all be long gone from here by the time anyone shows up. And I'll turn my phone off once the guy shows up. Well?"

David found himself the focus of their attention. He found himself frowning thinking about what Katerina had admonished them with. Not knowing what to believe, he relented. "Fine, go ahead and do it. Just remember to turn off your phone as soon as the ride gets here."

Ellen quickly turned on her phone and accessed the app. "OK, it says that the car will be here in ten minutes. The hotel is just a couple of miles down that road. I'm reserving our two rooms." Fingers twitched over the phone screen..

"If a black, windowless van shows up, I'm not getting in." David couldn't tell if Pete was serious or not.

What did show up in ten minutes was a boxy import car with ground effects. A young Latino man rolled down his window. With an accented voice, he said, "Ellen?" over the Reggaeton that was playing.

She glanced at her phone to confirm. "Our ride's here."

David held the door open for her as Pete went around the other side. The three of them squeezed into the back seat. The young man said, "I can change the music."

David said, "No, it's fine." The phone went off and his sense of unease started to dwindle.

"Everyone in? Buckle up." The driver turned to look back at them.

"Yeah, we're in," said David. Being crowded together had them all touching each other but David didn't mind, sitting next to Ellen.

She took his hand.

David felt her warm hand in his and felt happy. He questioned why he hadn't started something with Ellen earlier.

The car left the parking lot and went down the street, away from the ocean. In David's mind, he was planning future dates with Ellen when suddenly, she let go of his hand and leaned forward.

"Hey, you just missed our hotel!"

An unnatural silence descended over them, muffling everything. No music, no engine, no noise of outside traffic reached David's ears. He felt like the time that he had gone in an anechoic chamber, the same deadness of sound.

"What's going on?" yelled Pete, trying to combat the silencing effects.

Ellen took her commemorative glass and threw it at the back of the driver's head.

The glass hit something invisible in mid-air just short of the front seat and tumbled down to the floorboard. The three stared at the glass lying at their feet.

"What the hell..." was as far as Ellen got before the backseat went pitch black.

Five

Definitely the Other Guys

D avid yelled. He yelled in fear, in rage, in frustration. He yelled until he felt his throat start going raw. Nothing. All sound disappeared into the thick, all encompassing black.

His hands frantically searched the space in front of him. A smooth surface that had some give before it became rigid met his touch. He tried feeling around the door to his side. No door handle could be found. Just a blank surface, slightly yielding to his fingertips, same as what was in front of them.

Distraught, he slumped back in the seat as he realized he'd made the wrong decision. A hand, soft and warm, sought his hand out. Their fingers entwined, a weight came down on his shoulder, soft curls brushing his face. Ellen's scent filled his nose. David tried to calm down and Ellen's touch comforted him.

In the silent darkness, David became aware that he could feel every motion of the car by the seat of his pants. It seemed to be starting and stopping, probably going through traffic. The motions seemed to be spacing out. A left turn and then a smooth ride for some distance, going through some curves before stopping again. David lost all sense of time in the inkiness. Maybe they were in there for ten minutes? Twenty minutes? He couldn't tell.

Another stretch of road and a right turn before going slowly going over some speed bumps. Ellen's grip tightened. Her fingernails would leave an impression on his skin.

The car was slowly weaving through something, slowly making way until it came to a gentle stop. A shift and a shudder of the car told David that the driver had gotten out and closed a door. They had arrived somewhere.

It wasn't long before there was a gentle nudge to the car, a subtle rocking from the side he was on. A smell of burnt metal reached his nose. As the car settled back down, David squeezed Ellen's hand.

Bright light flooded the backseat, blinding David. He heard Ellen's sharp intake of breath and Pete's cry of surprise. The muffling curtain had been lifted.

"Come out slowly with your hands above your head," a voice on a megaphone commanded.

David's eyes watered as they tried to adjust to the illumination. The whole side, doors and jamb, had been taken off, leaving it all open. Something that looked like an industrial robot with four or five joints held something that looked like a high-tech pencil in its three fingered claw. The entire side of the car was on the floor a few feet away, toward the engine.

Blinking, he could just make out a squad of men in the relative darkness behind the light panel that shone in the car. They had weapons pointed at them. He didn't recognize them but he had no wish to find out what the weapons were. David raised his hands and stepped out onto the cement floor.

A man from the shadow stepped up to him and pulled him away from the vehicle. He patted David down and searched his pockets before relieving him of his wallet. Looking over his shoulder, he saw Ellen being patted down. Cell phone and purse were taken from her. They gave her a shove to move her out of the way. An additional guard stepped up to the car, waiting for Pete.

"Hey!" David started back toward his friends when he saw how Ellen was being treated.

A blow across his stomach with a baton stopped him short. He doubled over, struggling for breath. His escort growled at him, "Next time, I'll turn it on."

"Silence!" came the voice over the megaphone. "You will now be taken to your cells. Any outburst or attempt to escape will be dealt with harshly!"

The three were lead away from the high bay by the dozen men in dressed in black body armor. Truncheons, a can of something, and a pistol attached to a belt completed the full paramilitary regalia. David could find no identifying insignia on them, just pips on some collars.

Going through a set of double doors, they found themselves in a brightly lit, plain white corridor. It almost hurt his eyes. The dark garb the men wore was in stark contrast to the hallway, their striding boots clumping on the freshly waxed white linoleum tiles.

Turning down an intersection, they marched to a series of sliding doors. The guards stopped in front of three of them and lined each of them up, one to a door.

David looked over to Ellen and Pete. Ellen looked worried and terrified. But Pete had a steely look in his eyes. David momentarily became afraid for his friend.

The door in front of him noiselessly slid open. A rough shove and he nearly tumbled into the awaiting cell. The door closed behind him with a solid thud.

Looking over the space, David saw it was about ten feet by ten feet. A shelf at knee height was attached to the left wall, big enough he could lie down on it. A toilet and sink were opposite it, against the other wall. And that was all there was.

A voice came over the intercom in the ceiling, proclaiming "Lights out!". The light panels dimmed. David was thankful it wasn't the odious black from their ill-fated ride.

Stretching out on the hard plank, he felt the emotions of the ride overcome him. In a fit of trembling, he fell asleep.

***

A sudden brightening woke David. Instantly, he recognized where he was. The car ride was etched in his memory. His body ached from the hardness of the bed and he had a crick in his neck. Surveying the empty room, looking for any way to escape, he was overwhelmed by how insurmountable the task seemed.

He wondered how long he would have to wait here.

Apparently not long. The intercom told him to get up and stand away from the entrance as the door slid open. A man with a small, short barrel weapon hanging from a strap off his shoulder pointed it at him. It looked like it could fire a lot of bullets fast. A different voice from last night barked orders through the speaker for him to come out.

David did not want to find out if he was correct. He came out right away.

An escort similar to the one that brought them to the cells last night waited in the hall. A quick glance sideways showed his friends had also been taken out of their cells. Ellen's eyes were red-rimmed. Pete's jaw had a hard line. He looked right at David as said, "You OK?"

A hard blow with a baton was administered to Pete across his thighs. Pete didn't flinch. He turned to face his assailant, looking like he might tackle him. The man backed up and the baton made buzzing noises.

"Quiet!" hissed the man with a pair of pips on his collar. "I don't want to hear a sound out of any of you. Follow!" The harsh voice left no doubt who was being addressed.

Down the corridor they went, back to the intersection and they turned away from the high bay. The three of them, surrounded by their dozen burly guards in black, marched down the hall. David wondered what could he, Ellen and Pete could possibly do to them, seeing as they were hopelessly outnumbered and outmatched.

The hall ended in a single, reinforced door. A swipe of the commander's key card and in they went. Simple concrete was beneath their feet and the walls weren't even covered in drywall. Exposed steel trusses overhead added to the unfinished look of the chamber. In stark contrast to the Spartan ambience, an opulent Persian rug with a massive, wooden desk sat in the exact middle of the room. Ornate carvings of what David recognized as astrological symbols adorned thick pillars. The legs supported a wide expanse of polished wood. The desk crouched, staking out its territory on the carpet. A monitor and various books and papers were on top of the desk. A bald, older gentleman, dressed in tweed and sporting a silver Van Dyke sat behind the desk. Three folding chairs faced the massive block of wood, carefully set back from the rug. The entire retinue stood by the door.

A minute went by, and another. David started shifting on his feet, wondering if the man realized they were there. Ellen sniffled a couple of times. Pete looked like he was ready to leap.

The man glanced up and said, "Have them sit and go wait outside." Looking right at the three, he said, "You're not going to interrupt me while I'm working, are you?"

David couldn't help himself and shook his head. The goons walked them to the chairs and once they were sitting, turned on their heels and walked out. David couldn't believe they had been left alone. He stole a look at Pete, who had the most predatory smile David could imagine on his face. Ellen seemed to withdraw even more.

The three sat quietly. A faint scratching from a fountain pen on paper was the only sound they heard.

"Well, are you..." started Pete.

The man held his hand up without even bothering to look at them. Pete fell silent. He continued to scribble on his papers for another minute or so. Finally, he looked up at them. Taking his glasses off, he rubbed them with a cloth.

"Wonderful invention, microfiber. Really gets my glasses clean. Wish I had patented it." Putting the spectacles back on, he continued, "You may address me as Robert."

Pete started. "Well, Rob, do you mind telling us why your goons are holding us?"

Robert's eye twitched and the slight smile he had disappeared. "Well, Peter, you have some information that I can't allow to get out. You recorded it on your equipment. Right David?" Another smile was pasted on.

"I don't know what you are talking about. You burned my apartment and destroyed the tapes," said David

Robert sighed. "We know you have a USB drive with the information. Where is it? You didn't have it on you when my men searched you. Come now, don't you want to leave?"

David hesitated, thinking about what to say.

"Don't tell him anything!" Ellen hissed. "They aren't about to let us out alive."

The smile faded from Robert's lips. "We know you had help. Why don't you tell us who was helping you? What is the name of your contact?"

David thought about it for a moment and said, "I, I don't actually know who she is."

Robert examined something on his desk before looking back up at them. "Seems true enough. Don't worry, we'll find her soon enough. She can't hide from us forever. And then we'll make sure your information never gets out." The man stood behind the desk, palms on the surface. "Where is she? The one you were talking to on the phone in Arizona? Is she nearby? Is she your contact? Don't you want to save yourself and your girlfriend here?"

David started to say something and stopped. Locking eyes with the man behind the desk, he bared his teeth. "Rob, go fuck yourself."

A momentary spasm of rage lit his face but it was quickly gone. Robert then sighed and sat down. Pressing some unseen button, he said, "You had a chance to be helpful, in these uncertain times. But you've now become just another loose end that we have to clean up now. Guards, get rid of them."

Pete crossed the distance to the desk in an instant as he launched himself at Robert. He went flying through the desk and the man before landing on the far side of it. The whole ensemble, desk, rug and man, became digital snow and reformed five feet beyond Pete. Ellen and David rushed to Pete, helping him off the floor.

Rob was laughing uncontrollably at them. "Oh, that was precious! I realize now how little you know about us. I take it your contact didn't tell you much about us?"

A defiant Ellen told him, "She told us enough. We know you are the adversary!"

"Oh ho! The Adversary! Satan himself! That is too funny!"

The henchmen had reached them and proceeded to restrain them. They grabbed the trio's arms, forced their arms behind their backs. David struggled but there were too many people on him. His wrists were zip tied together. David and Ellen were lifted up and pushed toward the door. Pete was given a vicious shove almost causing him to fall.

"Don't worry, we'll find your accomplice. Nobody can hide from us!" Rob's parting words came between gales of raucous laughter.

Mercifully, Rob was cut off by the closing door. Straight down the corridor they went, back into the highbay where they'd been brought in last night. A black, windowless van, its side door open, waited for them. A single bench seat stretched across the back.

"Get in!" ordered the squad leader. Pete faltered stepping into the van and was prodded in the back with one of their sizzling batons. He went rigid and fell straight down, his head almost impacting on the car door jamb. He was hauled up and tossed into the van by the two men flanking him. Ellen climbed in and David followed suit and the door slid shut.

David and Ellen sat on the floor, by their friend when the front doors opened. In climbed two men wearing identical black suits and ties. One man, the driver, had his jet black hair slicked back. The other man had long blond hair in a pony tail. No sooner had they gotten in than the familiar dead sound feeling overcame the cabin. The driver adjusted his sunglasses and backed the van out, past a roll up door and into an office complex with low buildings.

David braced himself for the lights to go out and the forced silence to descend on them.

Instead, the van pulled out of a chain-link enclosed office park, onto a road. David could see the skyscrapers of LA through the windshield. Experimentally, he pushed against the side of the van. The same surface from last night greeted his fingers.

Pete's chest heaved as he struggled to pull air into his lungs. He shook his head and righted himself on the floor. "I agree with you, Ellen. We're screwed." Pete was barely audible.

"We'll figure something out," yelled back Dave. "Ellen, how did you know they weren't going to let us go?"

Ellen had already brought her hands around her feet to her front. "They didn't feed us. You don't feed something if you are going to get rid of it."

David followed suit and soon they both were helping Pete off the floor and into the seat. Sitting in the middle, Ellen started to cry and rested her head on David's shoulder. David held her hands in his.

Soon, they were on a highway, heading away from Los Angeles. They went through the hills and the terrain opened into a vast, desolate plain. David looked at the driver. He couldn't be sure since he couldn't hear him, but it looked like he was whistling.

***

The landscape became more desolate, desert as far as the eye could see. Their clothes acquired dark circles of sweat. A nagging thirst grew in David. An occasional car could be seen going the other way. But remembering how they had been ignored just a couple of days ago, he didn't feel confident in a rescue. But it was a better chance than what faced them now. David's mind raced as he tried to figure out what to do. He saw Pete biting at his restraints. Pete must be getting desperate thought David. He really hated the forced hush that was over them. It reminded him of being in an airplane.

Looking out the front window, he saw another highway mile marker go by. From the signs he had managed to glimpse, they were on their way to Las Vegas. He doubted they would make it that far.

Ellen got right by his ear. "I'm so sorry. I really thought we were safe when I called for the ride. That's not how computers work, how networks work."

David held her hands and squeezed them. "It's alright. How could you know? How could anyone know?"

"I'm afraid." Ellen looked away. She put her head down.

"So am I. I have a plan." David bent over Ellen, toward Pete and spoke so they could hear him. "When we stop and get out, I'm going to rush them, try to tackle one of them. You both start running in opposite directions. I know we're in the desert but I've been seeing cars go by. Stop one any way you can. Get back to LA and the building. Find Katerina. I got you into this, I'm going to try to get you out."

"I'll help you," said Pete.

"It's probably best if only one of us gets shot, Pete. Double the chance of one of you making it."

"Hey, I don't plan on dying!" Pete brought his bound hands down hard on his knees while flexing his elbows apart. The plastic tab in the knuckle snapped, freeing him. Pete grinned like a madman.

Astonished, David looked at his own set and brought up his arms. Pete held his hand up and motioned to David to give him his wrists. Grabbing hold of the tie end, Pete pulled it, tightening them to the point that David thought his circulation was being cut off. Letting go, Pete nodded at David.

David followed Pete's example. The plastic piece holding the ties together snapped. Ellen did the same.

They stuffed the plastic ties into the crack of the seat and held their hands behind their backs. Surprise was their only advantage.

Soon the van slowed and pulled off onto a dirt road leading away from the highway, through an embankment. They rattled down the road for a little bit. The moisture in their clothes made them uncomfortably rub against the vinyl bench as the jolts threw them here and there.

All too soon, the van came to a halt and the man with the ponytail got out with a gym bag in one hand. The driver twisted in his seat and pointed a gun at them with one hand, a fob in the other. As soon as he did that, the forced quiet was lifted. Real silence assaulted their ears. The door to the van beeped while sliding open by itself.

"Get out! Don't try anything," commanded the driver.

Looking at Pete and Ellen, David nodded. Peering out the door, he saw a dust cloud hanging in the air, back by the embankment. Nothing else was around. He couldn't even see the highway from his vantage point. A feeling of desperation flooded him. Thirty feet away, the rider had the open gym bag at his feet and held something that looked like a double barrel shotgun with some blinking LED's attached to it. David didn't know guns well but the two barrels looked comically large.

"I said, get out! I don't want to be breathing you in all the way back." The driver motioned at them with his pistol.

The three carefully made their way out, maintaining the fiction of being restrained. Slick hair got out and went around to join the other man. The driver held his weapon in the direction of the three.

"You're going to shoot us with a shotgun, right by the van?" Pete tilted his head. "Won't that be, messy?"

The man with the double-barrelled weapon shifted his aim slightly and pulled the trigger. A large group of cacti just behind the van immediately turned black and, as the forms started to wither, became wisps of smoke that dissipated in the hot, desert air. A strong smell of ozone filled David's nostrils. An evil grin appeared on the man's face.

"What mess?"

Of course, nobody liked the reply that the hatchet man gave them.

Six

Rescue

A hot breeze blew the pungent, metallic smell away. Pony-tail guy raised his weapon and looked down the twin barrels at them.

Standing in between his friends, David cast a look at each of them and arched his eyebrow at them and spoke, barely above a whisper. clenching his teeth. "Get ready." He hoped they heard him.

The slick hair man raised his hand, pausing the other man. He lowered his pistol and fished around in his front pant's pocket. His compatriot looked confused. Finally, Slick withdrew the key fob and pointed it at the van. Pressing a button on it, the side door started to close, beeping as it crawled shut. It sounded preternaturally loud to David.

The gunman rolled his eyes and sighed as he waited for the go ahead sign from the driver.

David saw his chance. The weapon lowered. "Now!" He charged his would-be murderers, headlong, arms wide. He would buy his friends a chance with his life. He saw the weapon start to rise. He lowered his head.

Something like a clap of thunder rolled across the desert, assailing David's ears. It startled him. He stopped well short of his target, surprised that he was still alive. He looked around.

Lying a couple of yards away was the body of the would be executioner, face down. Or rather, what would have been face down if he hadn't been missing his head. A growing pool of blood watered the rocky scrabble. The driver made a tactical mistake then. He turned to look behind him. He tumbled as another shot resounded across the landscape.

David turned and looked at his companions. The distance between them had grown as they had rushed apart according to plan but now, both stopped their escape attempt. They were standing still, staring at something behind him.

Whirling around, David saw a lone figure on the crest the long mound that hid them from the road. The figure slid down to the desert with a large rifle in their hands and started walking toward them. A long, loose skirt billowed behind her. A large straw hat hid her face in shadow.

He put his hand above his eyes to shelter them from the sun and get a better look. "Katerina? Katerina!" He waved eagerly at her.

The three stood dumbly in the bright light and sweated while they tried to make out her intent. She reached them in a few minutes and marched up to the bodies. She checked each of corpses. She gave a satisfied grunt when she saw the result of her handiwork.

"Katerina, I'm so glad to see you." David forced a weak smile on his face. She came right up to him and threw her arms around David's neck and gave him a perfunctory kiss on the lips. She let go of him and drew back. She looked him right in the eyes and slapped him across the face.

"You idiot! What were you thinking? What were all of you thinking?" She looked at all three of them in turn. All three of them found things to look at beside her gaze.

David rubbed his stinging cheek. "I'm sorry."

"Sorry? Did you think these people were playing? Did you think I was kidding? They tried to kill you, multiple times already!" She poked David in the chest with each punctuation, accentuating the point. "What part of not attracting their attention did you not understand?"

"In all fairness, they have some way of getting information that isn't normal. Computers don't work that way. They hacked into multiple systems and correlated information across them in real time." Ellen had made her way to David's side and stared at Katerina, her voice full of defiance and fire. "Besides, it wasn't his fault. I'm the one who called for the ride."

"No Ellen, I'm the one who told you to do it. It's my fault." David was still feeling guilty for what happened. He glanced up at Katerina.

"How did you even find us?" asked Pete.

Katerina pulled David over and spun him around. She put her hand on his waist and ran it between him and his pants.

"Hey!" said a startled David.

She pulled out a thin, brown fabric patch, shaped like an ellipse.

"You bugged him? Way to go, Kat!" said Pete.

"And a good thing too! I barely made it in time. Another second and poof!, you'd all be gone!"

"Yeah, what the hell is that thing?" Pete walked over to where the gun was lying by the assassin and bent down to retrieve it.

"Don't mess with it!" Katerina yelled at Pete. "It's got some sort of failsafe built in. If anybody else tries to use it, it blows up, leaving a big hole in the ground."

Pete stood up and backed away a couple of steps. "We can't leave it here. If it's that dangerous, someone could get hurt if they ran across it."

"Put it back in the gym bag and we'll take it with us," said David. "Hold the bag open, Pete. Katerina, can we safely pick it up?"

A quick nod from Katerina and they slid the weapon into the bag. Picking up the dusty, now heavy gym bag, they walked back slowly in the heat to the cut in the embankment. Just on the other side, a four door sedan waited for them.

David wondered what had happened to his minivan. "Where are we going now?"

"You promise not to run away again?"

"I promise."

"We're heading to San Francisco, to meet with Dr. Shtern. After your little stunt, we had to close up and leave in a hurry. He says he found something."

David was impressed. "That fast?"

"He said they weren't trying to hide it."

"We have some stuff to tell you, too. We met with some sort of big shot. Sort of."

"Really?" Katerina popped the trunk of the sedan open. A familiar grey box was already in it. She place the sniper rifle and the gym bag next to it. "Get in. You can tell me all about it while I drive. We've got a ways to go."

***

Dusk had already settled on San Francisco when they arrived. These last few days left David feeling whiplashed from all the highs and lows. He knew he wasn't cut out for this. But guilt over the fact that he got his friends into this predicament kept him from giving up.

They'd spent the long ride talking about what happened. David mostly spoke while he sat in the front seat. Ellen and Pete would clarify from the back. They racked their brains to come up with every detail about their meeting with Robert.

"That's technology that doesn't currently exist. Even how they tracked us shouldn't be possible, with what we have. Not even some mythical three-letter agency can do that in real time, anyway," said Ellen.

"And what about that weapon?" added Pete. "It looked like it just vaporized the cactus."

"What else do you guys know about them? You're holding back. It almost got us killed," said David.

Katerina pursed her lips. She started, "First off, you running away is what almost got you killed. But I'll try to fill you in. From what we know about them, they've been around for a long time." "

"Long time? Like how long?" said David.

"Early 1900's. Before World War One, in fact. Or something like them, anyway."

David cocked his head. "Are you serious? How is that possible?"

Katerina shrugged as she drove. "I don't know. The records are incomplete. Almost like they've been tampered with. So I don't exactly trust them."

"Are they part of some government?" asked David.

"They aren't part of any government, as far as we can tell," Katerina continued. "But all the reports have encounters with individuals, with the luxury of hindsight, as having 'inappropriate technology'."

Ellen looked thoughtful. "The desk thing? We can create holograms from scratch now. But not full motion, not transmitted. Not yet anyway."

"That's the pattern. Nothing outrageous, mind you. Just stuff that's slightly ahead of it's time." Katerina kept her eyes on the road the whole time.

"Whoa, that means that gun is around the corner too!" Pete's eyes went wide with realization

"Exactly. Somebody, somewhere has the basics of it already. Frightening, isn't it?" Katerina gave a tiny shudder.

Ellen leaned forward. "What else do you know about them?"

"Not much more, I'm afraid. I've been searching for them for a few years now. People don't usually survive an encounter with them. You were very lucky."

The toll of the day and now this knowledge overwhelmed David. "How do we even fight them?"

"We have a few surprises. And they confirmed what they were after. Somehow, we have to get whatever is in that signal out to everyone." Katerina sounded confident.

"I don't think we can just email it or upload it to the cloud. If they can override a ride app on a phone, they can probably do other things, like delete or change what we send," said David.

"I have an idea. I'm going to need a laptop." Ellen mimicked typing in the air.

"That, I can get you," said Katerina.

***

They met with Dr. Shtern atop a hotel by the convention center. The dim, cavernous room had enormous circular windows overlooking the city. The bartender relaxed against the counter behind the bar with her arms folded. David marveled at the emptiness of the bar, given his prior experience at Sullivan's, until he thought about the night sky being so prominently on display.

He was drawn to that view by a few familiar bright friends dotting the upper panes and was glad to see Shtern sitting in an upholstered armchair by the expanse of glass. Pulling one of the chairs away from the low, round table where Shtern was sitting, he angled it toward the window. From that vantage point, David looked out over the darkened streets. There was plenty of traffic with the yellowish lights of the headlights chasing shadows as lines of cars travelled in their gridded order. He wondered how much of the world was going to change in response to what was on the transmission he had unwittingly captured.

Katerina and Shtern were engaged in conversation. The doctor, a bit away from everyone, was going on about something. David ignored them, lost in the enormity of what Katerina had revealed. Mankind had waited so long for a word from Others. He could just make out Arcturus, over to the west, the source of their current problems. David let the soft murmur of their conversation wash over him as he stared out the faceted picture window.

"... in 1974, correct? Hello, David. Are you joining us?" said the Doctor.

David turned around. Everyone was looking at him.

"I missed your question. What was it?" he responded back.

"The message. That we sent. This response followed a similar format. It had the number of bits equal to three prime numbers, forming frames in the message. I have the data here." Shtern slid a USB drive across the table toward him.

David eyed it with suspicion. He hesitated before picking it up and said, "The last one got me in all sorts of trouble."

"And now's your chance to get back at them and get out of trouble." Katerina sounded downright cheerful.

Holding the USB drive in his fist, David looked right at the Doctor. "What did the message say?"

"The first frame has a numbering system on it and what I am assuming to be some definition of measurements and a map of our solar system. With the third planet high-lighted with a picture of a radio dish by it. The next three frames are broken up into two sections. The first section of the next three frames has numbers that look related to some of the measurements on the first frame. The second section looks like a random string of data. Parts of it are in common across the three frames. I have no idea what the last frame means. It's got a number of pictograms on it. One of them is a circle with something in it." David realized that Shtern sounded like his most hated professor when he was lecturing. The man threatened to make this discovery sound boring.

"Do you have it printed out?"

The doctor snorted. "I do, in fact. Here." He fished around in his briefcase and pulled out a folder that he placed on the table in front of David.

David's hands trembled as he picked it up. Opening it, he looked at the first page. There, in black and white, was a crude pixel picture. His heart raced as he realized that, in his hands, he held a communication from the stars. "This was in the data? For real?" He spoke just above a whisper.

"Yes, of course it was."

"Wow, just wow!" David felted humbled.

"Can we see it?" Ellen and Pete craned their heads, trying to see.

David closed the folder and passed it to them. "We have to get this out. We just have to."

"Who's going to believe us?" Ellen had the folder open with Pete looking over her shoulder, her eyes wide as she flipped through the pages.

"Believing us won't be a problem. We first have to get it out to everyone. You said you had an idea?" Katerina leaned in, closer to Ellen.

Ellen leaned back in her chair and closed the folder before putting it on the table. "Yeah, I need a fast laptop and a connection to the Internet. And time, of course."

"There's an office I suppose you could use. Nothing fancy. But I doubt you're used to better. I don't know how much time you'll have. That depends on you staying out of sight. Unlike last time." Shtern managed to sound angry and condescending at the same time. David wondered if the man ever said anything kind.

"The more time I have, the better. I'll be able to get more copies out."

Shtern nodded.

"There's more." Shtern seemed very relaxed for the news he was saying.

A small thrill ran through David. "What do you mean, more?"

"I ran an FFT on a small portion of the signal. Sure enough, I found this data ten hertz off the carrier, just like our message that we sent. But I also got a spike at a higher frequency. There's more information hidden in the signal. That's going to take some time to tease out."

"Will you be joining us in the office?" Katerina studied the pictures in the folio, not looking up to speak to Dr. Shtern.

The doctor got a look of disgust on his face. "Oh no! Far too risky. I'm headed to San Jose where I can blend in easier. I need some serious computing power."

"Can you get us what we need by tomorrow?" Katerina wasn't done with him.

"That shouldn't be a problem. But everything is closed tomorrow. You mentioned that they can spy on computers and networks? You start sending stuff out and you'll stick out like a sore thumb to them. I don't need to remind you what will happen next. If you wait until Monday, there's a better chance you'll blend in." Dr. Shtern paused for a moment. "Besides, I have an idea for a device that you might need. That will take me all day to get tomorrow. I'll also get you some burner phones, so we can stay in touch. "

Ellen nodded in agreement. "That's a good idea. Judging by what happened yesterday, I'm inclined to believe it."

"Of course it's a good idea. I'll get you everything and leave it in the office for you." Shtern curtly finished. He got his briefcase and left without even saying good-bye.

Ellen waited until he was out of earshot. "He's a real charmer."

"What do we do now?" said David.

"We relax, have a couple of drinks, eat some dinner." Katerina waved at one of the bored waitstaff.

"I can get behind that!" Pete enthusiastically said.

David was suddenly ravenous.

"Can we get some clothes too? We've been wearing the same outfits for four days now," said Ellen.

"We can take care of that tomorrow."

***

David felt refreshed the next morning. The comfortable bed and sheets were such a luxury after the last few days. And the hot shower was heavenly, even if he did have to put his dirty clothes back on. He hoped to remedy that soon as he put his well-worn black sports coat back on against the surprising San Francisco chill.

They had all agreed to meet in the lobby in the morning. David tried to get there early. He had noticed a coffee shop off the lobby of the hotel. He figured a danish and a cup of joe would do him good. Pete was already down in the lobby, at the business center on a computer.

Alarmed, David went over to him. "Hey Pete, whatcha doing?"

"Just reading some news. People are not handling this well." Pete looked up at David. "Don't worry, I didn't check my email or sign in or anything like that." Pete closed the windows and got up.

"I was going to get some coffee. Before our adventure."

"Sounds like a great idea. Let's go. But I gotta tell you, I'm sick of adventure. I've had enough. You seen Ellen or Kat yet?"

"Nope, not down yet."

"Maybe you and me can grab some money from Kat and just go shopping on our own. That way, we'll be back quick."

"I don't think it's a good idea to leave Ellen or Katerina together, alone."

"Yeah, you're probably right. And here they come."

A smiling Katerina, dressed in yoga pants and oversize hoodie, got off the elevator. David was surprised to see Ellen wearing a oversized sweater, obviously Katerina's. Her lips curled in a smile. It made him happy to see her like that.

Katerina marched right up to him and gave him a hug. "Good morning." David looked at Ellen, alarmed at how she would react. "Are we ready to go?" She released him from her embrace and hooked her arm in one elbow.

"Sure we are." Ellen came up to David and took him by the other arm. David was too astounded to say anything as they walked him out the door. Just before exiting the hotel, David looked over his shoulder. Pete longingly gazed at the coffee shop and followed.

They spent the morning shopping. David reassessed his previous comment about the two women. Glancing at his male friend, he noticed that Pete had a big grin on his face, particularly as David got manhandled between the two women.

Lunch came and he got a chance to sit down. Flanked by both women. Pete sat opposite of them. David was beginning to get resentful of Pete's ever-widening grin. But some beers arrived and after downing one while waiting for their food to arrive, he began to unwind. The good food and another beer helped ease his anxiety.

Pete got up to use the bathroom. "Old age calling," as he put it. Ellen grabbed one of the shopping bags and said she was going to change into something other than her shorts and tee-shirt and not to go anywhere.

While the two were gone, David looked at Katerina. Her first beer sat warm and half-full, next to her plate. She seemed to be looking around every so often.

"David, can I ask you a question?"

"Uh, sure."

"Back in the desert, looking through my scope, I thought I saw you start running toward the gunmen. What were you thinking?"

David took a sip of his beer. He spoke clearly. "I thought that I had to give my friends a chance at getting away."

"You would have ended up dead."

David shrugged. "I was going to end up dead anyway. If I managed to help them live, then I thought that was a fair trade."

Katerina looked at him, slightly nodding her head. Silence, interrupted by the cutlery against the plate, descended on the two.

"Why so quiet?" Pete pulled his chair out.

"Oh, hey, not at all. We were just talking while you were gone. And I got hungry." Katerina took a sip of her neglected beer.

Pete looked questioning at David. David shrugged and took a bite of his meal.

"Did you know there's a spa at the hotel?" Ellen had changed into some pants and blouse with a light jacket "Come on, Katerina. It'll be relaxing. We can get matching manicures."

Katerina's eyes went wide with horror. "I don't know."

"It'll be fun. And it will keep us in the hotel."

"Go on, Kat. You two can bond and relax." Pete turned his smile on Katerina.

"I guess." Katerina resigned herself to defeat.

"Hey, that's what friends are for!" Pete lifted his glass. "To friends!"

They all lifted their glasses and toasted. David felt at ease.

Katerina paid their bill. Gathering their packages, they all left the restaurant. Pete told them off-color jokes. They were all laughing, even when a light malfunctioned and turned green while they were in the middle of the crosswalk.

David felt that he was ready for whatever came their way. The start of the week would be the start of him taking back his life.

Seven

Relief

The ride to the office in the morning was short in distance but long on time. Several demonstrations were going on, spilling into the streets with people intent on garnering converts. Some groups had signs proclaiming the end was near and an equal number had signs welcoming the new rulers of Earth. Every light conspired against them leaving them mired in the crowds.

David couldn't help to stare out the windows. "This is crazy!"

"What exactly did you expect in a big city?" Katerina slowly drove the car down the street separating the two opposing forces. The police tried their best to corral the masses to the sidewalks.

"I don't know. It wasn't this bad back home. I thought people would start calming down."

Katerina tapped the brakes. A demonstrator had stepped out into the road. "You missed the fun times in Indio."

Pete's lips silently moved as he looked at the messages being thrust at each other and them. "This is why we need to get that message out. It'll give people hope."

"We don't know what it means yet." Ellen leaned forward and gripped the back of the seat behind Katerina. Her nails were freshly painted. "Only the first frame makes sense. We need to figure out what the other parts mean."

"I'm going to get help from the astronomers that were studying the Eyes. I know someone there." The way ahead cleared for Katerina and she started to distance them from the crowd.

"What about the fact that we're being chased by psychopathic murderers?" Pete cheerfully added.

"We have to be careful not to attract their attention. They can come down hard on you, like a sledgehammer on an eggshell." Katerina slammed on the brakes as the light changed to red.

"And we're the eggshells." Pete laughed at this.

Katerina frowned.

Soon they pulled into a parking garage and took the express elevator up to their floor. Katerina led them to an inside office. Past the door was a single, large room with a familiar mesh covering the ceiling, walls and floor. A couple of desks occupied the space. One desk had a black, plastic box about the size of a piece of carryon luggage, with handles on either end. The other had a brown paper bag on it and a charcoal grey, beefy looking laptop. A yellow Post-It note was affixed to its closed cover.

Ellen gravitated toward the laptop, Katerina toward the black luggage.

"Sweet!" Ellen looked at the logo and flipped the laptop open. "This is some high-end shit! I bet it's got a discrete GPU!"

"Like what you need for games?" said David who stood by her.

"No, doofus, so I can run the calculations I need. I've got a bunch of stuff to download so let me get started." She pulled an office chair over and pulled the note off of the top of the machine. "Dipshit set the password to 'password'," she said looking at the note. And with that, Ellen got to work.

David stared at her for a moment as her fingers flew over the keyboard. By the looks of it, she was going to be busy for a while. He wandered over to where Katerina and Pete were standing. The top half of the case had been removed and placed on the desk, next to the bottom half. He could see the word "RELIEF" stenciled on top. He leaned in to look at the exposed components.

There were two cylinders of unequal size laying side by side. The smaller one had an insulated line running from it to the other cylinder. The larger cylinder had caution stickers all over it with warning to stand at a distance. Thick wires ran into either end of that cylinder. A toggle switch that said "Arm" and a keypad with an LED display over it completed what was visible.

Katerina had her hands on her hips, looking impressed. Pete stood next to her, mouth agape.

David spoke up. "What, what is it?"

"This is our ace in the hole." Katerina waved her hand over it. "It's an EMP bomb."

David gave a low whistle. "How does it work?"

"Flip the switch, punch in the delay and get the hell out. Or my personal favorite." Katerina held up a small fob. "Use the remote."

"Isn't it, well, bad to use this in a city?" Pete seemed genuinely concerned.

"This is a small one. According to the specs, it's only supposed to effect three or four blocks," said Katerina.

"I hope we don't have to use it," said David.

Pete looked thoughtful. "That's some serious weaponry. Have you ever used one?"

"No."

"I hate to think what would happen to all the machines around it. People could get hurt."

Katerina grimaced. "It is a last resort thing."

An hour went by. And another. Pete and Katerina had taken Relief to the car while Ellen worked on her project. David sat by her until he saw the other two return. Grabbing the paper bag, he passed out the phones to everyone.

Handing Katerina a phone, he quietly asked, "Where do we go next?"

"The airport. It should be safe. I want the quickest way to get us to New York. The consortium studying the Eyes is headquartered there. I know the director and I believe he'll help us. After that, the UN, I would imagine."

"I can't believe my data has caused all these problems."

"Which reminds me. Here." Katerina dug in her pocket and pulled out David's old memory stick. "This is yours."

David forced himself to take the drive. "Uh, thanks?"

"No problem. It is yours, after all. Still, I'd keep your eye on it. I wouldn't let it get into the hands of the adversary."

David nodded solemnly.

Katerina then leaned close to David. He could feel her breath on his face. "I wonder how much time Ellen needs? We probably should get going." She smiled her thousand watt smile at him. David felt his heart skip a beat.

"Well, wonder no more!" Ellen stood up and stretched. "I'm done! And not a moment too soon! Let's blow this taco stand."

"Ellen! That's wonderful!" David backed away from Katerina and turned toward Ellen. "What did you do?"

"I was able to find the components on the Internet. A little shell scripting, a little Python and voila! I generated an image of each of the frames that I XOR'ed that with a one-time pad that I randomly produced. I then published the pad and the encrypted picture on Freenet and sent out emails to newspapers saying if you look at these two blocks and xor them together, you get something interesting." Ellen looked pleased.

"What's to stop them from finding those two files and corrupting them?" Katerina had a small frown.

Ellen smile broadened. "I automated the process and it does it over and over again. I even publish fake ones so they can't tell the real ones from the fake ones."

Katerina seemed impressed. "That's brilliant."

"The longer we let it run, the better. More copies get sent out. I set up an email to collect some of the instances. Now, I think it's time to go." Ellen put her arm around David's waist and led him toward the door. "Coming?" she called out over her shoulder while she walked out the door.

Katerina halted as though she was thinking of something but Pete caught up with her and they followed.

In the hallway, they stopped at the elevator. David pressed the call button when everyone had caught up. He turned to face the group.

"I'm so glad that we all are getting along. I know we had a rough start, but we got a lot done today. And we did it by working together. That makes me happy. I'm glad that you guys are my friends. This is how we start hitting back at them."

The elevator dinged and David heard the door open behind him. He turned to go in while thinking of how to convince people to look at what had been published on the Internet.

Hands on each of his shoulders yanked him hard toward the rear. His feet slipped and he tumbled backward, his head almost hitting the floor. "Ouch! What the..." He saw a look of horror on both Ellen and Katerina's faces, the people attached to the hands that had pulled him back.

"Dude! Look at the door!" Pete, his eyes round, pointed at the elevator.

David's gaze travelled to the open door. Blackness filled the frame.

"Oh shit..." Slowly, he got to his feet with the help of the two women. He took a step toward the door. He wanted to see if the elevator was anywhere in sight.

"Don't!" hissed Katerina. "Don't go near the door! The safeties have been overridden!"

"What? How? I mean, how did they find us?" He looked around. His eyes settled on a small, smoky, translucent hemisphere in the ceiling. "Cameras?"

Ellen looked dismayed. "Cameras are all over the city. They must be tapping into the security feeds somehow." She waved her hand to encompass all of San Francisco.

"How did they even know to look for us here?" said Pete.

"It could be anything. Any access to the Internet could be enough for them. Even from appliances, IoT, that sort of thing."

"Oh oh." Pete had an alarmed look on his face. "Yesterday, I checked some news sites. But I didn't use any of my accounts. I thought that's what they were looking for."

"We all have digital fingerprints. You just have to sift for them." Ellen's expression changed to alarmed.

"But how are they picking up a video feed?" Pete frowned.

"If you have a sensitive enough receiver, you can pick up any signal. It happens all the time to radio telescopes." David was re-evaluating the capabilities of these people.

"We're fucked," said Ellen.

"We just have to plan for it. Come on, down the stairs! Those are manual things and they can't control them!" Katerina ran toward the stairs. The crew followed her.

"Is it getting warm in here?" Ellen fanned herself while Katerina studied the door's locking mechanisms.

Pete reached his hand up toward one of the vents. "I think they're blowing hot air now."

Smoke started to come out of the vents. Katerina kicked open the door and they started down the stairs. A couple of floors later and the sprinklers came on, dousing them with foul smelling water.

"Of course," said David. "Watch out people. The floor is slippery now." They slowly made their way down the steps in the hot. stinking, humid air to the parking garage exit door.

Coming out, Ellen paused for a second when she saw a camera and extended her middle finger at it. They got to Katerina's automobile and got in.

The gate wouldn't lift for them at the exit. Katerina gunned the accelerator and broke through the bar.

In the street, she merged into the rushing traffic at speed, narrowly avoiding getting hit. Horns blared.

"Whew, hey, Katerina, I know we have to leave but can we be careful?" David gripped the crash handle over the door.

Katerina spoke through gritted teeth. "They are trying to delay us. They probably have someone on the way."

A traffic light halted them.

"Are we on our way to the airport now?"

"Yes, we have a flight to catch. We should have plenty of time."

"Couldn't we have just sent the Consortium an email with Ellen's stuff?"

Katerina frowned and nodded. "I should have thought of that. I should have given you those emails. I'm sorry Ellen."

Ellen shook her head in a succession of tiny, quick no's. "Yeah, I don't think I want to go back and change the program now."

"I was trying to think, how do we get the news agencies to open the mail you sent them?" asked David.

Pete craned his neck from the back seat to look at the traffic light hanging over their lane and pointed at it. "Say, isn't this traffic light staying red a little too long?"

David looked out the window. There were traffic cameras mounted on the poles. His mouth opened. "Oh no!"

Katerina had a grim look on her face. "Hang on!" And she floored the gas pedal.

The sedan leapt into the crossing traffic. Tires screeched to a halt and cars fishtailed around them. A slight tap on the rear quarter panel as they crossed the intersection and sped toward the next light which was cycling to red.

"We're not going to make it!" David yelped while he braced against the dashboard with both hands.

Katerina had a steely glint in her eyes. "Oh yes, we will!"

The sedan continued to gain speed and it roared through the intersection as the light turned red.

"Watch out!"

Ahead the cars were already stopped at the light as they approached at break-neck speed. She pumped the brakes and furiously spun the wheel sending the car down an alleyway. Righting the wheel, she came out on the next street over, hitting the gas when she cleared the corner and turning on the street. The oncoming traffic swerved out of the way.

"Oh fuck! We're going the wrong way!" screamed Ellen. Her hands were up in her face attempting to block the view.

"I don't think this is a good idea!" David's heart pounded in his chest. "And I'm thinking maybe going to the airport is a bad idea. If they can do this to us, on the ground, imagine what they could do to a plane."

Katerina cut over to the side and got off the one-way road. She roared down another alleyway and turned onto yet another street. This one, thankfully, was going the right way.

"I think we need some relief. Kat?" Pete sounded calm.

"I think you're right, Pete." Katerina thought for a second. "We need to ditch this car. There's a place a few blocks from here we can do that."

"You have a plan?" asked David.

"I do. I'm hoping that Shtern is a creature of habit."

Half a dozen or so harrowing blocks later, they pulled into a multi-story parking garage. Katerina slowly drove around each of the floors only going up after inspecting each car.

"What are you looking for?" David looked at each car too, unsure of what she was searching for.

"That." Katerina pointed at a car. A shiny black and chrome car with rectangular tail lights was in the space.

Pete was agog. "*That's* his car?"

David looked at Pete and wondered what was causing Pete to get excited. "Is it a good car?"

"Are you kidding? It's a classic muscle car. Look at the triangular back windows. It's got an SS emblem on it. It ..."

"It doesn't have electronics that make it go," interrupted Katerina. "We're going to need that."

Pete snapped his mouth shut. "Right."

"What's the plan?" said David.

"You and Pete take Relief up to the top floor and arm it. Ellen, help me unload and go park this car. I'm going to break into Shtern's and hotwire it."

***

David's arms were tired from hauling the heavy box that housed Relief up the stairway. There was no way he going to chance an elevator. Finally, he pushed open the door to the top floor of the parking garage with his back and took a deep breath of the cool air.

"I wonder if we are going to make it out of this alive." Pete's own labored breathing drew his sentence out.

"I don't know Pete. I'm really sorry I dragged you and Ellen into this. They seem really determined to get rid of us. We've been barely staying a step ahead of them."

"But Kat is helping us. And Ellen got the data out. We'll figure out what to do to get them to back off." Pete and David put the box down in the middle of the parking floor, under a clear, blue sky.

"I think it's going to have to be something drastic. What, I don't know."

Pete nodded. He lifted the cover off the box. David reached down and flipped the switch to the "Arm" position. The small box vibrated. "Do we put the cover back on?" said Pete.

"Yeah, I think so. And we lock it. I don't think Katerina wants it accidentally getting unarmed. Disarmed. Whatever."

They put the cover back on and David thumbed the combination wheels. They went back down the stairs to where Katerina and Ellen should be waiting.

The throaty sound of a big block V-8 greeted them. The driver's side tinted window rolled down and Katerina said, "Get in!"

The two men raced to the passenger side of the car. David opened the door and Pete tilted the front seat back forward and slid into the expansive back seat with Ellen. David pushed it back and got into the bucket seat. A gear shift with an 8-ball on it was between him and the driver. A little green cardboard pine tree hung from the rearview mirror.

Katerina tossed him the remote to Relief. "I don't want you to press it yet. If necessary, we want to be as far away as possible. Otherwise, all the cars on the street are going to block our escape."

David held the remote gingerly. "Where are we off to?"

"Oakland. We have a train to catch." She put the car into gear and eased off the clutch.

"Won't they be looking for us?"

"Maybe. But maybe changing cars will give them the slip and we won't have to use Relief."

They slipped into traffic on the street without a hitch. The automatic gate had opened for them just like it did for the line of other cars ahead of them. They casually turned onto the street after leaving the garage. The lights seemed to be behaving. They managed to go a few blocks and were waiting at a light. The highway on-ramp beckoned a couple of lights ahead of them. David was starting to feel hopeful.

"There's something happening behind us." Pete's words were an icy dash. "Looks like the lights are going crazy." David turned around and saw the traffic lights rapid cycling through all the changes.

"Hit it!" commanded Katerina.

David looked at the remote's single red button. Holding his breath, he pressed it.

***

The button press caused a radio wave to be emitted from the remote. It travelled in all directions at the speed of light, reaching the top floor of the garage and fell across on the antenna built into the case that housed Relief. The onboard processor decoded a series of modulations in the wave and recognized that it was meant for it. In a few nanoseconds, it decided to act. A number of relays were closed, dumping all the current stored in a bank of capacitors into a coil built from a high temperature superconductor kept cold by the liquid nitrogen in an accompanying Dewar. The current, wound around and around the coil and built an enormous magnetic field surrounding a copper sleeve with a slit in it.

The field bled into the copper tube and become constricted by it since copper isn't magnetic. Despite the cold, the windings of the coil started to fuse under the onslaught of the current. But that's alright; they weren't meant to be used twice.

A timer that was started when the radio signal was first received became zero. The magnetic field reached full strength. A different relay closed, detonating the explosive jacket around the larger coil and, more importantly, the copper tube. The tube collapsed in an instant, pinching and cutting the magnetic lines of force, converting a portion of the explosive power into part of the effect.

Even though the magnetic field can't be seen, it was still very much a physical thing and now, a ten Tesla field was severed and not allowed to collapse back into the now gone coil. A very powerful pulse propagated out at the speed of light centered on Relief. Originally built to tackle military rated electronics, it wrecked even greater havoc on unprotected consumer grade electronics. Electric currents far in excess of what the electrical components could handle were induced in the circuit board traces in proportion to the distance from the device. Indeed, every wire around it became an antenna for the pulse, picking it up and sending it down their length, effecting far-flung systems, damaging things beyond its intended area of effect. In a modern city as connected as San Francisco, half the city shut down as systems fried and safeties kicked in.

***

Letting out a gasp, David looked up from the remote. The traffic light over them was out. Cars rolled to a stop all around them as their computer controlled engines cut out.

"I guess we weren't out of the zone," said Katerina while she weaved around the dead cars. They got on the highway and rumbled across the bridge toward Oakland.

Eight

Journey into the East

I t took them the better part of an hour to cross the bridge and reach the train station. Traffic was backed up and snarled although David couldn't tell if the lights were still working against them. It seemed to be affecting everyone. When they finally pulled into the parking lot, several police cars were there, running their lights.

Pete stared out the small back window. "Uh oh, this doesn't look so good."

David nodded.

Katerina found an empty space away from the front of the station and parked. Turning to her passengers, she said, "I'm going to go in and see about buying us tickets."

Ellen leaned forward putting her face between the seats. "They probably know what you look like now. There's bound to be cameras in there."

Katerina's mouth formed a moue. "Do you have a suggestion?"

"I do. Buy the tickets over the phone. Then, we drive."

Katerina grinned, showing her teeth. "I can see why you keep her around, David."

David smiled back weakly.

A few minutes later and the purchase of four tickets on the Zephyr, they were back on the surface roads, headed toward the Interstate. Again, heavy traffic slowed their progress.

From his backseat post, Pete kept looking around. "Doesn't this seem odd? Is traffic this heavy around Oakland all the time? It's not rush hour. And why would have the police been there?"

"Hang on. Maybe I can get a local station that'll explain what's going on." David reached over and pushed the radio button. A tune about somebody watching the singer blared out of the speakers. Hastily lowering the volume, David then went for the tuning knob. He watched the orange needle go between the numbers on a little glass plate. Static faded as a different station frequency was found.

A loud, screeching tone played several times. A loud voice spoke. "Do not panic! Please do not leave your homes. Shelter in place. Wait for the all clear to be sounded. Currently, about half the city was affected by the unprecedented terrorist attack. Police are..." David switched it off. Wide eyed, he looked at his companions. Ellen was holding her hand over her open mouth. Pete looked upset, wringing his hands. Katerina kept mumbling to herself, "3 to 4 blocks, 3 to 4 blocks."

They drove in stunned silence, journeying into the east.

Some hours later, just past Reno, one of the phones that Dave had on him started to vibrate. David pulled it out of his pocket. With trepidation, he flipped it open.

"You set Relief off in the city? What the hell is wrong with you people?" Dr. Shtern was talking so loudly that the entire car could hear him.

"Everything around us was being used by them. Traffic lights, elevators, sprinkler systems, everything. We didn't have a choice."

"And you couldn't come up with something better to do than to set it off in the middle of San Francisco?"

"We were in danger."

"What a day. It's taken me all afternoon to get back from San Jose, thanks to your idiocy." Doctor Shtern paused, his voice almost normal now. "That's strange. I thought I parked here. Where is my car? It was right here." David could clearly hear the Doctor.

"Uh, yeah, about that..."

"WHERE IS MY CAR? YOU TOOK MY BETSY?"

It was crystal clear in David's mind how the Doctor's face looked at the moment, red with anger and veins pulsing, spittle coming out as he heard the inchoate words sputtering out. He closed the phone. "I think you're going to have to talk to him later," he said with a serious face to Katerina.

They kept driving the stolen car, further from the owner.

Late that night they finally pulled into a motel along the southern shore of the Great Salt Lake. They were grateful to stretch their legs so they walked down the street to eat some fast food tacos that nobody liked.

Ellen took a bite of her taco and spoke with her mouth full. "I thought spies were all about the glamorous life."

"Pass the hot sauce. Ha! That's funny." Katerina unwrapped her own food.

Pete swallowed and paused in his eating. "So what three letter agency do you work for? NSA? CIA? ONR?" He clearly was unwilling to let the question go unanswered.

"Pshaw, none of those."

"Of course, what else could you say?"

"David, my honor is being impugned. Defend me."

David chewed and took a sip of his drink as the other three looked at him. "Guys, I have it on good authority that it's classified." He quickly took another bite, the loud crunch of the shell a punctuation to his comment. The other three guffawed.

Later, as they headed back to the motel with Pete and Ellen ahead of them, David spoke to Katerina. "I know it was funny, but I wonder what other secrets you're keeping secrets from us. That's going to catch up, sooner or later. It might end up hurting someone. It might hurt you. We're all in this together."

Katerina stopped. David halted alongside of her. "David, is that a concern you have? Toward me?"

The other two walked ahead, oblivious to David and Katerina stopping.

David felt his ears heating up. "Yes, I do care about you. And I'm glad that we all are getting along. That's important to me. But secrets have a way of dividing people. I'd like to keep Pete and Ellen happy."

"You mean, your girlfriend?"

"She's not my girlfriend." And David started walking again toward the other two who had finally stopped when the noticed their missing comrades, leaving Katerina to catch up.

***

The next morning as they drove on the back roads toward the east, the car radio delivered grim news. There had been a plane disaster yesterday and a train had derailed overnight. The twin accidents had been so terrible that rescuers were having troubles finding the bodies. In light of the attack on San Francisco, people on the call in lines had an edge of panic and many questioned if the aliens responsible for the Eyes were involved. Everyone in the car felt disheartened.

Ellen slumped in the corner of the backseat. "It's like they can reach out and touch any computer system."

"We suspected that, but never really had proof." Katerina responded while never taking her eyes off the road.

"And then they sent people in to dispose of any survivors? They are evil." Pete ground his teeth.

"It looks that way. We have to do something and soon. I don't know what." Silence reigned for many miles in the car after David spoke.

At a gas station, when David exited the restroom, he found a five dollar bill. He couldn't believe his good fortune and immediately knew how to spend it.

An old woman sat on folding chair by the entrance to the gas pumps, an orange bucket by her side. While Ellen and Pete shopped for some snacks and Katerina pumped the gas, he went up to her and bought a red carnation.

He walked up to Katerina with the flowers behind his back while she put the pump handle away. "I have something for you."

Katerina cocked her head. "With what? How?"

He presented one of the flowers to her. "Found some money. Just a little something for you because you have helped us so much."

Katerina half smirked. "Are you sure that's why?"

"I have other reasons."

Katerina took the flower. Her lips pressed flat and her brow started to knit together. She stared at the flower for a second, her hand made a slow movement to the side but she stopped and brought it up to her nose. Her eyes softened. Speaking through the bloom, she said, "Thank you." She put the flower on the dash and walked to the store to pay for the gas.

David smiled. Ellen came out with Pete in tow. She was staring after Katerina. Her eyes squinted and she shook her head.

Snacks and gas secured, they continued on the byways. Ellen didn't mention the flower on the driver side dash.

The group pulled into a fast food burger place for dinner that night. Crowded into an uncomfortable booth, the four of them had their trays partitioning the table between them. Each had their hamburger and fries arrayed before them.

Pete, who sat next to David, had dumped his fries on paper wrapper from the sandwich, a small puddle of ketchup next to it. "Do you guys know how close we get to Chicago?"

"It wouldn't be far out of the way. But it is a delay. I was hoping to get to New York as fast as possible." Katerina's fries were in their cardboard container, with a little paper cup full of ketchup next to it. Her hamburger was held in the wrapper.

Ellen squinted at Pete. Her mouth had just taken a bite of her meal which had sandwiched a good portion of the fries between the buns of her burger. "What's in Chicago?"

"I don't know, Pete. It's not quite on the way. Why are you asking?" David's own tray had fries scattered on it. Ketchup from a paper cup had been squeezed out onto the tray's paper lining. He had his hamburger on top of its crumpled and flattened wrapper.

"Well, I've been trying to get ahold of my mom ever since the Eyes appeared. I'm a little worried about her. Last time I tried to call her was the night your apartment got broken into." Pete dipped a fry into the vinegary tomato sauce. He had a hopeful look on his face.

"I hate to point this out, but we didn't do so good in the last big city we were in." Ellen spoke between mouthfuls of meat and potatoes. "And we don't have Relief with us this time around."

"We don't have to go into the actual city. It's outside," Pete added.

David thoughtfully chewed his food. "I don't know. Would it help us?" He looked at Katerina across from him.

"It might keep them from figuring out that we're headed to New York." Pete took a bite of his cooling meal.

Katerina snorted. "They know. It's where the consortium is, after all. Where else would we be heading?"

Pete would not stop. "Maybe it will throw their timing off?" Katerina answered with a shrug.

Pete was persistent. "I don't think she's doing well. Dave, you remember when she came for a visit when you first moved in?"

Whatever Pete was doing was working. Dave felt guilty. The prospect of hearing Pete go on for a couple of days while they got closer to Chicago gave him a case of anxiety.

"David, how can you say no? Pete's been our friend for a long time, much longer than we've know her." Ellen cast a quick glance at Katerina.

David asked Katerina, "When will we reach Chicago?"

A sigh escaped her as she ate. "Barring any incidents, we'll be by Chicago in two days, probably around late afternoon."

"Thanks, guys, for considering it. I wouldn't have brought it up but I don't think it would be a good idea to call her, under our present circumstances."

David nodded. His friend was right. At the moment, visiting her was probably the safest solution to Pete's problem. He would feel better though if an expert agreed. "Do you think it's safe, Katerina?"

"You're asking me now? I suppose, if it's quick. Hopefully, we'll get in and out before anyone notices."

"For fuck's sake! Our friend is worried about his mother!" an exasperated Ellen blurted out.

Katerina stared at David with a tired expression. David couldn't help to sigh.

"OK, we'll go see your mom."

"I really appreciate it. You won't regret it." Pete's smiled from ear to ear.

***

A couple of days and 1000 miles later, the cityscape of Chicago rose from the plains. Dave looked at the tall buildings to the north and wondered how the masses of humanity were dealing with the knowledge that they had published. The radio ran stories about the mysterious pictures received via email and a statement had been issued about the potential that a 138'th star had been present.

Listening to some forgotten song, David thought about the small and very human problem they were trying to solve of visiting Pete's mom. If they couldn't do something so trivial, what did it matter what the larger issues were?

"Pete, do you know how to get there?"

"I can look it up. Is that safe to do? Ellen?"

"I think so. Just don't look her up, just the place. Here." She handed him one of the burner phones they had. "Just toss it after you're done."

"Lead the way, Pete," said David.

They reached a suburb and crawled north. A massive, black building towered in the horizon to the northeast of them. Pete's directions got them to a modest nursing home. Parking at the visitor spot, they went in, in search of Pete's mom. Pastel colored walls were decorated with art-work, ostensibly created by the residents. Some of it looked quite good to David's untrained eye. Wandering down the wide, antiseptic smelling hallways, Pete found the room that the reception desk had indicated. He stopped at a closed door and gave it a small knock.

A rheumy, gravelly voice answered, "Come in."

Pete lifted the latching door knob and carefully swung it into the room. Inside, a diminutive silvered haired woman sat in an armchair watching TV. She was dressed in colorful, flowered Hawaiian shirt with bright green pants. She peered through her thick glasses at the people now in her doorway.

"Petey?" an excited voice proclaimed. "I'm so glad to see you. What brings you here?"

"Mom? How have you been? I've been trying to get a hold of you. But the line to the home was always busy. I guess everyone has been checking up on people ever since the Eyes."

"The Eyes?"

"A couple of weeks ago. They were up in the sky."

"The sparklies? I don't understand why people are making a big deal of them. It's not like there's little green men on the White House lawn."

"Oh, Momma!" Pete crossed over to her. He bent down to wrap his arms around her frail shoulders. A happy smile broadened on his face. Straightening up, he turned to the other three by the door. He held out his arm toward them and said, "These are my friends. Ellen, Katerina, and David, of course. Guys, my mom."

"You can call me Sarah. Pete! Did you drag these poor people out to see me? All the way from Florida?"

"I moved out to Arizona a while back. Remember when you came to visit?"

"Your father loved Florida. He said he loved the heat and the humidity." Sarah's eyes wandered about the room. "Who are these people in the doorway?"

Pete's previous joyful look gave way to a more pained expression. "My friends, Mom."

"Hello, nice to meet you," said Sarah.

Ellen stepped forward and gently took her hand. "Hello, Mrs. Dainbridge. I'm happy to finally meet you. Pete talks about you all the time."

"Likewise dearie. Who are the other two?"

"I'm Katerina, ma'am. It's a pleasure to come here to see you." She gave a small wave to her.

"My, she's quite a looker. Is she your girlfriend, Petey?" Sarah turned to look at Pete.

Katerina snickered. Pete's face turned bright red. "Mom! Please? She's a little young for me, don't you think?"

"A pity."

David finally came forward. "Hello, Sarah."

Sarah squinted at him through thick glasses. "Do I know you?"

"We met a few years ago when you came out to visit Pete in Arizona."

A pained looked crossed Sarah's face. "I'm so sorry. I get a little forgetful nowadays."

"No problem." David looked at Pete. Pete's attention was focused on his mother. He could see tears welling in his eyes. Sudden inspiration hit him. "Pete, would you like to take your mom out for dinner?" He heard a sigh from Katerina.

Sarah grew excited. "That would be wonderful! We could catch the early bird special at Morrison's."

"I don't think there are Morrison's Cafeterias anymore," Pete gently responded.

"Nonsense, we ate there last week."

"Of course, Mom."

***

They found a suitable cafeteria a little distance away. Sarah seemed very happy and talked non-stop about Pete when he was growing up.

"His father bought him a BB gun when he was a little boy. Wanted to teach him gun safety. He told Petey that it was a big responsibility and that he could only shoot in self-defense and for food. Remember Petey?"

"Yes, Mom, I remember."

"What did you then do?"

Pete rolled his eyes. "I shot a bluejay."

"Did you learn your lesson?" said Sarah.

"Yes, I did. Bluejay tastes terrible."

A laugh burst out of Ellen. Katerina smiled and shook her head.

David grinned at the tale. "Speaking of terrible tasting things, I'm going back to get some dessert. Anyone want some?" Ellen and Katerina shook their heads in the negative. He pushed his chair back and got up.

"Great idea. I'll go with you and get Mom something." Pete also got up. The two of them left the women chatting.

"Dave," Pete said, picking up a metal tray and perusing the desert choices, "I'm really grateful that we were able to check up on my mom. Thanks for the dinner idea."

David had his own tray. He had selected a sundae cup of chocolate pudding with ersatz whipped cream on it. "Don't mention it. I hadn't realized how much she had ..." David struggled for a suitable word.

"Declined," said Pete.

"Yeah, I'm sorry man."

There was a growing commotion at the front door. David peered past Pete to see what was going on. Pete ignored the goings on. "I've been worried for her. I couldn't get through to the home."

"Oh shit." David pushed past Pete and started running toward the door, the pudding cup somehow still on the tray. Pete turned and dropped his tray and ran toward his mother.

A man in track suit and familiar looking gym bag pushed aside the hostess and reached into the bag. David could not move fast enough. The man pulled out an ugly, familiar double-barreled affair while the bag fell to the floor. He stepped off the carpeted area, his footsteps loud on the tile, purposefully striding toward him between the rows of food. David shouted at Katerina and Ellen to get their attention. He put the tray up as if to hit the assailant with it, the dessert cup falling off, twisting as it fell.

Back at the table, Katerina was in the act of standing and reaching for something while Ellen shouted and moved to shield Sarah. Pete was almost at the table. The fancy, glass desert cup shattered and sent pieces skittering across the ceramic tile. David was in point blank range of the weapon. He felt the blood drain from his body. He had to give Katerina time.

The would-be killer pulled the trigger as the metal tray contacted the end of the barrels. There was a startled yell quickly cut off. Reflexes took over and David dropped a burning hot tray. It clattered on the floor, scorching the pudding that had spilled.

David blinked. He looked down at his stinging fingertips and wondered what exactly had happened. Katerina reached him and in a smooth motion, picked up the armament and slipped it back inside the gym bad. A strong smell of ozone filled the dining hall.

A silence fell over the crowd of early diners. They had all seen a man disappear.

Pete's mom stood up and started clapping. "Bravo! Bravo!" A scattered response built into a crescendo. Katerina took a bow and she nudged David.

David looked up and heard the applause. Following Katerina's lead, they took their bows in unison.

"We need to leave. Now," Katerina whispered through the clenched teeth of a false smile.

Pete and Ellen already had Sarah in between them, arms through her elbow. They all made their way to the exit and hurried back to the home.

Back at the nursing home, they got Sarah back to her room. Pete had just sat her down when a nurse stuck her head in the door. "How was dinner?"

Sarah gave a vacuous smile. "It was wonderful. A dinner and a show."

The nurse gave her a thumbs up. "Great, I'll go check you back in."

As soon as the nurse left, the smile vanished from her face. Pete crouched down, eye level with his mother. "Mom, you OK? That was a little unintended excitement."

"I'll say. That man was trying to kill you. What have you gotten yourself into again, Pete?"

The four looked at one another.

"We can't tell you, Mrs. Dainbridge. But it is very important. And dangerous," said Ellen.

"You knew it wasn't a show? Why did you start clapping?"

"Petey, dear, I'm old, not stupid. Besides, it looked like you all could use a hand. Please be careful." She held Pete's hand in between her two hands. Looking into his eyes, her eyes became unfocused.

"Petey, what are you doing here?"

Pete's closed his eyes for a second. "Just visiting. Take care, Momma." And he leaned down and kissed her.

As they left the room, David heard her say, "What a nice couple."

***

They hastened away from Chicago, on the interstate in the deepening evening, trying to get in as many miles as they could at once. David thought he understood what drove Katerina to put distance between them and what had happened in the cafeteria. But even she had limits and David started to worry about her.

Sometime after midnight, above the sound of Pete's snoring that threatened to drown out some ditty about being on the road again, he told her, "Katerina, you're tired. Let's just find a place and call it a night."

"Just a little further. We've got to get someplace safe."

"It won't do us any good if you finish the job they started."

Katerina reluctantly nodded. "You're right. Keep an eye out for a place. I am tired. I really hate days when people try to kill us."

David couldn't decide if she was being serious.

Soon enough, they pulled into a seedy motel out in an isolated stretch of road, just off the interstate. A couple of adjoining rooms were acquired, the boys in one, the girls in the other. Nobody was in any mood to talk.

Tired as he was, David just couldn't get to sleep. He found himself staring at the ceiling over his bed. while his mind raced as the events of the day played out, over and over again. He turned his head to look at Pete in the next bed over. Pete's regular breathing let David know he was in gentle repose. He wondered about Sarah's remark.

David quietly got up and went for the door. Wondering if the conditions were favorable for doing a little stargazing, he gently left the door ajar behind him. The warm air of summer greeted him as he stood at the railing. Looking up, he saw countless stars blazing in the night sky. They looked beautiful to him. The past events melted away and he reclaimed some of his innocent wonder of them.

He heard a slight sound from behind him. He turned and saw the door to the girls' room open. Katerina's face peered out. She had a raised eyebrow.

"I'm sorry, I didn't mean to wake you," David said apologetically.

Katerina shook her head, sending cascades through her gleaming black hair. "You didn't. I just couldn't get to sleep," she said softly. She looked back in the room and came out, leaving the door slightly open. She wore a long tee-shirt with a baseball team logo and knee-high argyle socks. "I thought a little night air might clear my head." She silently padded over next to David at the railing.

They stood silently for a moment. David saw Katerina fidgeting. Her heel was going up and down in rapid fashion, sending slight waves through her hair. He looked out on the parking lot. "Do you need to talk?" He slightly turned toward her.

Katerina grew still. "I have a lot of thoughts running around in my head. First. I am really sorry about what happened at dinner. I let my guard down and you almost got killed."

David shook his head. "No, you were right. We shouldn't have gone. Thankfully, we're all still here." David forced a smile.

"That could have ended so badly. They must be getting really desperate."

"I know."

Katerina's voice became very soft. "What did you think you were doing?"

"I, I guess I figured that I had to give you time. Time to do, you know, your thing. To protect everyone." David felt a hard knot in his stomach.

Katerina nodded slowly. "I see you understand how they work. They wouldn't have left any witnesses."

David felt a shock of horror even though he knew it to be true. "After they took down a plane and derailed a train, yeah, I have no doubts. Pete is right. They are evil."

"But that didn't happen. My mother always told me not to borrow trouble. And, thanks to you, we now have a counter against that weapon. Do we have any burner phones left? I need to talk to Dr. Shtern. I need to tell him what we found out and see if he has anything for us."

David nodded back. "Yeah, I think we have one burner phone left."

"I'm really sorry about what happened." She massaged her temples.

"Hey, it's OK, Katerina. We're still here. We survived."

Katerina put her hands on the railing and looked up at the night sky. David watched her pretty face as her eyes travelled over the heavens.

"You know, I was telling the truth when I said I liked to look at the stars. Somehow, that all seems so long ago," she said.

David put his arm around her waist. She stiffened and then relaxed and leaned against him, her warmth adding to the warmth he felt. She rested her head on his shoulder.

He pulled back and squarely faced her. Her gray-green eyes searched his face. He leaned in closer to her, intoxicated by her scent. Katerina did not pull back. She met him halfway, her lips parted, unlike the other times she had kissed him. He felt her tongue with his, tasted her mouth. David pulled her tight against him, his arms wrapped along her back, her hands on the small of his back.

Still holding each other, David broke their passionate kiss. "I don't want to end this, Katerina," he whispered in her ear.

Her reply was low and sweet. "I like when you say my name."

They looked at each other longingly. Their thoughts ran down the same path as, simultaneously, they turned their heads to the car below them in the parking lot

David took her by the hand and led her down the hall, down the stairs, feeling very much like a teenager.

Nine

Hello

In the morning, David, Ellen and Pete waited for Katerina in the small motel lobby while she talked to Dr. Shtern.

Ellen filled a coffee cup at the station. She smiled at David from across the room. "Do you think she'll be long?"

David carefully studied the display with brochures for the local attractions. He spoke without looking up. "I don't think she'll be long."

She casually came over to stand by him, picking one out and examining it. "Some of these look interesting. You think maybe we could come back and visit?" She beamed at him.

Fleeing to the small desk with a computer monitor on it labeled business center, he experimentally moved the mouse that was on there, next to the monitor. "I guess it depends." He examined the screen that lit up.

Ellen looked puzzled. From across the small room, she said, "Is something wrong?"

He tried to smile at her. "No, nothing at all."

Ellen cocked her head. She looked like she was about to say something but couldn't quite figure out what.

Pete interrupted the awkward conversation. "Hey, do you all think we can get breakfast?"

David almost sighed in relief. "I sure hope so. We always seem to have long days, on the run."

Katerina just then pulled open the door and walked in. "Well, that was unpleasant."

"Do we have a plan now?" said David, a little overeager to his ears.

"We're supposed to meet him in a service plaza on the New Jersey Turnpike. He said he had an update for us."

"So, do we have time to eat?" asked Pete.

"Yes, we have time."

Katerina found them an old-fashioned diner, the kind that looks like a silver trailer and the waitress calls everyone "hun." David couldn't decide between the eggs and bacon or the pancakes. Katerina had oatmeal. Ellen watched him over her eggs and toast. Pete had the sampler breakfast that came with a plate of scrapple. He offered his compatriots a taste. "It's really good!" he said but had no takers.

***

Their route across the state ensured they saw a lot of forest. Small towns would appear beyond the dashboard and disappear in the rearview. Latin rhythms emanated from the speakers, asking the recipient to change their evil ways just before David turned it off. It would have been an enjoyable drive if they didn't have more pressing matters at hand.

Finally, the trees gave way to civilization and sprawl. The skyscrapers of Manhattan appeared and grew in their view before they turned south on I95. They headed toward their rendezvous with the doctor. Across the border in New Jersey, they pulled into a service area and parked.

The four got out, tired as they were from days of driving.

"I'm getting a Nathan's," were the first words out of Pete's mouth as he stretched.

Ellen stared right at David before turning and following. "Hang on, Pete. I'm coming with you." With a glance back, she left David alone with Katerina.

Katerina watched them go. "Are you going to tell her?"

David could feel his cheeks harden on his face. "Yes. I have to. Just didn't seem to have a good time to do it."

"We'll be stopping soon. Hopefully for a while. You should tell her then."

He nodded at her remark. Turning to face her, David said, "Did Shtern say when he'll get here?"

"Not really. That's not his style. You're supposed to wait for him. If you couldn't tell."

That made David lips curl in disapproval. "Of course. What do we do after that?"

"Make some more phone calls. See if we can set something set up for this evening or tomorrow morning."

"I never realized that being a spy could be so," David thought for a second, "mundane."

"Shows what you know. You still haven't met a real spy."

David arched an eyebrow at that comment. He was thinking of an appropriate remark to say when he saw Pete and Ellen marching back to the car with Shtern in tow. They looked unhappy.

"Speak of the devil," said David.

Shtern ignored his remark and started berating them. "I ran into them and not a minute too soon. The fools were about to go into the building. Didn't you realize that they have a camera feed from inside on their webpage, for crying out loud?"

"Last contact was in Chicago. We're pretty far from there." Katerina sounded defensive.

"Yes, but where else but New York would you go? The investigation is being run from the UN. And these people seem to have a lot of computing resources. National actor levels. I'm sure they could sift through all the feeds, looking for you."

Ellen squinted her eyes at that remark. She seemed like a thought was germinating.

Changing the subject, Katerina said, "You said you had something for us."

"Of course, because I'm nothing more than a glorified delivery boy." Anger flashed in his face. He closed his eyes. Slow, regular breaths followed until he opened his eyes again. "How's she doing? Betsy, I mean."

"Betsy?" Katerina looked confused.

"The car. You know, the one you stole."

Eyebrows arched and her mouth opened. "Ah, yes, it's...she's fine."

"Here's the keys to her." He held out a lucky rabbit's foot with a pair of keys dandling from it. "Take good care of her. I want her back. Preferably in one piece."

Katerina took the set from his outstretched hand. "Thank you very much. We'll take good care of her."

"You better!" A couple of deep breaths later and he continued, "I ferreted out the additional signal after you left San Francisco. I'm not sure what it is. It doesn't form a picture of any sort. It just seems like random information. I can't imagine that it got in there accidentally. I put what I extracted on another drive for you. I got some more phones. And I even got another laptop for you, whatever your name is. It's heavy so I left it in the car."

"Gee thanks," said Ellen.

"Don't mention it. Don't use it on the Internet, sweetheart. You can understand that, right?"

Ellen scowled at him but he seemed oblivious to her gaze.

"I analyzed the other frames. In particular the last frame. It's a warning of some sort. It has all sort of circles and lines all over it. Very busy compared to the other frames. You probably should get a semiotics expert to examine it. You know what that is, don't you?"

"Maybe our friends at the UN have resources."

"Huh. Good luck with that. Bunch of buffoons. Besides, do I need to remind you that you have no friends in this?" Shtern was being deadly serious.

David was taken aback with the last remark.

"What about defense against their weapons? We managed to acquire another one for you." Katerina had opened the car door and pulled out the gym bag from the previous encounter.

"We're working on something, based on the description you gave us. This additional weapon should help. It'll be a while before it's ready so don't be a hero and get yourself killed. Who's coming with me? I have stuff to give to you."

"Ooh, ooh, I'll do it! You haven't insulted me yet," Pete smiled at him.

The doctor glared at Pete. "Fine. Grab the gym bag. The quicker we get this over with, the better. I've associated with you too much already. I could get compromised. Katerina, enact directive twelve dash five from now on."

Katerina stiffened. "Are you sure?"

"I'm not willing to find out differently."

"Very well."

The doctor left with Pete following him, gym bag in tow.

"He's charming as always. What's 12 dash 5?" Ellen made air quotes.

Katerina frowned. "It says do not communicate back. Expect no extraction."

Concern grew in David. "That doesn't sound good."

"It isn't," Katerina said flatly.

Ellen's eyes went wide. "We're getting cut off?"

Katerina nodded.

***

They ended up back in Newark, in a gray, grimy building in a row of similar buildings, crowded together on a block. Katerina called it a "safe house". David didn't know if she was being ironic. At least it was spacious.

Katerina walked into the living room from her bedroom. "I've made some calls. We meet with the head researcher tomorrow. They are very interested in talking to the source of the pictures that some of the newspapers are reporting."

"I'm glad Ellen's idea worked. We just need to figure out what they mean," said David.

"Have you thought about them at all?"

"I have an inkling. But I need to verify. I think those are timings from pulsars. They are giving us a position in space. I don't know why. We did something similar for the Golden Record on Voyager."

"What about the rest of the stuff on the frame?"

"I don't know. That's still a mystery."

Ellen, who was working on the laptop, looked up from her place on the couch. "I've been looking at that stuff, comparing it across all three frames. There's some sort of structure there. Some of the information repeats across all of them."

"Oh?"

"Yeah, look." All three crowded around the display on her lap. Three windows full of symbols were lined up next to each other. "I converted the bits they had in the transmission to bytes so I could look at it easier. This is the hex representation. And this is it in ASCII, just so I can scan it easier."

Something bothered David. He turned to Ellen. "Why would their stuff be in bytes? Isn't that just something we made up, for our computers?"

"The data length was a multiple of eight. I figured I'd try that. Seems to be working. But look here. And here. And here." Ellen pointed at a row of text in the same place on all three windows.

"That's the same on all three?" David leaned in, to take a closer look.

Ellen nodded, setting her curls into motion. "The first two bytes of each message also match across the three frames. I can't help to think that's important somehow."

"What are they trying to tell us?" said Katerina.

Pete's head popped out of the kitchen door. "Dinner's ready." Delicious smells wafted their way.

Ellen put the laptop down on the coffee table. "Yum!" and she made a beeline toward the kitchen.

Dave started to follow when Katerina put her hand on his arm.

"When are you telling her?"

David wanted to ask her if she thought it was a good idea, but one look at Katerina's face made him instantly reconsider. "Tonight, after dinner."

***

That night, fireworks sounded outside, aliens be damned. David sat in his room and listened to them, people celebrating their independence and only caring about what they put into the sky. Katerina's look before dinner made him resolved to talk to Ellen. He crossed the living room where Pete slept on the couch and went to Ellen's room. It was next to Katerina's.

Knocking on the door jamb, he saw Ellen sitting on the edge of her bed, inspecting the pictures from the frames on the pillow. The papers with the codes in both decimal and hexadecimal were in her hands. She was mouthing something while in rapt attention. He studied his friend and suddenly felt very bad for her. But he couldn't lie to her. He cleared his throat. Ellen looked up and smiled.

"Uh, good evening," he managed to get out.

"Hey David, how are you doing? You've been so quiet all day. You've hardly said a word to me."

"I didn't realize that." David could feel his face growing warm.

A slight scowl transformed her face. "David, you're a terrible liar. What's going on?"

David tried to look at her and keep a relaxed face. "Ellen, I wanted to talk to you for a bit. I'm just tired and on edge. I'm not meant for this." He wasn't sure what he was meant for.

Ellen nodded. Her eyes softened and she said softly, "You have had it bad. You lost everything back home." She glanced at the spot next to her on the bed. "You can just sit by me. We can have that talk, if you want."

She wasn't making this easier. "That would be fine." David joined her and sat at the foot of the bed. The frame creaked under both their weight. "What were you looking at?"

"I was studying the first frame. Their use of a binary system made me think of putting things in bytes. The next three frames all have a section with what you think are coordinates and then a section with a stream of digits. Some of those digits match."

"And you translated that data into hexadecimal, so you could look at it easier?"

Ellen nodded her head. "Yeah, I wondered if the signal got corrupted. But it seemed unlikely that all three would get messed up in the same way. And look." She handed him the papers and pointed at the first couple of digits. "Remember how I told you about the first two bytes matching across the frames? It just happens to be the length of the information that follows, across all three. I don't think that's an accident."

Despite David's initial reason for coming to talk to her, he found himself getting drawn into her analysis. He held the papers in his hand, studying the digits, trying to make sense of it. "I wish they had been clearer. What's the point of saying hello if you can't answer back?"

Ellen froze. "What did you just say?"

David furiously thought back. "I said, why say hello if you can't answer back?"

"Holy fucking shit!" She looked like she had just been struck by lightning. "That's it! Here, this part's different. Unique to each of the frames. Probably the destination address. But this part is the same. On all three frames. That's us. And this part is the payload followed by a different number that I bet is a checksum. Do you realize what this is?"

David stared blankly at her. He shook his head.

"It's a structure. It's a ping packet, a hello, a sign on for a network."

He slowly started to understand and with his own flash, leapt to a conclusion "Wait, so the coordinates are ..."

"Where the routers or whatever they are on the Galactic Network are located."

David reeled from the implication. "That means that The Eyes weren't a warning, that we're being watched. The Eyes meant that we are been seen."

"They sent us a message to join them."

They looked at each other in astonishment. Ellen's lips started to curl into a smile. David felt relief wash over him. He felt his own cheeks tighten as a smile spread uncontrollably over his face.

Ellen put her arms around him and hugged him tight. David felt so happy and relieved that he just hugged her back. Their laughter rang out loud in the apartment.

In a second, Katerina and Pete crowded the doorway.

"Well, you two seem happy," said an amused Katerina.

Ellen blushed and coughed while she let go of David. "Yeah, I think we just figured something important out."

"Are you two going to spill or do we have to drag it out?" said Pete from where he stood behind Katerina.

"It's probably the best news we've ever had, if true," said David.

"Now, I'm really interested. We could all use some good news." Pete pushed Katerina into the room and followed her.

"Ellen figured out that the message is an invitation. And this data," he held up the papers of the three frames, "are a login for some sort of galactic network."

Pete's eyes light up. "That's amazing. Ellen, you are brilliant. Let me finish the dishes and we'll celebrate!" And he turned and walked out.

Ellen managed to turn an even deeper shade of red at the praise. "We don't know if that's true. We have to test it out."

"Don't be so modest. You did a fantastic job. Way to go Ellen," said Katerina.

"This will really help calm things down. People will see The Eyes in a different light," said David.

Ellen nodded her head vigorously. "They sure will. I hope this won't be kept a secret."

Katerina looked at David, tilting her head at him. "Speaking of secrets..." She let it hang for a second before turning and walking out.

David's euphoria evaporated. "Ah, Ellen, I hope that we can continue to be friends."

"Of course." She was still beaming at him. "Why wouldn't we?"

"Well, sometimes, things change."

"I keep hoping for the better, between you and me." Her eyes shone with expectation.

He shuffled his feet and stared at the floor for a second but he forced himself to look at her. "I don't think that's going to happen."

Ellen's demeanor transformed instantly. "What do you mean?"

Heart pounding so hard that he couldn't almost hear himself, he said, "Katerina and I, we ..."

"Stop." Horror and anger played across her features. And hurt settled into the lines of her face. "Don't say it. What? Or should I say, when?" Her eyes brimmed with tears. "You know, it doesn't matter. I'm happy for you both. Congratulations."

David never wished so hard to be invisible in his entire life. "I'm sorry."

"Don't be. Could you please shut the door when you leave? Now."

David nodded and walked out, closing the door to her room.

The fireworks continued for a long while.

Ten

The Calm Before the Storm

The city bustled in preparation for the weekend. In an office building by the East River, a stone's throw away from the UN Building, a group of David's fellow astronomers labored, checked data, cross referenced observations and, in general, tried to decipher the secrets of the celestial lights that had appeared a couple of weeks ago. Undoubtedly, their weekend would be filled with work as they were driven by a need to allay the fears of billions. Any news from them would be welcomed; good news even more so.

Even so, the ride over was very quiet. Any attempt at conversation was met with silence. Ellen spent all the time staring out the window. She hadn't even said good morning to Pete. They all hurried into the office, as though to escape the confines of each other's company.

A tall, overweight, older man, hair thinning but clean shaven met them at the door. He wore a pink polo shirt and a white lab coat with the words "Mumbler of Technical Stuff" embroidered in red over his left breast.

"Katerina, how are you?" said the man in a refined British accent. "It's so good to see you. It's been a few years since Tel Aviv."

"Hello Dr. Nicholson. I haven't been there since the conference."

"Please, Dr. Nicholson is too formal, especially after what we went through. Just Cornelius will do. I take it this is the chap you were telling me about?" Cornelius stuck out his hand, towards David. "I'm absolutely thrilled to meet you."

David took the offered hand and shook it. "Uh, likewise. Please just call me David."

"David. Very well. We are fascinated by the pictures that the newspapers have been printing. Katerina tells me you are the source of them, no?"

"Yes, I happened to be conducting a hydrogen survey and had my equipment pointed toward Arcturus."

"A lucky break for us. I'm afraid we were all distracted by the bright lights and didn't see the important dim star. Congratulations on keeping your head screwed on tight."

David felt heat grow around his ears but managed to say, "Thank you."

"So," Cornelius turned to the rest of the group, "who are these other stalwarts?"

"They are my friends, who helped me get across the country. We drove from San Francisco." Katerina introduced them. "This is Pete, keeping us sane and Ellen, who has some information and theory about the messages."

Pete waved at Cornelius. Ellen stared at the floor.

Cornelius nodded and waved back at them. "My goodness, quite a journey. I understand there has been some trouble recently. Dreadful thing. All across the country too, by what I've heard."

Katerina agreed. "It was a mess."

"Well, I sincerely hope that things start to calm down. Your pictures, once we've confirmed them, would help a great deal. I can't say that all this chaos is good for us, as a whole." Cornelius turned to faced David again. "Do you have the raw data? Your consortium partners never received your tapes."

David nodded. "Yes, I do. It's all on a memory stick."

"Splendid. Shall we get started? I imagine it will be a full day for you. I'm sure the oversight committee will want to talk to you. Ah, Harry! Would you please come here?" Cornelius waved a passing man over.

Harry was tall and a had broad shoulders, with a rugged, handsome face. He looked like he regularly worked out. "Yes, Dr. Nicholson?"

Ellen's mouth hung open. She made no attempt to hide the stare she gave him.

"Harry, would you please show our guests around? I have some business to attend to with this gentleman. Please get them anything they need."

"Of course, sir. Shall I give them the VIP tour?"

"By all means."

***

David started the transfer of the data and spent the morning discussing his equipment and how he ended up capturing the signal. He also told Cornelius about his theory that the frames were describing a position in space. Cornelius promised to look at the catalog of pulsars to try to figure out where they were being directed to. Overall, it was a very productive time.

After the busy morning, with the assistants scrambling to confirm and research the maps, David went in search of his compatriots. He found Pete in a meeting room, feet up on the table, drinking coffee.

"Where did everyone go?" he said as he surveyed the room. He saw a couple of piles of stuff around the table.

Pete put his feet down and straightened up. "Katerina went to meet with some security folks. Ellen stepped out with Harry to get some coffee. How did it go?"

"I'm supposed to come talk to the advisory panel this afternoon. I need Ellen to tell them her theory, about the hello packet."

Ellen came in at that point, talking to Harry. They were leaned close to each other. She had her hand on his elbow and was laughing at something David didn't catch.

David thought she sounded happy. "Ellen?"

Ellen looked up, a smile fading from her face. "Oh, David, what's up?"

David felt his brow furrow before he managed to relax it. "I need you to tell the investigation panel about the network thing you discovered."

"Of course. What time?"

"They said two o'clock."

Ellen glanced at Harry, who gave her a nod. "Perfect. I'm going to lunch now. We'll be back by then." Ellen gathered her things and walked out with Harry.

David let the scowl that grew on his face settle there. "That was a bit odd."

"Yeah, those two have been eyeing each other all morning long. Talking about being a fifth wheel. But she was feeling terrible earlier. I'm glad she seems to have cheered up."

Instant guilt assaulted David. His face went slack and he deflated. "My fault, really."

Pete shrugged. "People follow their hearts. Someone was bound to get hurt in that situation. I'm just glad it's over. I think that the longer that it dragged on, the more hurt the other person would get." Pete took a sip of his coffee.

David comforted himself by thinking he had done the right thing. Just then, his stomach growled. "Speaking of lunch, you wanna get that hot dog you were looking for earlier?"

The two left the room, heading for the exit. On the way out, they ran into Katerina who accompanied them on their quest for the New York staple.

"Kat, did you tell them about the bad guys and what they seem capable of?" Pete stuffed his mouth with a dog, sauerkraut, onions and mustard, of course.

"I did, but I'm not sure they believe me. It's making me worried." She looked momentarily guilty, an unusual thing for her. "Where's Ellen?"

"She went to lunch with Cornelius' assistant, Harry."

Katerina frowned at the information.

"I did mention that she needed to be back by two, to talk to the panel of advisors." David wiped his mouth with a napkin. "She is in a bad position."

Katerina nodded. "I suppose it's to be expected. I need to have a talk with her."

Coming back to the room they had by squatter's rights, they waited for Ellen. David and Pete sat at the table. Katerina stood by the far corner, phone in her hand, talking. Just before two, Ellen sauntered in, sans Harry.

"Well, hello everyone." Ellen had a smile on her face.

"You seem rather happy." Katerina did not have a smile on her face. In fact, it looked like a frown was forming.

She smiled a little sheepishly. "Why wouldn't I be?"

David started before Katerina could respond. "How was lunch?"

"Really nice. Harry took me to a little shawarma place. I liked not feeling like I was being chased. But we had to get back so he could go help analyze the data you gave them."

"You two seem to have really hit it off," said Pete.

"He seems to like me. And he's a computer guy."

"Really?" David could understand Katerina's discomfort.

"Everyone deserves a little happiness, don't you think?" She glared right at David.

David snapped his mouth close.

Katerina spoke softly to her. "I'm not saying you don't. I just think you should be careful and wait a little, that's all. I don't think we're out of danger."

"Being careful and waiting didn't work out so good for me last time." Ellen kept her tone even.

"Hey, look at the time! Don't you two have a meeting to go to?" said Pete.

Ellen let out a breath. "Yes, we do. Come on, David. Let's go find the room. I wonder what they'll think about my theory that it's a hello packet." She turned her back on them and walked out.

Katerina looked studious. "I think this is going to get uncomfortable."

David couldn't agree more. Getting out of his chair, he headed for the door where he could see Ellen in the hallway. "Ellen, do you need a copy of the data on paper? We can get it printed from a computer that they gave me."

Ellen looked back at him, past him. She shook her head. "No, I'll be fine. Let's not keep them waiting, we have important things to do." She didn't wait for David to catch up.

David threw a quick glance back at Katerina. She had sat down and leaned her chin in her left hand that rested on the table. She was looking right at them. David quickly turned his head and caught up to Ellen. He led her down the hallway, toward their appointment.

***

The interview was with a panel of experts from various fields. They listened intently to David's theory about the data referencing points in space, similar to the Voyager plaques. Cornelius added that they were currently looking for matching pulsars in their catalogs and having some success but that there clearly were ones that they didn't have. They also listened to Ellen's explanation of how the data that followed the spatial references appeared to be structured similarly across the three frames and that it seemed like a network packet of some sort, with a different destination for each one. All present agreed that those were extremely reasonable conclusions and should be further investigated.

"It's almost like they want us to understand what they are saying. Which doesn't explain the last frame. What are they getting at?" The man identified as a computer expert looked at the paper in front of him.

"We're not sure what it is but we think it's a warning. Of what, we don't know," said David.

They did have a semiotics expert. She was examining the last frame. "It has the feel of the type of symbols we came up with for long term issues. Like the nuclear waste problem. They are simple and direct."

"What problem are they warning us about?" chimed in another member of the panel.

The mathematician of the group keyed their calculator. "We don't know. We are assuming that this sequence of bits here is associated with the circle there. So it stands to reason that would be a measurement of some sort. And according to the measurement laid out in the first frame, it comes out to about Earth's diameter. If our assumptions are right, that is."

The previous member who spoke said, "And we all know about assumptions."

That got a round of chuckles out of the rest of the panel.

David waited for the panel to fall silent. "Why does it have a dot in the middle of it? Or is that corrupted data?"

"Again, assuming the three sequences by it are measurements, the numbers are about one inch, six inches and a very large number, somewhat larger than the observable universe. We think. There is a high probability that we're wrong."

"What is so dangerous about a six-inch rod?"

The questions hung in the air.

***

The ride back to the safe house was uncomfortable, made all the more so by the torturous and circuitous route going all over Manhattan. They finally made their way to the Holland tunnel to cross the Hudson River. Katerina said that you couldn't be too careful. They threaded their way through the surface roads of Jersey until they got back to their grimy block and parked. At least it was still light out, but not for much longer.

"Is this really necessary?" said Ellen before anyone had a chance to get out. "I mean, you gave them the data already. The cat's out of the bag. There's no point in chasing us anymore."

The doors opened and they clambered out.

David looked over the roof of the car at Ellen. "I did give them the raw data. But because I was distracted, I forgot to mention the other signal that Dr. Shtern found."

Ellen stood in the street blocking the open door of the car. Katerina waited to close the heavy door. But Ellen turned and moved close to the car and rested her hands on the roof. "Well, you can tell them tomorrow. I assume we're going back tomorrow. We're not letting a little thing like the weekend stop us, right?"

"Yes. I have to anyway. They were talking about addressing the General Assembly on Monday, just before we went to lunch."

"I'll go with you. I'd like to leave a little early tomorrow and swing by a phone store. I really want to get a new one."

Katerina confronted Ellen from behind the door. "What is wrong with you? We're not out of the woods yet. We're all still in very real danger. The threat hasn't been neutralized yet."

Ellen started yelling at her. "Says who? A super secret agent who won't even say who the fuck she works for? I'm done with your bullshit!" Ellen tore the door out of Katerina's hand and slammed so hard that the whole car shook. She walked away, crossing the street and dodging garbage on the sidewalk as she rapidly moved away from them.

"Ellen!" yelled David. He sprang to the front of the car to go after her when Katerina reached him and put her hand on his arm.

"Let her go. She needs to blow off steam. I'll apologize to her when she gets back. She might be right, after all. But I'm still not satisfied that we're out of the woods."

David looked after Ellen's retreating figure. "Is she safe?"

Katerina gave a half shrug. "Probably? I mean, this is Newark."

David felt alarm rising in him. He broke free of Katerina's grip and chased after Ellen. "Wait up!"

Ellen was already a fair distance down the block when she stopped and turned. "What is it?" she said in an angry tone when David got in earshot. "What do you want?"

"Nothing," he said, catching his breath. "I just didn't want you walking alone."

"I'm a big girl. I can take care of myself. Or did you come here with some more pity?"

"What? No! I'm, I'm just concerned about you. What's happened that you're so angry?"

"Really? Do I have to spell it out? Maybe I was just too trusting. Maybe I'm tired of running and tired of being lead around, dancing to someone's tune." She stood in front David, hands on her hips.

"Excuse me?"

"All this is because of that bitch."

"I'm sorry, I don't think Katerina was ..."

"You realize that if she hadn't stopped the break-in to your car, they would have been done with you."

David felt startled by the change of tack. "But I still had the data on the USB drive."

"Which they wouldn't have known about if you had given me the phone when I asked for it."

David shook his head. "They would have figured it out. She's been trying to protect us."

Ellen scrunched her face. "Speaking of which, I sure hope you used protection. And to think I actually liked you. Go back to your little spy. She has you wrapped around her finger." Ellen looked around as dusk started to fill the streets. "Don't worry, I'll be back. I literally have no other place to go." And she turned and walked off.

***

They ate a quiet meal, the three of them. Pete made it and brought it to the table. Despite the delicious smells, David didn't feel hungry. Ellen's empty chair accused him. David recounted what Ellen had said. Katerina stared at her plate, utensil in hand, and sat silent.

Pete leaned in, over his plate. "Look, man, there is no telling what would have happened. And based on what we know of them, they're not exactly the forgiving kind. No let bygones be bygones with them."

David stabbed a piece of food with his fork and held it hostage on the plate. "I suppose you're right. They don't seem to like loose ends."

"Yeah, I don't think that they would have left you alone. It would have been a matter of time before you ended up face down in a ditch. Or worse. Poof!" Pete's hand mimicked an expanding cloud.

David gave a slight nod. "Speaking of which, I wonder if Dr. Shtern has made any progress on a defense against that?"

And awkward silence met his question. Both sets of eyes turned to look at Katerina.

Pete finally broke the quiet. "Kat? You OK? You haven't eaten or said a word the whole time."

Katerina didn't look up from her plate. She gave a heavy sigh and let her shoulders slump. Thoughts seem to play across her face in rapid succession.

"We're not supposed to contact him. So I haven't heard anything." Katerina sank further into her chair. "Maybe she's right. Maybe I'm right. Who knows anymore?"

Pete looked at her. "Well, what I do know is that we all made choices and now we have to deal with them. And ignoring them isn't going to help us. I'm thankful you're here."

David gently took her hand. "And I'm glad you're here too."

Katerina lifted her head. A slight smile was on her face. "You're a good man, David." She squeezed his hand. "You too, Pete. I promise I'll do my best to get you out of this. All of you. Even Ellen."

The front door opened and Ellen called out, "I'm back. Any dinner left?"

"Excuse me." Katerina released David's hand. "I'm really tired." She got up and left the two men in the dining room. She brushed past Ellen, who jostled her in the doorway. Neither of them said a word to the other.

"Smells good. Is this another of your fine meals, Pete?" She pulled a plate out of the cupboard and sat at the table with the two men. Serving herself some of the cooling dinner from bowls on it, she started to eat.

"Ellen..." said David.

Ellen held her empty hand up in warning. "Not a word. I don't want to talk about it. I just want to eat my dinner."

Pete pushed back from the table. Standing up, he headed for the door. But he stopped just short of it and turned. "I feel bad for you that things didn't turn out the way you wanted. But we're all still in this together," he said, before leaving the room.

Ellen paused long enough to look at David and with her mouth full said, "You have something to say too?"

David's sucked on his lips. He simply said, "Yes, I'm sorry I dragged you into this. I didn't mean to hurt you." He then got up and left Ellen to eat her dinner alone.

Eleven

The Weekend

The morning started with Katerina and Ellen getting into a row. David heard them and hurried to see what was going on.

"We have burner phones already. I am not taking you to get a new phone," said Katerina.

Ellen had her arms crossed against her chest. "I'd like to be able to give my phone number out, so people can reach me."

"That's a huge security risk. You'll be found in an instant. I can't let you have that."

"Like you couldn't let me have David?"

Katerina turned red and her mouth hung open. She snapped it shut, turned and left the living room. Pete looked at Ellen and hurried after Katerina.

David couldn't believe what he had just heard. "Ellen, that was uncalled for."

Ellen angrily snapped at him. "You don't get a pass either. It takes two, you know."

David's face burned. He returned Ellen's hard stare. He considered his words and was about to say something he would probably regret when Pete came back in with Katerina in tow.

"I know everyone is upset at the moment," Pete started. Ellen snorted. "But we all still need to work together. I believe, like Katerina, that we are all, and I do mean all, still in danger."

Ellen started to say something but Pete continued. "I know you guys have to work things out. But, please consider that we all started as friends and tried to help each other. Things have changed but I believe that we can still get along." He gave everyone a slight smile.

Ellen seemed to reconsider. "Fine. We need to get going, I'm sure." Unceremoniously, she headed to the door. David sighed and followed her out. They waited at the car, in detente, for the other two.

The ride to the office was very quiet.

David had to go meet with his peers. He wasn't sure about leaving the group in such a fragile state but Cornelius sent Harry looking for him. He told Cornelius about the second set of data that had been discovered. Immediately, an effort was launched to look for it.

He spent the rest of the morning looking up pulsars, trying to match what was in the data so he could find the position in space.

Lunch came and went. Harry took a break from analyzing the data with David to take Ellen out. They were gone for quite a while. She returned with a new phone in her hand.

Katerina saw it, put her head down and just rubbed her temples. She whispered to Pete.

"You shouldn't have a cell phone. You know it's a security risk," said Pete. Katerina just glared at Ellen across the table.

"Guys, please don't do anything to each other." David got up and left to meet with the other astronomers and experts.

Talking with Cornelius, he asked, "Have you isolated the other signal yet?"

"Not yet. Harry, have the signal processing results come back?"

"Yes, Dr. Nicholson."

"And?"

Harry looked up from his screen. "We haven't found anything at the higher frequencies. Just the original stuff."

David felt confused. "Are you sure? Did you run an FFT to see if there was anything at all?"

"Yes sir. The software takes a while to run and I can run it again. But we didn't find anything."

"Did the file get corrupted?"

"If you have the original, I can plug it in here and check that." Harry held his hand out.

Chagrined, David remembered that he had left the USB stick back in his room, a casualty of the early morning dustup. "I'm sorry, I left it back in my room. Can you check some other way?"

Harry thought for a moment. "We saved the original hash. I'll check the file against it." Harry's fingers pecked away at the keyboard. "The hash is the same," he said after a moment, his eyes reading something on the screen.

"How can that be? Why would he lie?" David stroked his chin.

"Who sir?"

"Never mind."

Cornelius looked frustrated. "I'm afraid that if we can't find any trace of it, we can't tell the General Assembly on Monday about it. That will be disappointing. Quite so," said Cornelius.

David gave him a series of small nods.

At the end of the day, David asked for a copy of the data. He promised that he would look at it at home.

When David got back to the meeting room, the rest of the group weren't talking to each other. He saw Ellen sitting at the far end of the conference table, playing with a phone while Katerina sat at the other end, staring at Ellen and drumming her fingers. Pete sat in the middle, elbows on the table with his head in his hands. Only the barely audible sound of Katerina's fingers hitting the table top could be heard.

David's step faltered. He watched everyone for a minute before breaking the silence. "Hey, what's going on?"

Katerina stopped drumming. "Your friend is being difficult."

David sighed. "Ellen, do you think it's a good idea? That's how they found us last time. Through a phone."

Ellen turned to them and put the phone down in front of her. She steepled her fingers over it. "Shall we think this through? This," she held up the device, "is a random phone. It could belong to anybody. It is not associated with me."

"Who is it associated with then?"

"Harry. Harry got it for me. It is one of the masses. Anonymous. It's no different from your burner phones that you had. Even with their magic way of getting information, there isn't a way to trace it to me."

David thought hard about what to say next. He could feel Ellen's gaze on him. "I think it would just make everyone else a little more comfortable, given our experience, if it wasn't around the safe house, that's all."

"You know what? Fine, I'll turn the fucking thing off when we leave here. And I won't use it in the safe house. Is that safe enough for you, Katerina?

Katerina pressed her lips together into a line. She opened her mouth as to say something and immediately closed it. Finally, she simply said, "Yes."

***

Pete made a really nice dinner that night.

"This is fantastic! Where did you learn to cook like this?" David savored the food. It brought back memories of his grandmother's cooking.

Pete didn't look up from his dish. He used his fork to pull a piece of chicken off. "When you get to be my age, you end up with all sorts of skills."

"Well, this is really good Pete. Thank you," said Katerina.

"Yeah Pete. This is like the best homecooked meal ever," said Ellen.

"It was my favorite dish, Chicken and Onions, and some warm fluffy rice. Mom use to make it sometimes when I had a bad day. Everyone loved it and it made us happy. It always brought the family together." Pete continued to eat his food without looking up.

The three other diners looked at each other and finished eating their meal. Only the sound of forks against the plates interrupted the quiet.

Ellen volunteered to do the dishes.

"When you're done, there's something I need your help with," said David while he scraped a stack of dishes and gave them to Ellen.

"Of course. What's it about?" Ellen started to soak the dishes.

"Well, remember when Shtern said there was a second set of data in the signal?"

"Yes?"

"We can't seem to find it."

Ellen frowned. "Did the data get corrupted?"

"First thing we did was check the hash."

"I don't think the Doctor liked us but I don't think he would lie to us."

"Me neither. That's why I'm asking you to help me examine the file. I brought a copy of what they had, to compare against my original."

"Let me finish these and I'll fire up the computer."

***

Ellen joined David in the living room. She sat on the far end of the couch from him, laptop on the coffee table. "Let's see the data." David handed her the memory stick. "This is going to take a little while. There's a lot of data."

"Yeah. Ellen, I don't know what to say. I do want to be your friend."

Ellen's hands dropped to the couch. She looked down at her knees. "I know. It still hurts though. I tried for a while, to get your attention, before..." She shook her head.

"I hope you're not going to stay angry at us."

Ellen sighed. "I'm not angry. I'm really not." She gave him a little smile. "Actually, I'm a little concerned and scared."

David encouraged her to continue.

"Katerina," Ellen paused. "Katerina is good at what she does. If she thinks we're still in danger, maybe we are. We've almost been killed a couple of times, for fuck's sake. It's starting to get to me. Probably shouldn't have gotten a phone. But I was so angry at the moment. At Katerina. And you."

David nodded. "I get it. I totally get it. I guess I even understand it a little."

Ellen gave a little sigh. "If we're still in the crosshairs, that means that there is still something in that data that we don't understand. I would have thought that getting it out would remove us from being targets."

David thought for a second, working out what was going on. "Like there's a reason that this information is important and we don't know why."

Ellen nodded. She opened the laptop and plugged the stick in. "It has to relate back to the Eyes. Which makes me wonder if it's wise to stir things up again. People are finally starting to calm down."

David felt his heart drop. She was right.

Ellen finished typing something on the laptop. "I got this started. It's going to take a while to crunch through everything. Now, if you'll excuse me, I have a phone call to make."

David frowned. Ellen must have noticed because she continued, "Don't worry. I'm not going to upset your girlfriend and turn the phone on in here. I'm going outside. I'll be back in a few." Ellen got up and headed out the apartment door.

David sat and watched the progress bar on the screen for a couple of minutes before Pete came in.

"Hey, watcha doing?" said Pete.

"That's a real good question."

"Oh oh, that's not a standard reply. Now what happened?"

David rubbed his forehead. "One guess."

"Hmm, yeah, Ellen. You were talking to her and she left?"

David nodded.

"Well, I can't say I'm surprised at her reaction. She's on a rebound with her new beau. If you value her friendship, you'll have to be patient. And let her know you're still want to be her friend."

"What if she doesn't want to be friends anymore?"

Pete watched David with sympathy in his eyes. "Dave, there are consequences to choices. Sometimes, you can't walk them back. You're going to have to live with it."

David couldn't figure out what he should do next.

***

Katerina came by while David sat alone, watching the computer screen. In her hand, she held a small, delicate clay cup with an iridescent glaze. She put it down on the table in front of him after she sat down next to him, touching him.

"That's really beautiful. Did you make it?"

Katerina nodded. David picked it up and studied it. "You are really good."

"I wasn't lying when I said those things when we met."

David gave her a big smile. She returned it.

"David," she picked up his USB drive and placed it in the cup, "since things aren't exactly a secret, I'd like you to come by my room tonight." She leaned close to him.

Ellen cleared her throat. "Sorry to interrupt. Call me when you want to go over the results."

Katerina straightened. "No need. I was leaving now." Katerina patted David's arm as it lay along the back of the couch. She got up and left the two of them.

"Ellen..."

Ellen held up her hand and shook her head. "No need. I get it. You and her have your life. I need to get over it, I know. It was all in my head, after all. I really do wish you two happiness." A wane smile graced her lips.

David tried to smile back. "How's Harry? It's Harry, right? I only see him when he's doing something for Cornelius."

"Harry's fine. Thank you for asking. I wanted to do something fun tonight. I need to get out of the house for a bit. You understand, don't you? We're not going in tomorrow, are we?"

"I, I do understand. I don't plan on going in tomorrow. I have a speech to write for Monday. Can I borrow the computer? Does it have a word processor on it?"

"Of course." Ellen sat by David, where Katerina had just sat.

"Let's see what we have." Ellen's eyes narrowed as she studied the results. "That's odd."

"What do you mean?"

"The SHA-256 values are the same."

"That's the hash we used to compare them, right? We knew that already, I thought."

Ellen's finger swept across the screen. "I'm looking at the actual data. They're different."

"What? What are you talking about?"

"Someone went in, fucked with the data and somehow, the hash didn't change. That's simply not possible."

David was becoming alarmed. "How can that be?"

Ellen pulled up another window on the screen. A full-on frown settled on her features. "There's more."

"More?"

"Yeah, more. I took the time to extract the original signal we found, the one with the pictures. That data matches perfectly. That signal still there. But the second signal, the one Shtern found, is gone. It's only exists on your drive now."

David found himself going crosseyed trying to understand what Ellen was saying. He finally said, "I don't understand."

Ellen finally looked up from the screen with a grim look on her face. "Someone went into the data and changed it in a way that is impossible while deleting one set of data and leaving the other set. We are so fucked."

"I think we need to call the others in."

Ellen nodded her head.

Soon, Pete and Katerina joined them.

"What's up guys?" said Pete. Katerina stood quietly in the corner.

"Ellen just found out something. Somebody has been messing with the data, in a way that's impossible. Is that the gist of it?"

Ellen nodded. "This isn't something that's a little ahead of us either, like the other tech stuff they've done. This is so far ahead of what we can do that it's magic. Beyond magic." Ellen's phone started buzzing.

"I thought you promised to keep it turned off here at the safe house?" Katerina said softly from her spot.

"It's in airplane mode. That was just an alarm. Harry is coming to pick me up. It is Saturday night, after all."

Katerina's expression left no doubt what she thought of that. She shook her head and left for her bedroom. David felt similarly but managed to say, "That's good. You don't mind if I go down with you and tell him what we found?"

Ellen started to protest but Pete cut her off. "That's a great idea! He was helping to run the analysis, wasn't he? I'm sure he'll be interested."

Ellen decided not to argue. "OK. I don't want to keep Harry waiting."

***

Outside, the three of them waited for Harry to show up. Pete had decided to come down because he didn't want to be left alone since Katerina had locked herself in her room, presumably to cool off.

"Where is he?" said David, scanning the street.

"I don't see his car yet," said Ellen.

"You didn't give him our address, did you?"

"Of course not. I told him to come to this street and look for our car."

"He's not going to be able to park." David surveyed the street. Every single spot was filled with all manner of cars from rundown vans, SUV's that had seen better days and an assortment of older cars. The street seemed busy tonight. But Ellen was right, it was Saturday night after all.

Their car stood out like a sore thumb, a shiny, restored muscle car.

David turned to Ellen. "Maybe going out right now isn't a good idea." She was looking at him, paying close attention to his words. "I mean, these aren't normal bad guys. There's something really scary about them. I'm worried."

"I see a car slowly coming this way," said Pete as he pointed down the street.

Ellen squinted at the car. "Yup, that's him." She got in the street by their car and waved. The car came to a stop at her feet.

Harry left the car running and double parked while he got out. "Hi Ellen. Good evening to you, sir."

"Hello Harry. Please just call me David."

"Yes sir. You're not here to see Ellen off, are you? I promise my intentions are good and I'll have her back at a reasonable time." Harry plastered on a broad smile.

"Ha-ha! No, I'm afraid it's something serious. You were helping to look for the other signal, to confirm it, right?"

"Yes, I was."

"Well, we looked at the original. Something very," David hesitated. He didn't want to sound melodramatic. "sinister is going on."

"Did you find a second signal? I spent all afternoon looking for that. I'm suppose to go in tomorrow and look some more. I haven't found anything."

"There's a good reason for..."

Ellen cleared her throat. "Harry, I'm sorry that I made you come all the way out here. David, you're right. After what we found, I don't think it might be a good idea for me to go out tonight."

Harry's face fell. "Are you sure? How bad can it be?"

David said, "It's very bad. I'm going to need to talk to Dr. Nicholson tomorrow, to discuss what we found. Before going in front of the General Assembly."

Harry nodded. "If it's that Earth shattering, then maybe you should talk to him right now. Do you have your phone? No? Let me get my phone out of the car and we can discuss it." Harry went to the driver's side door and got in. He took the phone off its mount on the windshield. Ellen had her back to Harry, looking past David.

David watched him. He thought of asking him who else had access to the data he had provided when he noticed that the street got quiet. Too quiet, in a familiar, disturbing way.

"Oh shit." David turned to look around. Pete was mouthing something at him and pointing back toward Harry's car. He followed Pete's arm to Harry, who had come out of the car with a pistol in his hand. He was almost to Ellen who still was looking at something behind David. Her eyes were wide with fear.

"Watch out!" David screamed at Ellen. Hands tore at him from behind. He frantically tried to escape them. Pete was being wrestled to the ground by a small crowd of assailants. Harry reached Ellen, wrapped his arm around her neck and pointed the gun to her head. All the fight went out of David. Harry pushed her down to the street.

David was being dragged toward the rear door of a van. Pete had already been shoved inside. A pair of thugs went to Betsy with what looked like large crowbars with a cylinder attached. They stuck them into the trunk and silently popped it open. David could just see them bending down over Katerina's grey case.

A flash and an overpressure wave knocked him and his kidnappers over. Sound returned to the street, a loud ringing hurting his eardrums, glass falling and shattering, trashcans rolling, car alarms going off. A tripod with a long, thin rod near one of the vans had been knocked over.

David was dazed. Hands picked him up and tossed him into the back of the van. The doors closed and the van rapidly accelerated away from the scene of chaos.

He looked around the back of the empty van. A figure lay prone next to him. "Pete!" David shook his friend.

Pete clutched his head and groaned. "I'm so fucking tired of getting manhandled and thrown into vans."

David felt relief at hearing his voice.

Pete sat up. "What happened? Where's Ellen?"

David felt worried. "I'm not sure. She was on the ground when they tried to open Katerina's grey box. It went off."

"There was a bomb in it the whole time?"

"Well, she did tell us not to open it."

"Serves them right."

David was a little taken aback by Pete's bloodthirstiness. "You OK? That doesn't sound like you."

"Man, the stakes are sky high. Think about what we just found out. You have the only copy of the data right now. Whatever is on it must be super important. They attacked us in the open, in the middle of the street. We have to protect the data at all cost. You don't have the data on you, do you?"

Panic and then relief when he remembered the USB drive was still in the living room, in Katerina's cup. He shook his head in negative.

"Well, that's the only good news tonight. I wonder where we're going."

Twelve

The Warehouse

Peering through the expanded metal grate that covered the back window, the tunnel that they used to get to the UN offices was left behind. David briefly wondered what their destination was as the route seemed familiar. Soon, instead of veering left, they continued into another tunnel.

They emerged and could see the buildings of Manhattan out the rear window. They went through more urban sprawl and an enormous cemetery. In the fading light, he saw a large Earth globe to the left, the continents polished metal with the meridians and parallels denoted by more stainless.

They tried the doors of their metal prison, particularly when the van had slowed down to go through a toll. But the handles just didn't work. No fancy, semi-possible technology guarded them. Yelling through the glass at the other vehicles didn't attract attention from any of the other drivers on the expressway. They might as well be invisible. Still, David felt hopeful that absent their technology, there might be a way to escape. Pete wasn't certain.

The setting sun had long disappeared from the back window when they turned south. Small towns and suburbs scrolled into the distance while they went along surface roads. The traffic was stop and go and when the headlight beams hit the back window, they frantically waved at the cars behind them. Nobody even honked their horn at them.

It felt like a couple of hours passed since they were taken off the street. David had no way to be sure. The traffic had died down now and the van pulled into a parking lot in the dark. Under the sodium lights, David thought he saw boats and the smooth, black surface of water. The back door opened and the smell of the sea filled the cabin. The ugly long batons of now familiar weapons poked inside. They sizzled in the night air, a blue incandescent spark at the tip. David could see a man motioning at them with his hand. Having no desire to feel what Pete had described as an unpleasant experience, David came out of the van. An entire squad of black garbed thugs waited for the two men. In the uncertain light, David thought he saw they now had patches on their uniforms. It appeared to be a red, grinning devil face, complete with horns.

Surrounded by all the armed men, they went into a dilapidated warehouse. Crossing the threshold with the threat of pain all around them, David wondered if he would ever see the outside again.

Once inside, the two of them were led to a small room that was attached to a larger room in the middle of the warehouse. Dim incandescent light bulbs hung sparingly in the volume making it difficult to make out the further corners. David thought he saw offices along the far walls but they were dark.

The detail paused in front of the door and a device with a long paddle was passed over them. The person that did the scanning appeared to be female but it was hard to tell with the armor. A quick glance at the display of the device and a nod was all the acknowledgement they got before they were unceremoniously pushed into the small room and the solid door locked.

Their makeshift cell had the appearance of a hastily converted office space. The ceiling was tiled, the floor had wide well-worn wooden boards and there was a light switch by the door. Two cots sat against opposite walls and a bucket with a cover between the cots completed the tableau. David heard the hum of florescent lights.

"Well, this is interesting. I may not be as smart as Ellen, but I get the feeling that we are stretching them thin." Pete's mouth broke into a grin.

"They could still decide to kill us at any point."

"Yes, and they didn't. They want something."

"The data." David stated it, not a question.

"Of course. I am assuming that after the surprise got them, they weren't able to sweep the area. And they probably had to deal with an angry Katerina."

David nodded. "We can only hope." A pang of concern struck David. "Do you think Ellen is OK? She was awfully close to the explosion."

"I don't know, man. I was being dragged away." Pete sat experimentally on one of the cots.

"Harry was on top of her, with a gun to her head."

"We did get told not to trust anyone."

"Yeah, but in the investigation consortium?" David sat on the other cot and looked across the room to his friend.

"Why not? Where else to better sabotage something? I bet Katerina has some choice words about their security after this." Pete stretched out on his cot.

"You're not going to sleep, are you?"

"I can't think of a way out of this that doesn't end up with us becoming expanding clouds of smoke. One thing I've learned in my travels is that you should get some shut eye when you can. I recommend you do the same. Maybe something will come to us in our dreams."

Pete rolled onto his side, facing the wall. "Turn off the light, would ya?"

David watched the back of his friend. He was too keyed up to sleep. Pete's breathing slowed and became regular. Sighing, he finally went to flip the switch and tried to get some sleep.

***

In the morning, David's nose woke him. The bright florescent lights overhead made him scrunch his eyes. A familiar, greasy smell filled his nostrils, rousing his stomach. He looked around for the source. A plastic tray was by the door with a couple of fast food breakfast sandwiches, wrapped in paper, along with two cups of coffee. A small mound of sugar packets and creamers completed the presentation.

David eyed the food with suspicion.

"Hey, glad to see you're up. I was waiting for you and just about to wake you," said Pete.

David pointed at the food. "Do you think it's safe?"

"Well, no, it's fast food. But I do think it's a message."

David nodded. He remembered Ellen's appraisement of a previous situation, long ago and far away. "I wonder what they are waiting for?"

"I have no idea. We talked to Rob and were on our way to be executed before. This is all new territory."

"I don't think Katerina is going to find us in time this go around."

The day wore on. At some point, orders were barked at them through the door to get on the cots and the door opened wide enough for another tray to be pushed in with some subs, chips and sodas on it.

David thought that they hardly had to bother with all the yelling. They'd spent most of the day reclining on the beds. Wild speculation filled their conversation, some hopeful, some dark indeed.

But after this last meal, Pete had taken to inspecting every inch of their jail. "Hmm," he said after standing on his cot and examining the ceiling.

"What is it, Pete?"

"I don't know. This looks like it's just a drop down."

David sat up on his bed. "Do you think..."

Pete experimentally pushed up on the square. It lifted easily. David's full attention was on Pete now.

He walked up to Pete. "You want to get on my shoulders?"

From the middle of the room, Pete's head rose above the supports. He had David turn in all directions. "The wall doesn't go all the way up in the back. Let me down and we'll move there."

Standing on a relocated David by the back wall, Pete's legs soon disappeared into the crawlspace. A hand reached down to help David up. They came down in the long room behind them. The far wall was invisible to them. David saw a ghostly green light coming from the right wall between dark masses. As his eyes adjusted, he could just make out rows of rectangular objects about as tall as his chest. They seemed to be packed against the walls and a couple of rows of them occupied the center of the room. There was barely any space between them. They quietly made their way to a gap in the objects against one wall where the tritium plaque was affixed to a door. It said "Exit". Standing in front of it, the two of them could make out each other's faces. David pressed his ear against the door. Faint conversation sounds could be heard, undecipherable in their content. He waved Pete away from the door.

Standing in the middle of the aisle, Pete leaned close to David and whispered, "I think these are filing cabinets."

Understanding now, he ran his hand over the nearest one and found a handle and button. Gingerly he opened it. His hand reached in and found the drawer packed with paper. Pulling a sheath out, he went back to the only source of illumination. He dared not look for a light switch. Under the sickly green glow, he saw it was one continuous piece of paper, brittle with age, that had been folded over. The first line on it jittery text that said WRU with a series of numbers. He wasn't sure what they were, it didn't look like a phone number to him. Struggling to make out the faded date, it appeared to be February 1971. It was difficult to read but seemed like instructions on investing in some new technology and some uses for it.

Pete waved to him and gave him a folder with some fan folded paper in it. "This one says it's from 1981. I think it's talking about operating systems."

"I have an idea. Help me find the oldest looking filing cabinet. I'll look in this row, you look in the next one over."

David started going down his row. The metal cabinets smooth skin become rougher as he went down the line, no doubt from rust. Toward the end, the cabinets switched to wood, by what his fingertips told him.

"Psst! Dave!" A barely visible Pete was waving at him. David went around to him.

In front of them stood a filing cabinet that was barely holding itself together. "This is the most broken down one I found," said Pete.

Dave grabbed the handle and gave it a gentle tug. The drawer hardly moved. He gave it a stronger pull. Still no movement. "Pete, hang on to the cabinet. I'm going to pull on it hard." Pete nodded and braced against the wooden form.

David pulled as hard as he could. Wood, dried, unlubricated and warped, protested loudly in dark. David and Pete froze. Their eyes cast back toward the door, to hear for any change. Ten seconds, thirty seconds passed and nothing happened. David started to relax. He reached in and grabbed the first paper there. Something was attached to it with some sort of metal fastener he didn't recognize. It was a paper clip holding what felt like a ribbon of paper is what he figured. He went back to the placard to read what was on it.

Under the dim light, he read in spidery handwriting, "Received another message today. None of the other operators will fess up to sending it. I think there's something wrong with the cable. There already were several in July. I intend to respond next time, to see if I can figure out who it is." The note was dated August 13, 1908. On the slender piece of paper, typed words said "CHANNEL CHECK RESPOND IF RECEIVED STOP"

David stared at the sliver. Pete nudged him and traded with him what he had found. This one was dated in the spring of next year. In the same handwriting, it said, "Planning the expedition is in full swing. I have the capital necessary, thanks to my benefactor's advice. I have acquired a navigator. We leave for Paris within the week. I expect to be gone until the fall. Hope all goes well. It is very far from any civilized place and winter there would be deadly."

A commotion was occurring behind them, beyond the door. There were some loud shouts of "Yes sir" that managed to penetrate into the room.

"Oh shit! We gotta go!"

They put the papers down on top of the nearest cabinet and ran to the wall they had crawled over. David intertwined his fingers to form a basket. Pete stepped in it and vaulted up to the top of the wall. Hauling David up, he dropped down as David pulled himself over the wall. They made noise as they banged into the wall, but it couldn't be helped. At this point, they had to be back in the room.

David scraped the cot over and reached up to the ceiling tile and dropped it into place as the door started opening. He dropped straight down on the bed, breathless as the door swung wide.

Two uniformed men with their familiar electrified weapons held at ready came in, followed by someone without a weapon sullying his hand. The man in charge looked at both of them suspiciously.

"Good evening. I have been instructed to take you to meet with the boss. We will not tolerate a repeat of the incident in California. You are to follow me."

Surprised, the two men got up and went out the door.

***

David looked around trying to memorize as much as possible while being marched toward one end of the space, past rooms lining the wall. In his heightened state, he could see the guards did have a patch with a devil on it. All sorts of wooden and brass machinery with a patina of verdigris seemed to inhabit this part. Through an open door he saw Rob waiting for them, ensconced behind the same heavy wooden desk on the same carpet. The only difference was a large, cylinder of crystal about a foot tall and about as wide on the desk, close to them and to the right of Rob.

Rob looked up when they entered the room. He gave them a predatory smile. "I see you gentleman are doing well."

"No thanks to you, you piece of ..."

"Now, Peter, you mustn't be an ungracious guest. While your accommodations aren't the best, I'm sure you would find them preferable to the alternative." Rob drew his finger across his neck.

"What do you want with us?" said Pete.

"I thought it was obvious."

"He wants the original data, that's what he wants," David said angrily.

"Got it in one."

"So what are you planning, you shit? An exchange?" Pete's sharp reply drew a cautionary nudge from one of the armed guards.

"See, Ellen isn't the only smart one in your group. We will contact them and convince them to hand over the data and all the copies."

David sneered at him. "As if they would trust you."

Rob gave them another smile. "No, Katerina definitely wouldn't trust me. Quite unfair since she hasn't even met me. But she would certainly trust you."

David was incredulous. "What makes you think we would help you?"

"My dear boy, what makes you think I need your help?" Rob picked up a small, black box from his desk and pressed a button on it. Behind him, a cloud of static formed a figure and in a second, David was looking at himself. "They've even talked to you already. Say hello David."

The doppelganger raised his hand and waved. In perfect mimicry, it said, "Hello David," before its arm dropped back to its side, lifeless. Worse than lifeless. Blank.

David's clenched his teeth. He could feel the strain on his jaw muscles.

"What's with all the steampunk machinery outside the office? Is this where your ancestor started?" Pete stared at Rob.

Rob's face didn't register surprise or even any emotion. "I see you actually got to read some of my family's records. Did you turn on the lights to make it easier? Not that I care." Rob gave a careless wave. "The fact is, this is where grandfather started his side business. Far enough away to not arouse suspicion but close enough to still be a telegraph clerk. There are some fascinating records in there." A slight chuckle escaped his lips. "But it doesn't matter what you know. Soon, none of it will matter at all. I'll be taking care of it when we leave."

Alarmed, David asked, "We're leaving?"

"Oh yes, this was just a brief stop. I just needed to send a message to your friends while we're still on land where I have the bandwidth. Guards, put them in the boat."

The armed personnel motioned at them to move out, giving them not-so-subtle nudges with the tips of their sticks.

Rob stood up and came around the desk. He motioned back at the desk and pointed at the crystal. "Make sure that gets brought aboard." Another man came from outside the room and went up to Rob and handed him a folder.

"You son of a bitch!" Pete started to move toward Rob but the guards were quicker. They tapped him between the shoulders with a lighted stick. For the second time, Pete instantly went down. He went rigid and fell forward.

"Pete!" David stopped and bent down to look at his friend. The mercenaries reached down and hooked David under the arms and dragged him up and out of the office. He looked over his shoulder in time to see them dragging Pete up and putting his limp form between two of them.

They went down the length of the warehouse to the front door. Nighttime had taken hold outside. The street was deserted amidst all the seedy commercial buildings. The group made its way to a dock that was across from them. A fishing boat rose up and down at the mooring.

Boarding it, Pete's unconscious body was handcuffed to a railing. David was added to the same metal pipe.

The sea had a slight swell. The smell of the ocean reminded David of another pier an entire continent away. Overhead, the first stars shimmered to life while the dock disappeared into the distance. Hope vanished.

Thirteen

The Canal

A head of them, in the growing darkness, loomed a freighter with its running lights on. Land had disappeared behind them. A ladder was illuminated on its side, their destination. The slight chop made David uneasy about climbing it. David glanced back from where they had departed. A warm, orange glow suffused the horizon from the direction they came from.

"Up you go!" shouted one of the crew while they uncuffed him from the railing.

David wondered briefly what would happen if he were unable to comply. A look at their ugly weaponry motivated him to try hard. He clambered up the ladder in the rolling sea.

Once he was on the deck another group of henchmen received him. They had disconcerting smiles on their faces and they pointed their batons toward the superstructure of the ship. A man waited for him. He gestured to David to follow him. A pair of escorts trailed him. They descended a ladder and went below decks, travelling a slew of narrow metal passageways and more ladders and through a number of watertight doors, confusing David as to where he was.

They arrived at an open door to a humid, mildewing cabin where he was directed to enter. Stepping through the door, David saw a bunk bed, a small table attached to the wall opposite the beds with a couple of stools and a toilet and sink in the back corner. He turned to face his captors and they shut the door on him. A series of loud noises followed, the locks and bolts being engaged.

Sighing, he sat on the lower bunk and gave a closer inspection to the room. Except for what looked like a speaker box mounted high in one corner and a conduit on the bulkhead that came down from the ceiling and ended in a light switch by the door, there didn't seem to be anything else on the white, painted metal walls.

David was not left alone for very long. The sound of the door locks being worked prevented him from being surprised by his jailors. Pete's semi-conscious form was pushed through the door and allowed to collapse on the floor. David quickly went to him, to help him, even as the bolts were put back in place.

Pete weakly lifted his head. A patch of drying vomit was on his shirt. "Dave, ole buddy, I'm not cut out for this anymore. I'm just too old."

***

The loud sound of the locks being drawn back woke David up from his uneasy sleep. David had helped Pete get cleaned up and put him into the bottom bunk the previous night. Staring at the close ceiling, he felt when the freighter got underway a few hours later. The loud constant grumbling of the diesels left no doubt where the cabin was located. It took bone-wearying tiredness on David's part to overcome the disturbance of his sleep.

A plastic tray with two sectioned plates was left at the foot of the door. David got down from his bunk and placed the tray on the shelf table. He went and shook Pete awake.

"Pete, breakfast is here."

Pete sat up and covered his mouth as he yawned. "Thanks man."

"How are you feeling?"

"Like shit. What's on the menu?"

"Looks like powdered eggs and a sorry excuse for bacon. A scoop of some white, grainy stuff with butter on it. Nothing like your cooking."

Pete cast an eye at the plates. "Grits. You mean grits. We can't be too picky now. Any idea of where we're headed?"

David shook his head. "No idea. Nobody talked. I'm tempted to ask next time someone comes by."

"Nothing to lose by it, huh?"

"Not anymore."

The two sat at the table and ate their food. Conversation drifted between the status of their friends, the UN meeting and what their ultimate destination was.

David looked at his friend. "I'm really worried about Ellen right now. I feel like it was my fault."

"Didn't you say Harry had her pinned down?"

"Yeah, close to the explosion. I hope she's alive."

"That would be terrible if she got hurt." Pete put a plastic sporkful of grits into his mouth.

"Yeah, it would. I know things were rough between us when all this happened. But I don't want anything to happen to her."

Pete thoughtfully chewed his food. "You and Katerina getting together happened to her. Supposing we get out of this alive, do you think that she'll want to be reminded of what happened between you guys?"

David frowned. "I suppose you're right. But we've been through so much together."

Pete gave a heavy sigh. "Yeah, we have. Stuff like this bonds people forever. People do forgive each other. Especially with everything that has happened. Maybe."

David nodded.

A few hours later, around lunchtime, the locks could be heard again. Another tray was put on the floor. Beyond the door, David could see an unarmed man, watching over the one who brought in the food. The man wore civilian clothes. David actually found it encouraging that they were being regularly fed. It seemed like there might be some long term plans for them. He told Pete his theory after the door had closed. Pete called him an optimist.

About what must have been mid afternoon, the door was opened and three heavily armed men stood in the corridor outside the door.

"You! The young guy. Front and center!" The guard motioned at David.

David stood up from the table. "Where are we going?"

"Shut up and come with us."

David glanced back at Pete and stepped out into the hallway. Pete gave him a thumbs up as encouragement. Walking in the midst of the men, they went forward and up a few decks. They arrived at another cabin door. Inside was a room, bigger than what he and Pete occupied, but not by much. This room had a fairly large table in the middle of it with two chairs. One chair, the one behind the desk, was occupied by a man in a suit. There were a number of cameras on tripods in the room. Also on tripods, one in each corner, was a rod. David thought they looked similar to the one he had seen outside of the apartment when they were kidnapped.

"Sit down," the man said quietly.

David thought about not complying but decided to play along.

"I have some questions for you. I do hope you cooperate. Don't bother trying to lie. We can tell. " The man motioned over his shoulder to a camera behind him.

David put his hands on the table and leaned forward. "No. I'm not going to help you."

The man smiled and lifted a finger in signal. A sudden, suffocating quiet descended on David.

Oh, oh, here it comes. David steeled himself against the expected blows. But nothing happened. Confused, he tried to ease himself back into the chair. That's when he found out he couldn't. Alarmed, he tried to stand up, to wriggle his fingers. Nothing. He was like an insect caught in amber. He glared at the man across the table.

"I see you need further convincing. Increase by one."

Something pressed down on him, all over him. Every square inch of his body felt an insistent weight trying to get inside of his skin. Breathing was becoming difficult. He struggled to fill his lungs.

"Perhaps another notch."

The pressure increased. David was left gasping for air. His lungs burned and ached at their emptiness. His vision started to go purple and he thought he was looking out of a tunnel. They were squeezing the life out of him.

Suddenly, the force holding him in place turned off. The muffled quality of sound went away and he fell forward toward the table. Only the fact that his hands were already on it kept him from hitting it with his head. He drew large, ragged breaths.

The man behind the table spoke. "A couple of clicks usually convinces people to cooperate. Go above that and bones begin to pulverize, insides liquify. But don't worry, we wouldn't do that to you. You would just have to watch it on someone else." The man smiled a toothsome smile at David.

David felt cold from the sweat.

"Now that we're clear, why don't we start? How many copies of the data on the USB stick exist?"

Gulping, David tried to regain some composure. But his hands were still trembling. "I made two copies."

"Two? Only two?" Quiet descended on him again.

Panicking, David rapidly spoke. "Two! It is a lot of data. It takes a while to copy and ..."

"I don't believe you." The man's calm tones were a complete opposite of David's. "I want to believe you. The machine says you think you're telling the truth. I think that I'll eventually trust you. But I wonder, if I apply a little pressure, if the true truth will come out."

David felt his breath wrung out of him. He sat, mouth wide open, trying to expand his lungs, just force his ribs out a tiny amount, anything at all, to feel air flow into his lungs. He felt dizzy from trying and his sight faded.

Suddenly, the pressure lifted and sweet oxygen flooded into him. He would have collapsed onto the table but was still in the clutches of the invisible field. It took him a moment to recover but he was finally able to focus his eyes on the man in front of him. He had never wanted to hurt someone so badly.

"Back with us? Good," said the interrogator. "Why don't you tell me how many copies there are?"

***

The door to the cell opened and David was pushed in. His legs felt like rubbery noodles. He struggled to keep his balance, to make it to the table. Instead, they gave way. Pete rushed to pick him up.

"Dave, you look terrible. What did those bastards do?" He led David to a chair.

"I tried to tell them the truth. But they wouldn't have any of it."

"What are you talking about?"

David braced his head in his palms, elbows on the table. He told what had happened. He included the threat to Pete.

"Shit! Don't worry about me! Don't give in to them!" Pete's fists were white.

"Pete, you would have done the same for me."

Pete took a deep breath before letting it all out and grimly nodding. He suddenly brightened and said, "Hey, I asked one of the guards where we were going. The guy who's dressed differently. He said we're going for a meeting with the big boss."

David immediately straightened his head, his interest piqued. "I thought Rob was the big boss. Did they say where?"

Pete shook his head. "Naw, the other guy told him to shut up."

"We know that Rob's family has been talking to someone for a long time. Are we on the way to talk to them?"

"Where to? Europe is where they went before."

"Yeah, why a slow ship? You'd think he could just have an airplane or something take him over. He's rich enough to have his own plane."

Pete shook his head and shrugged.

***

The next morning, David and Pete were already awake and up by the time the door announced it was being unlocked. They stood by their bunks while the person who didn't wear the armor or uniform everyone else had came into their space with a tray in his hands. He stood by the door, gauging the two prisoners. Plates with breakfast heaped on them filled the tray.

"Come in. Just put it on the table." Pete waved him in.

The turnkey seemed to hesitate, unsure of the casual greeting.

"I don't think our plastic sporks are really too much of a threat."

"You could try to escape," said the man.

"To where? We're on a ship. In the middle of the ocean, right?"

The man shrugged. "Yeah, that's true. Somebody would find you and hunt you down as soon as you got to the deck."

"Exactly, my good man. We really can't go anywhere, even if you left the door open."

"Huh, I bet you'd like that!"

"And miss our Michelin star cuisine?"

The man snorted at the remark. Pete motioned at the tray he was holding. "Do you want to give the food to Dave?"

The prison guard looked down and almost seemed surprised he was still holding it. David held his hands out as if to take the tray.

"Just back up. I'll put it on the table. Don't try anything!"

"Of course not. I'm Pete, by the way. What did you say your name was?"

"I didn't" was the short, curt answer. He placed the tray on top of an already crowded table and carefully backed out of the cabin before engaging the locks.

Pete looked after the man for a moment before turning to David. "What's for breakfast?"

David looked at his companion. "You sure that's a good idea?"

"It's always a good idea to make friends."

David shrugged and went to the table. "Looks like eggs, ham and toast."

The two ate in relative silence, the thrumming of the engines filling the space.

"Pete, have you thought that we're probably not getting out of this alive?"

Pete paused and looked up at him. "Dave, I've done a lot of things in my life. Some really dangerous, some mind numbingly boring. I never thought I'm getting out of this alive." He gave David a feral grin. "However, I am going to try to maximize the time I have here."

David felt a roil of emotion welling up in him. "I don't know how you do it. You probably accomplished a lot in your life. I didn't do squat."

"Hey, what I've done is peanuts compared to you, my friend. I'm not the one who recorded the alien secret message."

David's heart skipped a beat. He put down his spork and he felt the blood drain from his face. "Yeah, about that. That was me not doing my job."

"What? Yeah, you froze up. A lot of people panicked."

"Well, not exactly." David looked around, rolled his eyes and let out a sigh. "I was doing something I shouldn't have been doing. I thought it was safe to do. I had no idea."

"What are you talking about?"

"I dropped some acid."

Pete had a confused look on his face.

"I took some LSD. I wanted to look at the stars, on the Summer Solstice. I was being irresponsible." David's ears burned in shame. He looked at his friend for some sign of understanding.

The corners of Pete's mouth curled up. His eyes crinkled and he seemed like he was stifling a reply .

"BWAHAHAHA!" finally erupted from him.

David frowned.

Pete's laughter died down. "I'm sorry, Dave, but you picked a great time to do that!"

"Yeah, I thought it would be a wonderful time for it, being the first night of summer and all that. I thought it would be 'significant'." Dave gave a little shudder. "Instead, I had these huge eyes staring down at me, dissecting me and all my life choices."

"It's cool man. If it wasn't for that, you probably would have aimed your equipment at the Eyes. Instead, something awesome came from it." Pete gave him an encouraging smile.

"Something that is probably going to get us killed."

Pete immediately became serious. "We're not dead yet."

At lunch time, the same guard dressed in what they thought of as civilian clothes brought them their meal. He put the new tray down and picked up the old dirty ones.

"Thank you so much, my good man. Say, would it be possible to maybe get a deck of cards or something?" said Pete.

The man paused. "We're going to be underway for a while. I'll see what I can do."

"You are a prince amongst men. Who do I thank for this?" Pete asked.

"Jack. My name is Jack."

"Jack. Thank you very much. We would really appreciate it."

Jack grunted at them and left with the used trays.

At dinner, a different set of armed and armored men brought them their food. They opened the door and one set it down just inside the threshold under the watchful gaze of the other before closing and locking the door.

***

A couple of days passed, marked by an accumulation of trays. One time, late after the last meal of the day, a detachment of men opened the door and told them to come out. They walked the labyrinthian passages up to the deck where a warm, muggy night greeted them. A thin crescent of the Moon was rising half way to the zenith. They were told to walk around the perimeter of the ship. There were floodlights every so often and a cameraman followed them, documenting their foray.

David glanced around, trying to avoid the bright lights.

Their circuit complete, they were lead below, back to the cell that held them, now newly clean. A pack of cards was the only thing that lay on the table.

"Looks like Jack came through for us."

"Yup." David was thinking.

"Katerina must be giving them hell, if they wanted to record us walking around."

"Mm huh. We're not going to Europe."

"Are you sure?"

"Positive. It was a little hard to see, because of the lights, but I'm pretty sure that I saw Arcturus over us. And if I'm not mistaken, Rigil Centaurus. Not sure about that one. It's not one I normally see." David shook his head. "I don't know where we're going, but we're not crossing the Atlantic. We're going south and west."

Pete thought for a moment. "Panama Canal?"

"That's what I would guess too. If we could only get word to Katerina. They could ambush the ship while it's crossing the canal."

The next day early in the morning, David felt that the ship had stopped its forward motion. The engines had a different sound. A gentle rocking by unseen swells moved the cabin. The engine would grow loud and the ship crept forward in fits and starts. Finally, the freighter became still and the sound of rushing water joined the idling engine sounds.

Whatever was happening seemed to occupy the crew as breakfast and lunch times passed without the sound of their door locks being used. The ship cruised along for a bit before repeating the cycles of holding still and the sound of water hitting the hull occurred a couple more times.

David was starting to get a headache from hunger when the welcomed sound of the door being worked rang in the cabin. A man holding a tray with a couple of sandwiches came into the room while Jack was just outside of the room. He held with distaste what looked like a normal machine gun, ostensibly to cover the two prisoners.

"What, no celebratory meal for crossing over into the Pacific?" Pete smiled at the man in the room.

The man put the tray down on the table and glared at Pete. Jack watched from beyond the door and tried to suppress a grin but he wasn't very successful. Leaving David and Pete to their meal, the door was locked once the armored thug left.

Fourteen

The Dinner

T he first morning in the new ocean roused them from their slumber with the now familiar clatter of bolts being disengaged. Their morning breakfast delivered, the two of them tried to figure out how to spend the time ahead of them. Pete broke out the cards. David would play a few rounds and lose interest in the game at hand and stare off into space. Pete dutifully proceeded to explain a different game. He seemed to know a lot of them.

"You really need four players for some of these," Pete said while he was shuffling the deck in between games.

David, only half paying attention to the rules being recited, looked right at Pete. "What are we going to do when we get back?"

"Oh ho! You *are* turning into an optimist!"

David felt exasperated. "I'm being serious. These people are obviously rich and power-ful, have technology that no one has and from what we found out, more compute power than anybody should have. I'm sure they would be very dangerous in a fight. Assuming we survive, how do you live with something like that? How do you go up against them?"

"Ellen figured out a way..."

"Don't say her name." David looked away. Instant guilt assaulted him.

Pete wrinkled his brow. "Why? I thought you cared about her? I know things were messy with her, but..."

"But nothing. Why did she have to start something with Harry? She just didn't take it seriously, that we were still in danger. She fought with Katerina about the phone."

"That's harsh, man. In her defense, you and Katerina did hook up. You two could have waited for a better time. And Katerina is part of the reason you got in trouble in the first place."

David looked down at the table. A deep sadness ached in him. "You're right. I wasn't thinking. So much has happened but it's not an excuse. I hurt my friend."

"Well, you should have done something to take care of that."

David rubbed his forehead and passed his hand over his hair. "Yeah, I should have done something. Anything really. It just didn't feel like we had the time. I wonder if it's too late."

"I think you should always make time to try to fix things with the people you care about."

"I mean, if we get out of here alive."

"Hey! What happened to the optimist?"

Both of them were silent. David rummaged in the bin of his thoughts, looking around the cabin.

Finally, he looked at Pete. "So what's this next game you want me to lose at?" .

"You wouldn't lose so much if you paid more attention."

***

At lunch time, a familiar face brought them their food.

"Hello Jack, how are you? We missed you. Thank you very much for the cards," said Pete.

"Hello, yourself. It looks like you two scored. You'll be having dinner with the old man tonight." He placed the tray down on the table by them.

"Really? What do we owe this to?"

"Something about celebrating crossing into a new ocean. Or some shit like that." Jack smirked.

"Are we to attend looking like this?" Pete waved his hands over himself. "Or do we get a chance to be presentable?"

"Yeah, we're supposed to get you some different clothes."

"Do you need our sizes?"

Jack gave an unpleasant laugh. "We know everything about you. They'll be brought later in the afternoon. Boss man likes to eat early. Make sure you're ready." His departure was accompanied by the requisite sounds.

"Oh boy, dinner with Rob. I can't wait." David was less than thrilled.

"This is our chance to find out where we're going and what's going on."

"A lot of good that is going to do us. If you don't mind, I think I'll just sit your little fishing expedition out."

"Tsk, tsk, one of the first rules of warfare is to find out all that you can about your enemy. Besides, I'm sure this is a command performance."

David couldn't help himself and his face contorted in disbelief. "You're just making things up now."

Pete gave a little chuckle. "Sun Tzu. But also, talking to him as a person may make him hesitate to just get rid of us."

"Hmm," was all David could think of in reply.

A few hours later, a detail of guards led them to the facilities onboard. They turned out not to be far from their room. David let the hot water sluice away the grime. He dreamed of just staying there. He felt that if only he could be under the stream of water long enough, the fears, the doubts, the worries would wash away. But his daydream was cut short by a gruff reminder that they had a dinner to attend. Regrettably, he finished and shaved with the provided razor.

Standing in front of the mirror, he appraised the razor. He briefly wondered if he should attempt to take it with him to maybe fashion some sort of weapon. A fantasy of the stupid sort as he realized he had no idea how to do that and even if he did, he didn't think he would get very far threatening Rob with it.

A different guard brought in two packages of clothes, wrapped in plastic. Threatening them with a shock stick made the two of them give him ample room as they sought the corner of the room furthest from him. The bundles were placed on the stools by the table. He growled at them to get dressed quickly as the boss liked to eat on time.

Pulling the packages apart, both of them quickly got dressed. The clothes were a little strange; they had no seams. But the pants, shirts and jackets fit as though they were custom tailored.

David was finishing knotting his tie when a knock on the door startled them. David and Pete looked at each other.

"Who is it?" David finally said.

"We're here to escort you to dinner," was the curt reply. David finished his tie and straightened his jacket. The two of them went to the door and said they were ready.

The four guards wound them through the ship, climbing decks until David felt sure they were in the superstructure. They arrived at the bridge of the ship. Large glass windows lined the wall on the left, overlooking the deck of the ship. A pilot wheel was on a pedestal in the center of the windows. Screens with various systems displayed on them covered the console that ran the length of the windshields. There was not a person in sight.

The remains of sunlight played across the deck. Soon, darkness would descend, cloaking the ship. In that light, the party came to a halt in front of a set of double doors that were ornately decorated with old astrology symbols. A pair of matched comets were the handles.

"Do come in." Rob's voice came out of a small box next to the door. A single LED glowed green on it.

The escort stepped back, away from Pete and Dave, away from the door, their weapons on their shoulders. David looked around, gave a small shrug and grabbed the tail of a comet. A single pull caused the door to easily open.

A large room, twice the size of the bridge, waited for them on the other side. A table that could easily seat twenty spanned the room from one end to the other. A carved and gilt chair was at left end of the table with two lesser chairs flanking it on each side of the table.

David recognized Rob's desk and carpet by the far wall. The transparent block from the warehouse was on the desk. As his eyes scanned the rest of the room, David felt his heart drop. In each corner of the room was a tripod with a rod on top.

Rob stood on the far side of the table by the throne at the head. He put down an envelope he was opening with a stiletto on the near corner of the expansive table and picked up a half filled martini glass. "Gentlemen, a pleasure to have you join me for dinner. Please, come in. Would you like a cocktail?" He motioned to a man in formal livery standing by a bar cart near the desk.

Pete wrung his hands. David saw this and put his hand out and shook his head. Pete took the hint and the two walked over to Rob.

"There is always too much work. Please forgive the intrusion of business with our pleasure." Motioning with the conical glassware towards them, he said, "My bartender makes excellent martinis. Proper gin with the right amount of vermouth. And olives. I highly recommend one or two."

David shook his head in negative.

"Very well. Your loss, really." He drained his glass. "I do hope you two aren't tiresome and can relax a bit. We're supposed to have a five course meal tonight. My chef has been working very hard. I've selected some wonderful wines to go with the meal. I'm rather proud of that." Rob seemed a little unsteady. David wondered how many martini's Rob had enjoyed already.

"I think we should go sit down. David, if you would be so kind to sit at my right. Peter, I'm not slighting you in the least, well, maybe a little, but David is the reason we are here. Come, come." Rob placed a hand on the armrest of the throne at the head of the table. The bartender came over and pulled the chair out for Rob. He pushed it in when Rob was ensconced in it. Pete was bristling but went around back and sat at Rob's left under the watchful eye of the servant. David pulled out his chair and sat on the right.

In his mind, David upgraded the man who helped Rob from bartender to manservant. The man went to the door and came back pushing a serving cart. With a flourish, he lifted a bell cover from a serving tray. Slices of French bread, toasted, with some creamy looking stuff and a piece of grilled stone fruit on top, were placed on his plate via golden tongs. The man then sprinkled tiny ribbons of basil, according to David's nose, on top of each of the pieces. The man then pushed the cart out of the room.

David stared at the food in front of him as though it were poison.

"Come on, eat! Here." Rob picked one up and took a large bite of it. "Delicious. Though I'm afraid this is the last of the fresh fruit on this trip. We don't get resupplied on long voyages."

With a bit of hesitation, David picked up one of the crostini and bit into it. An involuntary smile spread on his face. Rob was right, it was delicious. The charred fruit was sweet and it was balanced by what David thought of as tangy cream cheese. The fresh basil added just the right spice. He quickly returned to his dour expression.

"This is quite good. Grilled nectarines with goat cheese is a good pairing. My compliments to the chef." Pete had eaten one.

"I'm sure she'll be thrilled. Ah, about time they brought the wine. Good help is hard to find."

A glass of chilled white wine was poured for each of them. Pete took a sip. David merely held the glass.

"Did you inherit the ship or did you buy it yourself?" Pete said.

David froze and carefully looked at Rob.

Rob swirled the wine around in his glass and took a sip. "I bought it. My grandfather started the tradition of having a ship for the family, with the money he made from listening to the advice that the Ghost gave him. My father had his own ship and now I have mine. With upgrades, of course. It's easier that way."

The waiter appeared again and cleared their dishes. He placed bowls in front of the three along with soup spoons. From the tureen on his cart, he ladled a jewel-like brown broth with what looked like little round balls of vegetables. A few white meatballs were added to each bowl from a separate dish. David hoisted a spoonful to his mouth. He could barely stomach anything under the stress that he felt.

Pete lifted part of the meatball to his lips. "The consomme is fantastic. And the chicken quenelles are nicely done. Not overcooked and rubbery."

"Yes, you would know something about fine dining, wouldn't you? I believe that she could have a star or two if she had her own place."

Wielding his tableware like a wand, Pete casually pointed it at Rob. "Why is it that your family has had ships?"

Between slurps of the bullion, Rob said, "It's the easiest way to update. And the antipode is much easier to reach than the original site. Come now, David, is the food not to your liking? You've hardly touched anything."

"I'm just not use to such fine dining. This is becoming a very memorable evening." David hoped he had said the right words.

"Ha, there's more to come. Would you care for some more wine?" Rob held his goblet up and the waiter obliged by refilling it. "It is surprisingly difficult to maintain a decent wine cellar on a ship."

"I'm sure it is. But I'm sure with enough money that's something that can be fixed, right? This is a very nice Chardonnay, by the way." Pete took another sip of his glass while he eyed Rob.

"Indeed. But thanks to my connections, it's something that I can easily afford."

David gripped the stem of the glass tightly. "Connections? I thought you worked alone?"

"I meant connections to the Ghost. Through that." Rob motioned with his glass toward his desk.

"Your desk?" David was puzzled.

"Ha ha, no. The crystal on the desk. It's Grandfather's legacy, what he found on his miserable expedition to the northern wilds."

David looked at the crystal. It seemed to be about a foot tall and as wide, a transparent block. Now that he examined it, he saw that it wasn't a cylinder, that it had sides to it. But it seemed to have an odd number of sides which didn't seem quite right for what David remembered about crystals.

Turning to Rob, he said, "That crystal, it's not natural, is it?"

"No, it is very much not natural." Rob snickered. "We call it the Inkwell. Grandfather actually used it for that. Even after he found out what it really was. He was a stubborn man."

David felt a million questions bubble up in him.

Old wine glasses were cleared away and red wine was poured into new glasses. A thick log of golden pastry, decorated with cut out leaves and vines was presented to the group.

"Oh good! The main course. I've selected a robust cabernet to go with it. I hope you enjoy it." Rob seemed almost giddy.

The attendant cut thick slices from it and plated it with a scoop of mash potatoes that had a slightly burned crust and green beans with bacon. A small boat of horseradish was added to each plate before being put in front of each of the guests. David looked at the perfectly red meat in its casing and the way it was presented on his plate with the intensity that a condemned man studies his last meal.

Pete looked over his plate. "I see your chef has gone old school with the whole steakhouse Potatoes Romanoff and green beans."

"You are an entertaining fellow. Perhaps I can find an opening for you in my organization, as a court jester."

Pete silently fumed.

Rob stabbed at his Beef Wellington with relish. "This is simply delicious! You really must try it."

David cut a piece for himself and tasted the buttery, soft morsel. "Yes, this is really good." Pausing to watch Rob eat his dinner, David asked after a while, "Why did you invite us to dinner?"

"I felt that a celebration was in order. We crossed over to a new ocean. New ocean, new opportunities. Also, the USB drives are now blank. They plugged them into a computer that we controlled."

Pete took another bite of his food. "So you called us in to gloat?"

"You are such a simple man. I am merely being a gracious host."

David felt the pit of his stomach drop. The only way this evening could get worse was by ending in their deaths.

Rob held his hand up, while chewing, and took a sip of red wine. "I realized that, given the obvious fact of what happened a few weeks ago, that my position has changed. My relationship with the Ghost, for better or worse, must evolve to keep up with the circumstances. In order to deal with the new development, I came to the conclusion that I might need someone who has a handle on this, has dealt with it firsthand, as a radio astronomer. You know, to listen for further messages and to talk back to senders. I don't want them getting suspicious,"

David felt a creeping sense of horror at the realization that the evening, had indeed, gotten worse. "Are, are you offering me a job?"

"In a manner of speaking, yes. I will need someone to speak to the new would be overlords. You would have considerable resources."

"You tried to kill us," Pete growled.

Rob shrugged. "That was before you showed your resourcefulness. A regrettable oversight on my part." He turned his attention to the food in front of him.

David thought hard about what Rob was saying. He looked at Pete who was concentrating, just staring, at his food. "Has your Ghost friend said anything about the Eyes?"

Rob snorted and looked at David. "I am my own man. The so-called Eyes are a great opportunity. Beside, I don't really need the Ghost. I can ignore them. The Inkwell is more than enough, even if it is a dumb terminal."

David was going to ask a question when Pete grabbed for his wine glass and accidentally knocked it over, spilling on the envelopes.

"Clumsy oaf! I am going to have to cut you off. No more wine for you," said Rob. Pete grimaced while he tried to wipe up the mess that he had made. The waiter came forward to clean the table and remove the plates.

A cheese tray was brought out after the dinner plates were cleared.

"You have to try the blue. It comes from a cheese shop in Seattle. They have the best mac and cheese there. I recommend it with a bit of honey."

David was trembling, though he didn't know if it was fear, tiredness or anger. "This has been a memorable meal."

"Yes, I suppose we should do something like this again, depending on your decision, of course. The offer stands, but don't think too long. I rather like you to accept. We'll be at the antipode within the week. I will have to finalize things then. Now, I do hope you saved some room. We still have the last course."

Soon, a hockey puck sized dessert was placed in front of David. It looked like an albino flan, drizzled with some dark red sauce. David hesitantly took a spoonful of the creamy object. It was not too sweet.

"Panna Cotta, my favorite!" Rob attacked it with relish. Pete just stared at Rob with seething hatred in his eyes. David hoped that Rob didn't notice it.

"I don't think I've ever had this before," said David.

Rob looked up at him, his eyes slightly out of focus. "Normally, we'd have a port, maybe a cigar. But this has been a long day for me. I'm sure you won't mind if we call it a night after this."

"I think that would be ..."

Pete's chair flew backward. He was up and moving toward Rob. A flash of steel was in his hand, the stiletto that Rob had been using as a letter opener. David was surprised by his friend and he started to cry out to warn him.

Pete never even got close to Rob. Suddenly, he froze in mid step, knife out and pointed toward Rob.

"Well, well, that is rude! I invite you to a nice dinner and you try to harm me." Rob chuckled evilly. "I guess you thought you were quick, huh old man? Now I'll just have to crush you like a bug." Rob gestured in the air.

Pete's face contorted but he didn't cry out. His eye bulged but somehow he managed to stare down at Rob with a frightening intensity.

"Wait! I accept the job! On one condition!"

"Oh?"

"You let Pete live. I'll join you, I'll be your radio astronomer."

Whatever was happening to Pete stopped. Rob seemed to consider Pete who was trapped like a fly in an invisible amber. Looking right at him, he said, "You're not worth the cleanup effort. Guards, come take this away." Rob waved his hand at Pete, dismissing him. Four burly guards stood by Pete and one of them took the knife from his motionless hand. With a guard on each limb, whatever was holding Pete was released and he started flailing. But the handlers were ready for his exertions. They simply carried the writhing man out as he yelled "You're an evil fuck! I'll kill you! You damned piece of shit."

The door closed on the group, leaving Rob alone with David. Rob smiled at David. "Welcome to the team."

David felt his blood run cold.

Fifteen

Working for a Living

A different cabin waited for David. One lone escort led him to the new location. A room with a single bed, a chair, a shelf with some toiletries, and a pull down table met his eyes.

"If there's anything you need, let me know sir," the man said.

David nodded and was left by himself to contemplate the deal he had struck. No sound of locks being engaged followed. He took off his jacket, loosed his tie and lay experimentally on the bed, the softness of it small comfort.

What have I done?

In the solitude of the night, a cold sweat broke out on his brow, the enormity of what he told Rob he would do staggered him. He felt sure any deviation from what was expected would be dealt with harshly. Trying to calm down by drawing deep breaths, his chest felt like it was shuddering from the onslaught of his beating heart. Nervous energy twitched his limbs.

Slowly, he felt parts of him grow still. At some unknown point, he drifted into an uneasy sleep.

***

In the morning, he woke with a start. He dreamt that he was suffocating and the act of gasping for air brought him to quick awareness. His hands clawed at his neck before he calmed down. He sat up, looked around, and tried to stretch his muscles.

Sounds of conversations just outside his door tickled his ears. Hesitantly, he tried the door handle. The door opened inward and he poked his head out, to find the source of the voices.

A small knot of men who weren't wearing armor and weapons were walking away from him. They were still dress similarly, all in black. David decided on the spot to follow them and stepped out into the gangway, shutting his door. He hurried not to lose sight of them.

Luck was with him. They headed to mess. Smells of food permeated the air and the men walked through a doorway. A good sized space held two rows of tables. The buzz of people eating and talking with the occasional sound of cooking filled the room. A cafeteria style buffet held warming trays with a stack of compartmented plates at one end.

David suddenly felt very hungry. He really hadn't eaten much at Rob's fancy dinner last night so he stepped in, crossed the room, and picked up a tray.

Immediately, every eye was on him and the sound died. Only the sound of something sizzling on a griddle in the back was heard. In his formal wear, he felt out of place to the uniformed personnel in there. He steeled himself against putting down the tray and leaving.

Drawing a deep breath, he filled his tray. The food was familiar, being what was brought to him and Pete.

At that thought, he stopped and almost faltered but managed to keep his composure. Looking around, he could see the diners had returned to their breakfast. Almost all. A single man stared right at him.

David walked straight to him and sat down. "Good morning, Jack."

"Huh, left your buddy behind." It was a statement, not a question.

Carefully looking at his plate, David pushed some of the food around with his fork. "I didn't have a choice. He would have been killed." David was surprised that he said that. He looked expectantly at Jack.

Jack raised an eyebrow. "Tell you what. Meet me here after lunch and I'll show you around. We can start with the quartermaster, so you can get some better clothes."

He finished downing his cup of coffee and picked up his tray, depositing it in a slot. Turning to David, he nodded and walked out, leaving him to finish eating.

***

Time crawled. Pacing back and forth in his room occupied his time. He examined every square inch of surface in the cabin. Twice. Briefly venturing out, he found the head and showers. He thought that at any moment, someone would tap him on the shoulder to take him away, his heart skipping a beat whenever he heard a noise outside his door.

Finally, he couldn't stand being in the cabin any longer. He retraced his steps and went to the mess hall to wait for Jack.

The room had been cleaned and the staff was preparing lunch. While he waited, food items were loaded into the trays and people started showing up. Everyone gave him a wide berth.

Previously, David thought everyone was male, due to the bulk of the armor. But now, sitting in their midst, he realized that a number were, in fact, female. And not everyone was in black, militaristic garb. The vast majority sported black dungarees, the sailors and everyone else needed to run things he figured. Everyone had a devil patch on their shoulder. All their clothes fit them very well. He wondered if everyone got custom clothes. David was keenly aware of how he stood out in his dress pants and white shirt.

When he started to wonder if Jack was coming, the man showed up. Jack wore neither of the uniforms, but rather simple black clothes composed of slacks and a short sleeve shirt. The only concession to the uniform worn by everyone else was a patch on his shoulder.

"You eaten yet?"

David shook his head and followed Jack to the line. Grabbing a plate, he looked over the selection, a far cry from last night. Thinking about the evening made him feel ill. He redoubled his resolve to talk to Pete.

"I know you can ..."

Jack interrupted his speech. "We'll go to the quartermaster. That way you can get stuff. Tablet, clothes, stuff for your job. I take it you have to do something for the old man, right?"

David nodded.

"Good, first we eat. Save your questions for when we are out of here."

David wolfed his food, then followed Jack as he went forward on the ship.

The quartermaster was adjacent to the third hold. It was a room similar in size to the mess, filled with shelves and containers. Near the back, a man sat behind a counter. The man reached beneath the counter and handed David a tablet when Jack explained that he was new.

"Just pick what you need from the catalog app. It'll tell you a delivery time and what shelf and bin it's in if you're allowed to have it." The man behind the counter dismissively waved at the tablet.

"Does it do anything else?" said David.

The man smirked. "You can get all the porn you want on it."

David blushed. He was about to say something to the man when Jack waved at him and said, "Come on, let's see where you're set up. Turn it on."

David walked away from the sneering man and turned the tablet on as they went forward on the ship.

"Good afternoon, David," appeared on the screen.

David stopped and looked at Jack. "How, how does it know it's me?"

"Fucking thing knows everything on the ship. I swear, it reads my mind. Ask it where your workshop is located."

A quick look at the screen showed the words, *"Your workshop is 12-AQ, fore of the first hold, two decks below the main deck."* He relayed the words to Jack.

"I know where that's at. It put you far from your cabin."

Jack took him topside and they walked the length of the ship in the hot sun. David looked at the blue sky. He hadn't seen it in a while. One of the holds had its cover rolled back. An arm composed of many segments smoothly lowered a pallet full of large cylinders with "Xe" marked on the sides. Despite the rolling ship, the cargo went straight down into the hold. David couldn't spot the operators among the crew. Peeking over the waist high wall surrounding it revealed tightly packed machinery. He ran after Jack, who was waiting at a hatch. Stairs went down into the relative darkness.

"We go down two flights and make a right."

Down the stairs they went to the second landing and through a door. A little way down the corridor, there were two doors on either side of the passageway. The door to the fore of the ship was marked with a placard, 12-AQ, his new office. Inside was a good-sized space, easily three or four times the size of his cabin. A desk and office chair were in one corner and the opposite corner held a high workbench with some instruments and tools on it. There was a tall stool in front of the workbench.

"There's a way to get to your cabin, going through the other door. But that makes you go through the holds. I don't recommend that. Anything else?"

David paused. He didn't know who to trust but he had to ask. "Is there some way I can check on Pete?"

Jack grimaced. "I thought you might ask that. That might not be a good thing to do just yet. Maybe wait a bit."

Starting and stopping a couple of times, David finally said, "Fine. I'll wait."

Jack nodded at him and left.

Now alone in his office, he sat at his desk and thought.

What can I do while I look like I'm making the transmitter?

A smile settled on his face. Of course, make another transmitter! He was going to need parts.

"Tablet, what do you have for electronic parts catalog?" he said out loud as he selected the app.

"There is a wide variety of parts available. Please specify type and operational parameters."

This was going to be interesting.

***

First thing he did the morning of the next day was verify what he thought were the locations of the alien receivers. Ellen called them "routers". Thinking of her brought feelings of remorse and worry in him. He pushed them down. Pulling up the published frames, he crossed-referenced the pulsars on the message. The tablet seemed to have every pulsar specified in its databases. Soon, he pinpointed the location in space for the first of the three routers. It happened to be 3.6 light years away, a mere stone's throw. All he had to do was make a maser operating at 21 centimeters capable of reaching the distance. He snorted at the likelihood of being able to do it.

Hoping for a different outcome, he mapped out the locations of the other two routers which proved even more discouraging. The two following frames denoted sites even further away, as though it were a challenge to the human race. He threw his hands up in frustration. All he knew was that at 21 centimeters wavelength, there was no way human technology could even begin to reach the closest one, never mind the next one or the furthest one out.

Turning to the tablet, he computed the energy required to illuminate the target at that distance. An overwhelming sinking feeling settled in the pit of his stomach. It was not a small number. An Apollo or Manhattan style project would be required, no, even bigger, with the stakes higher than anything before in history. The prize being talking to aliens.

Who could put a price on the most precious commodity of all, knowledge? Though it did occur to him, they set the bar pretty high.

Half-heartedly, he punched in the requirements for the maser, wondering what the tablet would respond given an impossible task. His eyes widened when it came back with a suggestion.

He read the specifications of the piece. Several times, to make sure it was there.

The part was ordered and he was told it would be available within the hour. David was very surprised that they would have that onboard. Buoyed by his little success, he performed a few more calculations and created a few diagrams. Soon a prototype design was scrawled out. There was a problem of scale but if he could build a small model, then it became a question of repeating the nodes until your ten mile wide array was built.

Over the next couple of days, he became a familiar sight at the quartermaster. Collecting the parts, assembling and testing the components, the project took shape. Two transmitters were built, one to talk to the stars and one to monitor and control the scale model. Early on, he realized standing by it when it was operating would be quite dangerous. While he built the radio controller, he selected parts that far exceeded what was necessary, pinning his hope no one would pay too much attention to what he was assembling. It was a foolish hope, to be sure, but he had to try to signal somebody, anybody. He only interrupted his work for meals when his stomach complained too much and slept when he could no longer go on.

All the while, he wondered how he could meet with Jack to find out how Pete was doing. The guilt of not talking to his friend filled his dreams with recriminations. David felt himself growing haggard while a collection of parts grew in the middle of his workspace.

The following day, he ran into Jack at lunch. David whispered to him if he had heard anything.

Jack took a good look at him and told him to meet him in the passageway in the first hold after dinner.

That afternoon was not as productive as the previous days. The appointed time came and David found himself in front of the door opposite his. Opening it, he saw an elevated, grated catwalk that ran from the door he came in to a distant wall where another door stood.

Inside the hold, all around the bridge, was machinery. Intricate, crowded machinery, jammed with all manner of pipes, fins, coils and who knows what else that presented an almost solid wall. David's mouth fell open. The smell of oil and ozone permeated the air, along with strange chemical odor. A harsh, red light not meant for human eyes gave the incessantly chattering machine a ruddy complexion.

David almost turned back but he could see a figure on the narrow walkway. He closed the door behind him and went quickly toward the man.

He motioned at the mechanisms around them. "Jack, what is this?"

"The reason I don't like going through the holds. That nobody likes to go through the holds." Jack pointed at the machinery. "It was started back in the warehouse and placed in the hold when it was still small. We built it up to a certain point and then *it* took over and started building itself." He shuddered.

It was hard for David to see clearly but there was motion in one part of the assemblage. What looked like an industrial robot arm with too many joints was taking apart a piece of the fantastic apparatus.

David gave a low whistle. "Is this what makes the stuff in the catalog? Wow!"

Jack ran his hand through his hair and scratched his head. "You didn't bring the tablet, I hope. When you get back, you should ask the tablet about it. Personally, all this gives me the willies. But since nobody likes coming in here, we can talk more or less freely. Look, I haven't been able to get near Pete. I'm not assigned to that anymore. And you get asked about it if you go around getting information that you don't need to do your job. But I do know someone I can ask. However..." Jack looked around and leaned in close to David, his voice barely audible above the din. "You gotta do me a favor. I want off this boat."

Surprised, David pulled back and took a good look at him. Jack was staring right at him. He looked sincere to David. This was dangerous territory he found himself in but what choice did he really have? Jack was expectant, waiting.

David nodded at him. "Alright, if I can get off this ship, I promise to take you with us. Us. That means Pete, too."

Jack thought about it and stuck his hand out. David shook it while wondering about yet another promise made.

***

Late that evening, seated at the table in his cabin, he pulled out the tablet, curious about Jack's remark. "Tablet, what is the machine in the holds?"

"*It is a stage one universal manufacturing unit.*"

So many questions came to mind. He started with the first one. "What do you mean by stage one?"

"*It produces the necessary components for subsequent stages to be assembled.*"

"What are the subsequent stages?"

"*Stage two is an autonomous resource harvester, stage three is a self-replicating mobile unit, stage four is planetary production unit for...*"

"Planetary production? What do you mean by that?"

"*Planetary production entails covering the surface area of the planet with mobile units working in concert to disassemble the planet.*"

"How long will it take to disassemble the planet?"

"*4.397 mean solar years.*"

"After stage three is done?"

"*After the update.*"

Rob had mentioned something about an update at the ill-fated dinner. He racked his brain trying to remember what Rob had said. "When is the update scheduled for?"

"*The update is scheduled to occur in four days.*"

Equal parts terror and disbelief fought for attention in his mind. His lips quivered as he whispered, "What are you?"

"*I am the Terminal Guidance Block, colloquially known as the Inkwell.*"

David stared at the screen for long minutes. He finally got up. Rob had to be told. Even though it was late, he would chance it. He had to.

Rob was behind his desk, opening a letter with a familiar stiletto. A cup of fine china with a saucer held some steaming tea next to him. The aroma of chamomile drifted from the cup. "What brings you here? It's rather late. I'm busy and don't like being interrupted."

Half way to the desk, David stopped. "I asked the tablet about the thing in the hold. Or should I say, the Inkwell."

Rob placed the ersatz letter opener down. He steepled his fingers and looked at David. "Yes, it's a wonderful piece of machinery. Very handy."

"Very handy? Have you asked what it's for? Do you know about stage four?"

Rob gave him a broad, toothy smile. "Yes, of course. How do you think I intend to get off planet? Play your cards right and I'll take you with us. You can even bring your girlfriends. We'll need breeding stock."

David was horrified. He felt his jaw drop. "What are you talking about?"

"Tsk, tsk. Did you find out what the purpose of stage four is? It's to make more Seeds."

The confusion that David felt must have been playing out on his face. Rob looked at him and impatiently motioned him closer. "Come here. Just watch. Inkwell, play recording one."

The eleven-sided, foot high block that was on his desk really did look like its namesake. It had a reservoir about an inch wide in the middle of its top face that went half way through it. David wasn't sure what Rob meant but while looking at it, the room went black and he couldn't see anything at all. Panic at remembering the previous black-out started to affect him. But the stifling quiet was missing. Looking around, he noticed tiny pinpricks of light all around. The feeling of floating in space was very strong especially as he thought he recognized some of the patterns as constellations. A gray surface, pitted and scarred with sharp shadows, lay at his feet. There were various dishes and tall trusses which he thought of as antennas on the surface of the elongated rock. The points wheeled about, centering on an unassuming yellow star straight ahead.

There was movement near the front. He went up on tiptoes, trying to make out what was going on. It looked like a thick cylinder was telescoping out of the front of an asteroid. A bright flash of light came from the end, seemingly pointed at the bright star.

While he puzzled over what he saw, a flurry of activity broke out over the surface. Shutters rolled back and small, brilliant specks came out at high speed, racing away from the surface toward something behind the camera. Involuntarily, he twisted around to see what was behind him.

Suddenly, white filled his vision.

David was momentarily dazzled. When he recovered, the view had switched to showing the yellow, target sun. It grew larger and larger until it filled the field of vision. Individual convections cells could be seen. A loop of plasma erupted in front of him and whatever was recording passed under it, skimming the fiery surface. The sun slowly fell behind him.

Ahead, darkness again, interrupted by recognizable arrangements of stars. Dead in the middle of the images lay a planet. David's blood ran cold as familiar blue and green markings resolved into view, leaving no doubt what it was. Watching, he saw the camera come over the Atlantic and fly over Europe. A vast plain of trees spread out before him. Whatever it was, it was still some distance up when another flash filled his sight.

The lights returned to the room. David blinked at the light. The Inkwell sat on the desk, unassuming in its malice.

He couldn't move his eyes away from the crystal, from the images that it had shown him. Rob's voice came to him. "That asteroid ship at the beginning was a Seed. It seeks out candidate civilizations, civilizations that it can use to create more ships, to spread out in the galaxy. At least, it did until it got destroyed by your new sky friends. More's the pity."

David looked at the evil thing on Rob's desk. "What if something were to happen to the Inkwell?"

"Ha! There isn't a power on Earth that could harm it. It once held the core of a star."

Sudden epiphany came crashing into David. The data from the last frame of the message made terrible sense. He gripped the edge of the desk to steady himself.

"You need to get out of my office. Like I said, it's late. Finish the transmitter to keep your star buddies off our backs."

***

David staggered back to his cabin and sat down with a sheet of paper in front of him. There was no way that he wanted the Inkwell to know what he was doing.

Not accessing the tablet to check on his values made it a little difficult, especially as it wasn't his area of expertise, but he trudged on, calculating the results by hand. He worked into the deep night until he had an answer he thought was right. The number he saw on the paper filled him with dread, made him fervently wish it was wrong. It probably was but in a way that underestimated the effect.

The last frame, the piece of the puzzle that no one had understood, was made clear. Rob had said that the Inkwell had held the core of a star in it. It wasn't just any star. The Inkwell had held a cylinder of neutronium and had dropped it into the Earth where it undoubtedly settled in the very center. The dimensions from the meeting at the UN fit what he saw on Rob's desk.

David's scratchings were attempts to calculate what would happen if whatever magic held the core together suddenly stopped holding it together. Apart from some wildly exotic particle interactions, it would release the energy of a six mile wide asteroid slamming into the Earth. David couldn't imagine that the consequences of that would be benign.

He sat back in his chair and ran his fingers through his hair. His head felt like it had a fever as a feeling of unreality settled on him and he wracked his brain, trying to figure out what to do. All he saw was an end to humans on Earth, either right away or in a few years.

Sixteen

Ellen's Story

Ellen knew exactly how badly she had fucked up. The hard, sharp pebbles of asphalt surface, worn and weathered by too many cold winters and salt, pressed into her flesh, the weight of her "supposed" boyfriend sat on the small of her back and the hard, steel barrel of the gun he held pressed against her temple. She had fucked up royally.

The awful, hushed quiet the enemy used before was the first hint that something had gone wrong. Now, it stifled the screams futilely issuing from her mouth. She could see Pete and David being hidden by a crush of people making their way to a van, the rear doors flung open. Shouts for help is what she figured David's open mouth meant.

A group of the enemy attacked the trunk of the car that had brought them here. There was a flash and a force pressed down on her, knocking the wind out of her. Instinctively, her eyes closed against the dust. She gasped for air and her eyes fluttered open, looking about. The dampening sound quality left the milieu though everything seemed surprisingly distant. Harry's weight shifted. Moans and cries started to filter in, no doubt from the attackers. Ellen didn't understand why things were so quiet in the aftermath. Contorted figures lay on the ground in her sight. A few were oddly shaped and covered in red. There didn't seem to be anyone else in sight. A couple of the further participants were attempting to get up. The van was gone. The back half of the car that brought them here was missing. Someone was going to be pissed.

She realized the gun was no longer in contact with her head. Hazarding a look, she turned her head toward where the barrel had been. The pistol's business end was pointed down, at the ground, the whole thing carelessly held by an outstretched arm, some distance from her. A finger was not tightly wrapped around the trigger.

Twisting under her captor's weight, she followed the arm up to a shoulder doused in blood. A large piece of black metal adorned Harry's forehead and jutted out the side. A scream bubbled up out of her and she pushed the corpse off of her before stopping and drawing a breath.

She heard a faint door slam and a quiet pop, pop, pop. Her eyes followed her ears. Katerina was standing on the steps to the safe house, weapon drawn and pointing, scanning the carnage. Hearing must not be working quite right, Ellen thought, because it looked like Katerina was yelling at someone and she couldn't make out what was being said. She followed the line of her pistol and saw a man with one of the double-barrelled rayguns in their hands sweeping it up toward Katerina.

Pop. He went down.

Katerina spotted her. She launched off the steps and ran toward her. A man tried to stop her and received a swift kick in the balls for his effort.

"Are you OK? Can you walk?" Katerina's neck muscles stood out, veins clearly visible. She sounded so tiny and far away. Ellen nodded.

"Come on, we have to go."

Ellen scrambled to her feet. Katerina put her arm around Ellen's elbow and the two rapidly walked away from the scene of devastation.

***

Hearing slowly returned to Ellen. She sat at a table, looking out the darkened window of a coffee shop. Katerina sat across from her. Two cups of coffee, steam no longer rising, were in front of them. Some time ago, police cars and emergency vehicles whizzed past the window, lights on and sirens blaring in the dusk.

Katerina did not look happy. Using her index finger, she tapped on the table to draw her attention. "What happened? Where are David and Pete?"

A shudder worked its way through Ellen. Shoulders drooping, head down, focused on the coffee cup, she reached for it. It was difficult to pick up as it swam around in her sight. Her stomach was in turmoil.

"Hey." Katerina tapped on the table again. Her words were short and harsh and her eyebrows were knitted. "Hold it together. You can fall apart later. What happened?"

Ellen sniffed once and nodded. "Harry was working for them. He put a gun to my head and pushed me down on the ground. I saw David and Pete being taken away. That's when the car blew up." Her throat was dry as that long ago desert so she took a sip of the coffee. It was cold and bitter.

"That was my gray case."

"You had a bomb in it the whole time?"

"I did tell you not to open it, didn't I?"

Ellen lifted her eyes tentatively. Katerina unblinking stare transfixed her. Involuntarily, Ellen gulped. Her voice sounded weak to her ears. "Now, what do we do?"

"We go to the UN office. I start pulling strings."

The chair scraped backward as Ellen stood up. "The data!"

Katerina held her hand up. "I grabbed the thumbdrive when I heard the explosion. But, yes, we start there. It's obviously an existential threat to them. We need to see about making that happen." She took a large sip of her cold coffee before getting up and tossing it into the garbage. "Let's go."

Ellen dumped her coffee and followed. Outside, they got a ride to the office where the enemy had lain in wait. The first thing Katerina did was roam the halls looking for Cornelius. She found him getting ready to go home.

"This operation has been compromised. I am exerting Executive Order 1337-b. I will need the employment history of everyone involved with this project. A team will be coming in the hour."

A stunned look played over Cornelius' face as he held his hat. "What are you talking about? We have a meeting with the General Assembly on Monday."

Katerina continued. "A little over an hour ago, we were attacked in broad daylight. A car was blown up. I'm sure it was on the news."

"I didn't realize we had anything to worry about. We're doing this for all mankind."

"Remember what we discussed in Tel Aviv?"

Cornelius mouth hung open.

Ellen spoke up. "Sir, we need to get a computer. And a SAN or NAS. Several in fact. We found out that the data we gave you was tampered with. Most likely by Harry. We need to make sure that original data doesn't get destroyed."

"I, I will see what I can do." Cornelius sighed and went and sat in his desk chair with a heavy plop. He reached for the phone on his desk.

A ringing came from Ellen's pocket. She fished it out of her pocket. Looking at the screen, Ellen felt the blood drain from her.

Katerina noticed the look on her face. "Who is it?"

"It's Harry's number."

"Answer it! Quick!"

Her finger slid across the accept button.

David's voice came out of the speaker. "Hello? Hello? Ellen? I don't have a lot of time."

Her heart leapt. There was a video call request on her screen which she quickly accepted. "David? Are you guys OK? Do you know where you're at?"

The phone framed David's face. Sweat glistened on his brow, his face ashen. Indistinct shadows were behind him. "No, I don't know. They made me get on to tell you that if you want to see me and Pete again, you'll have to destroy the data on the drive."

"Give me that." Katerina took the phone from Ellen. "Tell them that we are going to need assurances."

David's eyes went up and down her face, studying it. "Katerina Eyal. I think they heard."

An impassive mask came over Katerina's face. "Excellent. We will consider their demands." She handed the phone back to Ellen.

Somewhat surprised, Ellen said, "How will they know we kept our end of the bargain?"

"I told them how many copies I had made." The image looked off camera. "They want you to tell them how many you've made. They can tell when you are lying."

Ellen was taken aback. "We haven't made any yet. There's just the two that were made."

David looked away and then back to the camera. "Good, good. They say you're telling the truth. Don't make any more, Ellen. Please keep this phone close to you. I don't know when I will be able to talk to you again." A hand came between David and the camera and the screen went shiny black.

The phone seemed heavier than it should be. Everything was dragging her down. How could things get worse?

""That wasn't David." Katerina's voice was flat, unemotional.

Puzzled, Ellen looked right at her. "What do you mean? He sure looked like him, sounded like him."

"He didn't act right. Specifically toward me." Katerina bit her lower lip and hesitated. "Considering, uh, our history?"

Ellen found out how things could get worse. She felt her jaw drop. "Oh crap. You're right."

Katerina looked right at her. "I'm going to need you to tell me everything you told Harry. About our group, about David and me. I think I would like to avoid talking to them as much as possible."

"I don't think I told him much." Ellen was quiet for a few seconds. "Yeah, I didn't say much about you two, in particular. I told him how you were bitch and wouldn't let me have a phone." Ellen's cheeks burned. "Sorry. I didn't exactly want to think about you two being together, you know." Ellen closed her eyes and took a deep breath. Holding it, she thought that her recalcitrance to talk about them was possibly the only good news today. She had to do something. A long sigh escaped her.

Opening her eyes, she locked gazes with Katerina. "What do we do to rescue them?"

***

Cornelius found an office and Katerina furnished a computer, cannibalized no doubt off of someone's desk. Ellen hastened to get setup and immediately downloaded development tools.

A few phone calls were made and Katerina furnished an IP address and port on a yellow post-it note. "You can access a SQL database of phone records here. I have to go talk to the team."

Ellen threw herself into the task. She pieced together a program, from scraps of other programs, to search the records. She would find where the video came from. But she didn't kid herself. This could take a while. A half a dozen other tasks were started, to aid the search.

"Ellen, it's really late. We need to rest." Katerina's voice broke her train of thought.

The screen in front of her held a multitude of windows, a couple already scraping sites. Regarding the results of her handiwork proved a bit difficult in the bluish florescent light. Her eyes protested and felt hot and itchy. The letters seemed oddly proportioned, a strange font for this. She waved Katerina off. "Just a second."

"Ellen, you're not going to make it go faster. I know you're an amazing programmer and it's the best it can be at the moment. Let's get some rest. It's been a long day. You can look at it in the morning, with fresh eyes."

A wave of despair hit her. Elbows on the table before the keyboard, as though in supplication, she held her head in her hands. "It was my fault."

She was a little surprised at feeling a gentle hand on her shoulder.

Katerina's voice was soft and low. "Maybe it was your fault. Maybe it wasn't. But everyone screws up eventually. We're just human. It's how you recover from it that really matters."

The hand came off. "Sometimes, there isn't a chance to recover. But that's not now. We're not going to let this be that time. I don't have to tell you we can't blow this. And as bad as it is, having David and Pete taken, I think you realize there's something else going on. Something much bigger at stake. And we need to figure it out."

Ellen's lips tightened. She blinked once, twice and nodded her head. In her core being, she knew Katerina was right.

"Come on." Katerina headed toward the door. "Let's get some shut eye."

Numb from sudden exhaustion, she pushed back from the desk. "Yeah, that's a good idea. Where are we going?"

Silence was her response and she followed in Katerina's wake, not really caring where they went.

***

Morning came, bright and unsuitably early. The pair stopped at the coffee shop in the lobby of the nearby hotel they were staying in. Ellen got their largest cup with a couple of extra shots of espresso. It slowly worked its magic, clearing out the cobwebs of troubled sleep.

Pausing in the doorway to the requisitioned office, she drew a breath and straightened her shoulders. *Let's do this.* She went directly to her waiting chair and wiggled the screen to life.

Katerina followed her and stood behind her, looking at the display. "What have you got?"

Her now fresher eyes scanned the results of her efforts. Carefully tracing the values across the windows, Ellen put a finger on an entry on the screen. "Huh, it seems to have gone all over the place but they didn't really try to hide it. It came from some place called..." She consulted a map in a window, "Freeport? It's on Long Island, on the southern coast."

Katerina bent right over her to look at the map. "That's not far at all. Can you get closer?"

"Hang on. It went through a cell tower. I'm trying to get the other nearby ones so we can triangulate."

Ellen forgot about everything for a while. She searched and wrote scripts and soon had a result overlaying on the map of the town. A sigh of satisfaction came from her. "I found them." She turned to look for Katerina.

Katerina was leaning back in an office chair, her cowboy boots on a table by the corner. She was looking at some papers in her hands. In an instant, she was behind her, looking at the screen. "Where are they?"

"It looks like a warehouse in the satellite pictures. Doesn't have a company name associated with it. Right by the docks, too."

"Can you find out some more about it?" A predatory look was on her face. It reminded Ellen of a hawk.

Ellen typed a few more things in her browser. "Oh oh. There was a fire there overnight. It burned to the ground."

Katerina pursed her lips. "Of course."

"Hang on." Ellen's fingers flew over the keyboard. She wasn't going to give up that easy. "What are you doing?"

"They had to go somewhere. That was just last night. All those people can't just disappear. You need something big to carry everyone."

Katerina's face lit up. "Something like a ship!"

"Bingo."

"You are good!"

Ellen's tips of her ears heated up. She pulled up another browser window. She squinted at the information being shown and zoomed in. "Well, shit. AIS said there was a ship offshore a few miles from the warehouse. It got underway about the same time as the fire. And then it disappeared. They must have turned the transponder off. Awfully ballsy."

"I've got some more phone calls to make. There's got to be a satellite view of it." Katerina left Ellen alone.

No sense of relief accompanied Katerina's proclamation. She had a sinking feeling that it couldn't be that easy. What else did they have up their sleeves? Where could they be heading?

She looked at the papers that Katerina had deposited on the desk next to her. They were pictures of the message frames. The last one, the one with the warning, was on top.

Curiosity got the better of her. What were the numbers? It looked like a long string of binary digits. She ran her finger along the sequence, typing the 1's and 0's in. Holding her breath, she hit enter. One point three seven eight nine and some random digits times ten to the fortieth power. *That's a big number.*

Looking at the last frame, she remembered that number being associated with a cylinder. Acting on a hunch, she calculated how many inch wide by six inch long rods would fit in the Earth. The number was nowhere close to the first number. Her forehead wrinkled in thought.

"Found something else?" Katerina's voice intruded.

"Not really." Ellen relaxed. "I was looking at the last frame of the message, again. It's like we're missing the point of it. Did you make your calls?"

Now it was Katerina's turn to make a face. "Yeah, there was a ship there, some sort of freighter. It disappeared."

"What?"

"It shows the ship in one frame. The next, it's gone. But seeing how that's all digital now, I believe our friends are up to their tricks again."

Ellen slumped. "They have a long reach."

"Yes they do. We have to figure out where they are going, so we can arrange a suitable reception for them." Katerina had a faraway look in her eyes, her teeth showed from slightly parted lips.

A surprised feeling came over Ellen. A fierceness came up from the depths of her being. *How dare these people!*

She turned back to her screen. She would find them.

***

The two of them settled into a routine. Get up in the morning, grab some java from the hotel coffee shop and walk to the office. Katerina set a very quick pace. Ellen would be out of breath by the time they got in. Once there, Katerina would go off to make calls, have meetings, make contingency plans and generally leave Ellen alone.

Ellen would stare at the screen, following lead after lead, looking for energy utilization spikes and network routes and datacenter usage. She dug deep for where their computing machinery might be located, the ever growing number of tabs on her browser testament to her effort to correlate capacity to location. She even wondered if maybe they needed a ship get to their secret undersea location. Eventually, she would end up slowly banging her head on the desk

As a break from that task, she tried to figure out where the ship was going.

In the evening, Katerina stood in the doorway to the office and ask if she had anything. Ellen would shake her head and the two would silently go back to the hotel, much more slowly than the morning. Ellen would order delivery now that things were relatively back to normal and cry herself to sleep.

And today, they had received a video of David and Pete walking around a ship at night. Immediately, she launched her digital bloodhounds. The call originated from a geostationary satellite. Somewhere in the Western Hemisphere was spectacularly unhelpful.

After almost a week of nothing but failure, the video was the last straw. Ellen couldn't take it anymore. Her dinner sat untouched on the table in her room. She decided maybe some alcohol would ease the pain. The hotel bar was conveniently nearby.

Walking out of the elevator, she halted and almost turned around. Katerina sat at one end of the bar, a drink in her hand.

Ellen sucked on her lips. She wasn't sure she wanted company but decided drinking alone was a bad idea. She walked up and pulled out the bar stool next to Katerina. "What are you drinking?"

Katerina looked tired, maybe even bordering on weary. "Mojito."

"I'll have the same," she said to the waiting bartender.

Katerina's knuckles went white on the glass. Small ripples could be seen in the drink. She opened her mouth but snapped it shut and closed her eyes Ellen thought she heard her mutter something.

"Katerina, you OK? Do you want me..."

She was interrupted by an upheld hand. Gray-green eyes opened and inspected her. Ellen felt that every detail and flaw were exposed to the gaze. She resisted the urge to hide.

Bent down, Katerina took a sip of her drink. Her voice sounded clear. "Look, I know we didn't start off on the best of terms. I made a lot of assumptions about you. I realize that you have no reason to like me now. But I think that we should try to get along, at least until we rescue the boys."

"I thought we had reached an understanding, back in San Francisco. We talked about it, in the elevator. We weren't supposed to try anything until after we were safe." Ellen's eyes narrowed. She clenched her glass.

Nodding, Katerina looked at her own highball. "It's not an excuse, but I'm tired of this life. I just wanted something normal and David seemed like that."

Ellen snorted. "David? You wanted normal and you went for David?"

Katerina spoke in low tones into her drink. "He has good points. In the desert, he was willing to sacrifice himself for you and Pete. He took on the gunman in the cafeteria to try to buy me time."

Ellen drew back. "Yeah, he did do that." She took a good swallow of her drink and faced the bar. Words just above a whisper came out. "I guess I didn't have a chance anyway."

Next to her, a squealed sounded as the bar stool top swung around. Ellen could feel Katerina's eyes boring into her.

The silence stretched out and Ellen grew even more anxious. Finally she couldn't ignore the attention being poured on her. She looked at Katerina. "What?"

"You are quite possibly the smartest person I know. And I know a lot of people. A lot of people find that very attractive. This wasn't supposed to be a competition, you know. This just happened to two people who followed their hearts. For what it's worth, I think we could just as easily be in each other's position. Of course," she gave a small sniff, "I don't think I would have gone out with Harry." She drained the rest of her glass.

Ellen deflated. She looked down at the bar, unable to face Katerina. Picking up her glass, she finished it in a couple of long sips.

"Bartender, another round for both of us."

Katerina raised an eyebrow. "Is this your attempt to 'bond' with me?"

"Uh, sure. OK?"

"Keep them coming and we'll see where we end up."

A fresh drink was placed in front of each of them. Katerina picked her's up and, putting it to her lips, drained it in one long swallow and put the glass down with a solid thunk. "Aaahh!" She looked straight at Ellen.

Ellen gulped. She picked up her own glass and noticed how the condensation accumulated into little drops that ran into each other and formed big drops that finally fell off the bottom and went splat on the bar top. *Fuck.*

She put the glass to her lips and tried to pour it down her gullet. Bits of mint hit the back of her throat threatening to make her cough and sputter. By force of will, she maintained the flow and finished the drink in what she was sure was record time for her. A slight "hic" escaped her as she set her glass down next to Katerina's.

"Sir, another round please."

Katerina's grinned at her, showing lots of teeth. Ellen found no comfort in her smile. And she almost gave a sigh of relief when Katerina merely picked up the newly placed mojito and sipped it.

The bartender approached and placed a small bowl of bar snacks between them. Ellen was suddenly aware that she hadn't eaten. Grabbing a few pretzels, she offered the bowl to her companion. Katerina took a handful and tossed it in her mouth.

Mouth full, Katerina said, "You've got talent. But you need drive to stand up to challenges. Resolve should be your best weapon. This is a long game we are playing." She took another sip of the mojito.

Ellen warily took her untouched drink in hand. The sweetness of it was not helping her increasingly distressed stomach. "I'm not about to walk away. It was my fault and I intend to do everything I can to fix it." She stared back at Katerina with what she hoped was a fierce look on her increasingly numb face.

"Hmm, talk is easy. You have to follow through."

Vigorous head shaking from Ellen followed. "No, you're still making assumptions about me. Only when you drop all assumptions..." She froze. Something in the back of her mind was lumbering forward, knocking aside thoughts and preconceptions.

Katerina peered at her over the rim of her drink. "Well?"

"Holy shit!" Ellen was dumbfounded. "They aren't human!"

"What?"

"Rob, or whoever he works for, isn't human. They're, they're aliens."

Katerina suddenly sat erect in her seat, razor focused on Ellen. "What are you saying?"

"All this time, we've wondered how could they be slightly ahead of us, where is their computing center, how can they tap into anything. They're aliens. And they are here, on Earth, not up in the sky."

"Are you sure?" Katerina's voice wavered.

"Positive. It was my most basic assumption. I bet it was everyone's." Ellen tilted her head back and stared at some empty spot on the ceiling tiles. "I bet I know when they got here. And I think I know where they are going. But I have to check."

"Of course." Katerina stood up. "Come on, let's go check."

***

The office was uncomfortably warm and dim. Two women got off the elevator and made their unsteady way down the corridor, leaning against each other, toward Ellen's office. Wobbling a bit, Katerina blamed the lack of food. Ellen couldn't disagree, causing her to giggle.

"Shh! The guards will know we're here."

Ellen stopped in the middle of the corridor and peered at Katerina. "Wait. We're supposed to be here."

Katerina gave a shrug. "Force of habit."

Ellen slowly shook her head before starting back down the hall.

Sitting at her computer, she flipped to one of the open tabs on her browser. Putting her finger on the screen, she went down a table. "You said they were here before World War One, right?"

"Yeah."

Her finger stopped moving. "Here it is. June 30, 1908. The Tunguska Event. I bet that's when they got here." She sat back and crossed her arms.

"Pretty smart. You got anything for the fifth message?"

"Hang on." Ellen went back and forth on the browser tabs with a calculator up. She ran some numbers. "No, no. What if that's the number of things in the rod..." Another page displayed and another calculation was performed. This time, she liked the results. Her head bobbed up and down. "It's a plug of something called neutronium." She felt quite happy that she had figured it out.

"That doesn't sound like something we have just laying around."

"Nope. Found only in certain stars. But, definitely alien tech."

"You said you thought you knew where they were going?"

"Right. I thought they might be headed to where it landed." She pulled up a globe of the Earth and stuck a pin into it. "But you don't need a boat to get to Siberia. The thing about neutronium is that it is super dense. If you dropped it on the ground, it would just go through the Earth and come out the other side in, like what, thirty eight minutes?" Rotating the globe over, she showed a spot in the South Pacific. She pointed to a spot about 800 miles west of Cape Horn. "That would be around here, give or take."

Katerina came over her shoulder and peered at the monitor. "There? Really? That is interesting."

Ellen looked up at her friend. "Interesting? Why's that?"

"Well, there's some sort of anomaly down there that affects all sorts of things. Compasses, electronic machines, satellites. But why would they have to go there?""

Ellen shook her head. "I don't know. Maybe they need to talk to it. But I bet you that's where they are going."

Katerina chewed on her bottom lip. She straightened up and slapped Ellen on the shoulder. Hard.

"You've done good. You've done real good." A grin, happy this time, went from ear to ear.

Ellen couldn't help to smile herself. "Can we go back to the hotel now?" Her smile was short lived as her stomach reminded her of its agitation.

"Sure, we can wait til morning to tell people. We'll grab a drink to celebrate."

Ellen groaned and slumped.

***

The next morning was painful. A hot shower helped to dull the hangover but Ellen was definitely on the lookout for some aspirin.

Her dose of survival juice acquired, she followed and didn't have to struggle to keep up this time. Katerina talked the whole way, which didn't help the headache. But Ellen liked the seeming normality of it.

Searching for Cornelius, they found him in the first place they looked, his office. He sat behind his desk.

"Good morning, ladies," he said in his polished British tones. He stood to greet them.

Ellen couldn't contain herself. "Good morning, sir. We were looking at the last frame. It's neutronium."

Cornelius smiled at them. "We thought of that. Apart from not being a sphere, there is no way that you could drop it into the Earth without us knowing. All sorts of instruments would pick it up moving around as it settled into the center."

Ellen smiled back. "What if you dropped it in back in 1908?"

Cornelius' mouth hung open. He fell into his chair. "1908? Oh dear. Katerina?"

Katerina nodded her head. "We have records of activity by this organization in that timeframe. It fits with what we know of them."

His face was ashen and his eyes became unfocused. "Oh my, oh my," he repeated over and over again.

The two women exchanged glances.

Ellen spoke up, interrupting his litany. "What's wrong?"

Cornelius looked at Ellen and Katerina, eyes darting back and forth between them. "Have you told anyone about this?"

"No, we thought we'd tell you first." Ellen looked at Katerina.

A very solemn Cornelius nodded his head. "This is serious. Very serious."

Ellen's elation at having discovered this was turning into something quite different. Her head pounded in earnest. "I don't like this. What is going on?"

"That much neutronium would cause quite an event. Like the dinosaur killer. Or possibly worse. It's not a sphere. It's more like a shape charge. Probably blow huge chunks of the planet into orbit as the neutrons come out at the speed of light."

Horror at last night's revelation set in. Ellen fumbled for a chair and came down hard. "If I came up with that, how long do you think it will be before someone else comes up with it?"

Katerina stood by Ellen, her face a study in stone. "Fuck. I have to make some very hard phone calls. Ellen, I need to use your office. Cornelius, Ellen, I am swearing you both in under the United States Secret's Act."

"I'm, I'm not an American citizen. You realize that people are going to figure it out. You published the frame."

"This is to give everyone time to prepare to avoid a global panic. I know all the governments will be contacted. We are at the UN, after all."

Cornelius nodded, seemingly satisfied at the moment.

Ellen's phone buzzed. Alarmed, she dug out the phone. There was an incoming video call request. "It's them," she said as she accepted the request.

David's disheveled torso and face appeared on the screen. His shirt was open, his arms were behind him and he glistened under the lights. "Did you get all the copies of the data?" Eyes darted off screen. "There are only two still two copies, right?"

Ellen nodded. "Yes, we have both copies."

David heaved a sigh of relief. "Thank goodness! Don't make any more. You're about to get a computer." He turned his head, listening to some indistinct voice. "They want you to plug the drives into it. Turn it on when you get it. They can tell when you lie."

The picture went dark but Ellen could still hear the audio of David pleading, "No, please don't..." just before the call was dropped.

It felt like a railroad spike was driven through her head. She held the phone on her forehead and just closed her eyes.

A hand rested on her shoulder. "Hey," Katerina's soft voice was close to her ear. "That probably wasn't David."

"I sure hope you're right."

Giving her a friendly pat, Katerina left to make her phone calls.

Ellen lost track of time, sitting in Cornelius' office. They stared awkwardly at each other. Neither of them were up for small talk or work. Several abortive attempts were made, but nothing came of them. She did ask and finally get some aspirin, though. That seemed to help the throbbing.

Mercifully, Katerina came back in. She did not look happy. "It'll be lunch time soon. I've been instructed to convene an assembly of the delegates as soon as possible."

"Are you delivering the news?" said Cornelius.

Katerina opened her mouth but the phone on the desk rang.

Picking it up and listening to it, Cornelius looked up at the two women and said, "There's a package that arrived for you, Ellen. Just like they said."

Soon, a laptop with a wireless access card sat on Ellen's desk, next to her monitor. Ellen stared at the laptop recognizing the trap that it was.

Katerina hovered behind her. She kept crossing and uncrossing her arms. A couple of times, she opened her mouth and thought the better of it and closed it. Cornelius stood in the doorway. He kept his arms crossed.

Ellen cleared her throat. "Do we have both drives?"

"Here's David's drive." In her outstretched hand rested the USB drive that had started this all.

Cornelius approached. "Here's the one that David made and gave to Harry." He handed the other drive to her.

Taking a couple of deep breaths, she grabbed the lid of the laptop and flipped it open. A few seconds later, a single window appeared in the middle of the screen. It said, "Connecting..."

Briefly, Ellen wondered if she would be able to trace this call. Those thoughts were put on hiatus when Rob's odious face appeared full screen on the computer.

"Rob. I was wondering when you would show up."

Rob smiled at her. "Now, now, I see you decided to be reasonable. Let's not walk back on that, shall we?"

Ellen bit her tongue. "Fine. I've got both drives right here." She held the drives up so the camera could see them.

"Are there any more copies?" Rob's eyes ran over her and looked at something to his right.

"No, these are it."

Rob nodded his head and looked up at the camera. "Good girl. Well, don't just sit there. Plug them in."

Ellen's anger made her fumble at the attempt but she got both of them plugged in.

"Excellent. Your boyfriend would be proud."

Ellen stiffened.

An evil chuckle escaped Rob. "Your concern is touching. In fact, I applaud it. Because of it, I got what I wanted."

Through clenched teeth, Ellen said, "Are we done?"

"Just a few seconds more, my dear. -- There, we have finished our business together."

"When do we get David and Pete back?"

"It will be a little while. But don't fret, they'll be back safe and sound. In fact, I think I will have them over for dinner."

The screen went black. Ellen slammed the lid close. "Can you believe that fucker? Katerina? Katerina?" Looking around, she realized that only Cornelius was left.

He answered back to her, "She left as soon as you opened the laptop."

Ellen's heart dropped. She felt that she could have used some support against Rob. Fighting the rising emotions, she grabbed the mouse to her computer. The LCD came to life. One of her windows was clamoring for her attention. Her jaw fell as she read what it was saying. "Katerina! Katerina!" She pushed back her chair and went looking for her.

She found her, back against the hallway wall, staring at the ceiling. Her hands were in her pockets, her long legs with jeans tucked in the boots propped her up..

"Why did you leave?" was the first thing out of Ellen's mouth. "I turned over both drives to Rob by myself. It was terrible. We'll never know what was on it."

Katerina looked thoughtful. She pulled her hands out of her pockets and intertwined the fingers of her hands in front of her abdomen. "You're done with them? Good. I'm calling the good doctor. The situation has drastically changed. It's all hands on deck. He still has a copy."

A spark of pure joy lit in Ellen's heart. "I totally forgot about him. That's fantastic. Now we have a chance."

Katerina nodded.

The spark grew into a roaring fire. "Oh, I was looking for you! I know where they are. They turned on their AIS. The ship is at the Panama Canal."

A wicked grin spread from ear to ear across Katerina's face. "You were right. Pack your things. We're going to San Diego."

Ellen felt triumphant. She would do whatever it took.

Seventeen

Antipode

A harsh knock on his door drug him out of his stupor. Stiff and aching from having fallen asleep at his table, David's body complained as he got up.

"I'm coming."

The knock sounded again. Mildly irritated, he yanked the door open.

Jack eyed him from head to toe. "You're late. You were supposed to be at work already."

Stifling a yawned, David said, "I didn't know anyone cared."

"Hmm. How is the prototype going?"

"It's mostly done. I think that I'll put it on a boat behind us, to test." David arched his eyebrow knowingly at Jack.

Jack nodded. "That's good. By the way, your little visit last night motivated the old man to come check on you. He's supposed to be by after lunch for a dog and pony show. You can put something together to show, right?"

David frowned. "What time is it?"

"Almost ten."

"Crap. Give me a minute."

Soon, the pair got to the deck. When they were some distance from everyone, David stopped and turned to Jack. "Any word on Pete?"

Jack walked over to the railing and looked out over the sea. David stood by him.

"Yeah." Jack turned to face him. "They have him in isolation. Blacked out and hushed, only turning it off for his meals."

David gripped the railing and trembled.

Seeing the emotion in him, Jack put his hand up and looked him straight in the eyes. "Hey, you're not going to try anything, are you?"

David shook his head. "No, the stakes are too high. Something has come up and we've got to do something or we are all screwed."

Jack's expression was stony. "You promised to get us off this ship. You're still doing that, right?"

With a nod from David, the pair walked to the workshop. Saying that he would check up on him later, Jack left him to finish.

Alone, David ordered a boat, to ostensibly put the increasingly powerful array away from them. The request was immediately put on hold. Disappointed that his request was turned down, David went to work on the scaled model. It was mostly done but he still had to connect his clandestinely overpowered radio to it. Wondering if his modified radio controller was noticed, he bolted it underneath the array. All part of his laughable grand plan for getting them rescued. He had no idea what good it would do but he had to try something.

His heart pounded in his chest and his fingers trembled at the thought of getting caught. Sweat made dark crescents on his shirt. Rob would be arriving soon and he had to be done. Time seemed to vanish. His stomach rumbled, reminding him of breakfast and now lunch missed, but he pressed on.

As he finished attaching the radio antenna, the door to the workshop swung open.

"I expect you have something to show me." Rob unceremoniously came into the room with an armed detail.

Wiping his hands clean, David forced a smile. "Just finished. Ready for the tour?"

Passing a critical eye over him, the boss man said, "Yes I am."

"Well, thanks to the catalog on the tablet, I was able to find these units." David held up a polished golden colored square mounted on bracket. "These all fit together nicely and I realized I could put together an array of them. I had wanted to make a square meter model, but that turned out to be too much work for me. I only got a quarter done." He pointed at the half meter by half meter assembly that was on the workbench.

"Why did you build a radio?"

"Well, even something this small is already really dangerous. I gave it a remote control, to turn it on and get telemetry from it. You don't want to be anywhere near it." David found himself holding his breath. Slowly letting it out, he hoped that Rob hadn't noticed.

Luckily, Rob was bent close to the golden array. He ran his fingertips along it. "Dangerous, huh? It has a certain beauty to it."

"It puts out over 800 watts or so, without even trying."

He turned to look at David. "That's a lot?"

"Well, it wouldn't instantly cook you but it wouldn't be pleasant. And it hasn't been properly collimated. It could put out radiation in all directions. Of course, it won't go too far in our atmosphere but the ten mile wide one would be built in space. That'll put a few 'U's in someone's display."

Rob nodded his head. "Are you ready to turn it on and test it? To see if it works?"

"Yes, but I'm not sure where to put it. Obviously, it would be a really bad idea do it in here. I ordered a boat to trail it behind us, so it's out of the way, but..." David bit his lower lip.

"I don't like it." A crossed expression played across Rob's face.

David hastily came up with Plan B. "With some work, I suppose I could mount it on top of the superstructure." He tried to keep his face neutral.

"I like that even less. What if someone spots it?"

"People don't usually have twenty one centimeter radios. Unless, of course, you're a radio astronomer." David plastered a smile on his face.

Rob seemed to be thinking. "Fine. Hurry up and get it installed on top. I want it tested today. I need to know if this will work as soon as possible."

***

Jack returned after Rob had gone with a dolly. Together, they hurried to haul and install the equipment on top of the ship's white, rust stained superstructure. David finished the connection between the array and the bank of surprisingly light batteries that he had brought up through the access panel. The batteries were something that he would have earlier thought impossible but now just another miracle of the thing in the hold. Jack was fastening the equipment to the metal of the roof with some sort of adhesive from a tube.

Scanning the horizon, David saw dark clouds approaching. A cold wind brought the fresh smell of the sea. David thought he was going to need winter clothes. Already he was shivering.

Jack looked up at the front. "Looks like a rough patch is coming. We better hurry."

"I want you to get a message to Pete. Tell him that we are really in trouble and I'm trying to figure out what to do. Tell him I'm trying to get him out."

"How the hell am I supposed to do that?"

"I don't know. I'm still working on getting us off the ship."

"I hope you figure something out soon."

They worked as fast as possible. Just before heading to the hatch, David connected the batteries to the transmitter on apparatus. The die was cast. He didn't know who would hear it, but it was something, a signal to anybody listening out there. It was the only thing he could think of.

He and Jack made their way to the pile of equipment left on the deck. Already, large, frigid raindrops were starting to color the wooden planks. Freezing air blew across the ship while it grew darker by the minute.

Turning his equipment on, he glanced up at the top of the tower before looking away. There was nothing to see, of course. He turned his attention back to his instruments, where the glow of the screen washed over his face.

"Well?" said Jack. "Is it working?"

A shiver ran through him as he studied the numbers on the screen. "Looks like I'll live a bit longer. Seems to be working perfectly, which is really a surprise."

"Hmm, I think you better tell the boss right away." The ship pitched at that moment. "I don't think you are going to be able to take the equipment down before the storm. You turning it off?"

David shook his head. "I need to burn it in anyway, to make sure that it lasts."

Having overcome that issue, David faced a different, more personal problem. His stomach was very unhappy with what was going on. He managed to get below, a guiding hand on the bulkheads to steady him in the rolling seas. Getting to his cabin was an adventure and he managed to send an email to Rob telling him the results of the test and how he needed it to stay on before collapsing in his bunk and being sick.

Jack came by later, after dinner time. David couldn't believe that Jack wasn't sick. Jack nonchalantly told him that everyone gets sick at some point, it just wasn't his point yet. A wave of nausea hit him and he threw up into his waste basket. Or, more accurately, he tried to. He hadn't eaten all day so all he could do was dry heave. It was a long and miserable night.

Toward the afternoon of the next day, the storm abated, much to David's relief. He hesitantly got out of bed and unsteadily made his way to the mess. Although his insides were still feeling sensitive, he felt he had to eat something. Sitting at the table, spooning chicken soup into his mouth, Jack came and stood in front of him.

"We need get back on the roof. To quote, 'Take that damn transmitter down.'" Jack grinned.

Throat suddenly dry, David struggled to swallow. His stomach was not quite settled yet but he had come upon two contradictory facts: He was starving and, now, he didn't really feel like eating. Leaving his soup behind, they went up the stairs of the superstructure and climbed out onto the roof with their tools.

"I got word to Pete," said Jack while he worked on one of the fasteners, swabbing some goop on the connection point. "He said be careful but please hurry. It's wearing thin."

David stood up from his task and faced Jack while he rubbed his back. "I haven't worked things out yet but when it happens, we are going to have to move fast. Is he being held where we were?"

Jack didn't answer. Instead, he was concentrating on applying more solvent to the strap holding the array down. David got annoyed and repeated the question when he heard a noise behind him.

A quick glance over his shoulder and he saw the unfamiliar face of a woman ducking back down the roof hatch.

His heart skipped a beat.

"Jack, we may have a problem."

Jack heard that. He whipped his head around to look at him. "What happened?"

"I think someone overheard me talking."

"Do you know who it was?"

David shook his head.

The look on Jack's face was one of resignation. His lips were a thin line and his brow glowed, despite the cold. A grunt from him and he went back to prying the straps off the deck. David went to the array and unplugged the batteries, tugging at the connections until they tore loose.

A couple of worry-filled hours went by as they finished the task of disassembling the test array and taking it down to the main deck. Night fell before he and Jack finished stowing the prototype back in his workshop. Jack left without saying a word, which David took as a bad sign.

Forcing himself to act as if there was nothing out of the ordinary, he strolled along the railing, leisurely stopping amidship. For some reason, the normal lights were off and only dim lights marking the hatches were on. Darkness pooled on the deck.

He gave a quick glance up and stopped. His breath was taken away. The storm had scrubbed the atmosphere and left the winter sky clear. All the stars of the southern sky shone fiercely in the dark night. Constellations he only dreamed about unfurled before him as he turned all around. The Milky Way spanned the vault of heaven in an unfamiliar swirl. Eta Carinae was almost straight ahead, high in the sky. The Magellanic Clouds, a bit to port, only half as high. And his old friend, Arcturus, dead north. He was drunk from the grandeur. But now, he knew that others roamed the space between them. A fierce resolve rose from deep within him. He would do whatever it took to ensure Man's place among them. He had to stop Rob, by any means.

***

Reluctantly leaving the spectacle of the night, David went below. He wracked his brains, trying to figure out what to do next.

His stomach grumbled, painfully. The headache he had been nursing all day long made itself known in earnest.

He realized that getting something to eat was a good thing to do next.

It was after dinner time for the ship so he walked into a mostly empty mess. There was only Jack sitting at a table. A brief nod from Jack acknowledged his presence.

He went to the meal line. Only cold sandwiches were out now, the kitchen having closed for the night. He grabbed one and headed out.

Jack stood up. David stopped when he saw him making a beeline toward him.

"David, whatever you had planned, we need to get going on it. Now."

"I'm not sure what to do. I had ordered a boat, intending to put the array on it. And then, well..." David shrugged and held his free hand up. "But it wasn't approved."

Jack bit his lower lip. "Let me see your tablet."

David took the sandwich from its surface, wiping the crumbs before handing him the tablet. "What good is that going to do?"

Jack didn't answer. Instead he held the tablet in one hand while his other hand traced out something hidden from David's view. He carelessly offered the device back.

Not understanding, David took it and looked at the screen. He couldn't believe what he was seeing.

"You have until morning to figure out what to do. The old man is going to be pissed, but I don't care anymore. I rather like this planet."

***

Arriving at his quarters, he sat down and absently munched on the sandwich he picked up from the mess hall. He had to keep his strength up for what needed to be done. Pulling up the catalog application on the tablet, he stared at the confirmation of the survival boat. It informed him that it would be ready in the morning. He wondered about Jack but he pushed those thoughts aside. There was no time for it. He had a lot of work to do, to engineer an escape.

He broke out the paper and drew what he knew of the ship. Carefully, he made a list of what needed to occur, starting with breaking into Rob's office, stealing the Inkwell, breaking Pete out, and escaping with everyone in the survival boat. All this before the report of what he was talking about to Jack made it up the chain to Rob, who would undoubtedly kill him because of it.

It seemed impossible.

He found himself wishing Katerina was here. She could have pulled it off single-handedly, no doubt in his mind. Maybe he should break Pete out first. Pete could probably talk his way off the ship, convincing people to let him go. But breaking him out would set off all sorts of alarms. Better save that for later. Ellen, of course, wouldn't have a problem. She would have figured out half a dozen ways to get the job done. Who was he? A radio astronomer, who just wanted things to get back to normal, who had trouble deciding what to have for breakfast, who accidentally received the single most important message ever.

He thought about that message, what he hoped it implied, that someone or something was willing to help.

Despite his earlier resolve, David felt unequal to the task. He doubted that he could pull this off. He buried his head in his hands. He needed a distraction, something to keep everyone occupied. But what? Various options played out in his head through the night.

Somehow, morning came and he had not been dragged away and executed. But something was going on. All night long, he kept hearing groups making their way past his door. At first, it had fueled his terror, but now, it filled him with curiosity.

Steeling himself, he went to the door and waited for the next set of clomping feet. He didn't have to wait long. He opened the door as the next knot of militia approached.

"What's going on?" he called out to the unit going by.

"We arrived but the boss thinks someone is following us," said one of the men as they sped down the passageway.

David had to stifle a shout.

Eighteen

Underway

Outside, a taxi waited to take them to JFK.

Ellen stood by the open door and looked over the roof of the cab at Katerina. "Shouldn't we pack or something?"

"No time. Besides, what do you have to pack?"

Ellen conceded the point.

She heard Katerina made call after call on the ride to the airport. The last one was to Dr. Shtern.

"Benjamin, listen to me. This is beyond grave. Beyond exceptionally grave. This is catastrophic. Not just for us. For everyone. For the world."

Ellen strained to hear his reply. Only rumble of his voice was discernible to her ears.

"I don't care what the regs say. There is no protocol for this. We figured out what the last message frame means."

Katerina closed her eyes while the phone reached a crescendo.

"Earth shattering. I'm being literal." Katerina relayed to him what Cornelius had said.

The phone mumbled, a bit softer now.

"Uh huh. Uh huh. Yes, bring whatever you managed to put together. We're on our way to San Diego. Yes. OK, see you at the pier."

Katerina ended the call as they went under the sign for the airport.

"What's going on?" Ellen said.

"The good Doctor has been busy. He has a few things for us, for when we meet our friends."

The taxi pulled up in the departures lanes.

Katerina opened her door. "Come on, we have a plane to catch."

***

Ellen thought she would have enjoyed the five-hour flight in first class more if she wasn't so terrified about what they were on the way to do.

Katerina seemed pretty confident, sitting next to her. "It's simple. We hop on a ship, take Marines with us, surprise them at their little rendezvous point and sink them."

"David and Pete are on that ship."

"That's why we have the Marines. To board and rescue them."

Ellen looked at Katerina with her mouth hanging open and shaking her head. She doubted it would be so easy. There was no end to the ways that she could come up with how things could go wrong. Badly. Foremost in her head was thinking they would be facing unknown alien technology that didn't have to hide.

But she had to admit, standing on the dock, alongside the warship, it was impressive. Katerina nodded approvingly next to her.

"She's a good ship, one of the best destroyers. State of the art. And fast. We're going to need that to catch up to them."

Ellen felt nervous. "Yeah, I'm worried about that. Being state of the art. That means that there's a lot of computers on it. Remember what they can do?"

A frown appeared on Katerina's face as she looked down at the cement of the pier before looking up with a grin. "Well, think of it as a challenge." She clapped Ellen on the shoulder. "You figured out stuff before that worked against them. I'm sure that you can figure something out again."

Dismay filled her. Her mouth fell open again and she questioned Katerina's grip on reality.

"Hey, there's Dr. Shtern." Katerina pointed and started walking toward a rented box truck. Shtern looked out of place in his suit among the crew unloading the vehicle. A pile of familiar looking grey boxes sat on the ground.

Katerina called out as she got closer. "Doctor, what do you have?"

"No good afternoon or how are you? Your manners have really gotten worse since you've been hanging around with these people."

Ellen choked back a response. Katerina just stared at him.

"Nothing?" He gave a half-hearted shrug. "All business then. I managed to get a dozen suits manufactured. That's all time and resources allowed. The gold and aerogel were expensive. They also tend to be a bit snug. Make sure the mesh covers the joints."

Looking over the boxes, Katerina said, "Will they stand up to gunfire?"

"They should offer some protection. But try to avoid that. It can harm the protective layers, leaving you vulnerable to their beam weapon."

Katerina nodded. "Noted. Got anything else?"

Shtern scowled. "What am I, a slot machine that you keep pulling the handle hoping for a pay out? Honestly, you've become no better than the vermin you've been hanging around with. Where are the other two rats?"

Ellen saw red. She was about to unleash when Katerina put her hand on her shoulder and spoke. "Of course not. You just always seem to get so much done. I was wondering what else you had time to put together, that's all."

"Hmm, well, I also got ten sets of hand held jetpacks working. You hold two of them, one in each hand, to fly. A little practice and you should be able to do it."

"Even with the suit on?"

"I wouldn't recommend it."

The crew had finished unloading the grey cases and were now closing the back of the truck and getting into their accompanying van. Katerina surveyed the stacks. "Thank you very much. This will be incredibly helpful."

Shtern nodded and started to turn. He stopped and turned back around to face them. "Oh, one last thing." He reached into his inside suit jacket pocket and pulled out a thumb drive. "This is a copy of the original data. I took the liberty of making additional copies, in case there is a later. I also put the second, isolated signal in a file in the top level directory. I named it in honor of the car you killed."

Ellen had enough. She snatched the memory stick from his hand. "I'll take that, you self-serving, pompous prick."

Shtern's eyes went wide. He started to redden, sputter and cough.

Ellen turned on her heels and marched down the pier, leaving Katerina behind to deal with him. She walked until she could no longer hear Shtern.

Katerina joined her a couple of minutes later. "Was that really necessary? I know he can be difficult to work with."

"He's a dick."

A sigh escaped Katerina. "Yeah. But I'm the one assigned to him because I can get along with him. Not a lot of people like working with him."

"I'm not surprised that people don't like him. Why do you put up with it?"

"I owe him my life. And I have a knack for dealing with super smart people."

Ellen was speechless.

***

As the setting sun tinted the sky, the ship finally slipped the bonds of the dock. Soon the harbor vanished over the horizon as they entered the open ocean. Sea birds flew overhead in the dusk, still bright against the sky.

Ellen was bone tired. It had been a long, long day starting on an entirely different coast. Now, she was out at sea. One more strange bed to sleep on. She missed her own bed and her games. Brief thoughts about the game she had started and left on her TV intruded. A sigh escaped her. She could understand why David just wanted things to return to normal.

A sailor approached her while she contemplated her adventures and told her chow was open. She realized she should probably eat something before turning in for the night.

At mess, she saw Katerina sitting alone at one of the booths. Not really feeling up to talking to her, or anyone for that matter, Ellen took her tray to the furthest table possible.

Soon, a dark shadow fell across her food.

"Can I join you?" A tray was placed on the surface opposite her.

Ellen's shoulders slumped even further. "Sure." She continued eating, not bothering to look up, carefully chewing her food.

"Ellen, can we talk?"

"It's been a really long, stressful day. I don't have any spoons left." She looked up at Katerina who had slid into the bench across from her.

"I understand. But I need to tell you some things because we are going to be very busy soon and we need to trust each other completely."

Ellen's anger flashed. "A little late for that, isn't it? I mean, I did and look what it got me."

Katerina nodded, small little nods. "First off, I am sorry. I knew that you were interested in David. I knew he was attracted to me. I used that to get him to come along. That wasn't a good thing to do." Katerina lowered her head and exhaled. "But I've seen him willing to sacrifice himself for his friends, for you."

She paused and looked at Ellen. "I meant it when I said it changed how I saw him. And now, assuming that we get out of this alive, I realized that I'm done. I've had too much adventure and just want things to calm down. Be normal, for a change."

Ellen couldn't help herself. A fascination was growing in her as she witnessed something strange occurring before her.

Katerina looked right in her eyes. "My selfishness hurt you. I am truly sorry. I hope you can forgive me."

Blinking slowly, Ellen considered Katerina's speech. Part of her was being cynical and thought that this was yet another act by the person who had a knack for dealing with smart people. She looked carefully at Katerina, searching for a sign that she was faking it. Surely, there would be a slight curl to the lips, maybe a little flush appearing. She studied her opponent's eyes, wondering if they were blinking too much or maybe a tear in the corner?

But, no, Katerina merely sat there, looking at her, maybe even a little expectant. Her lips were a thin line, her eyes sought understanding in Ellen's face. She seemed just like she did all the time, solid, efficient, blunt.

"I forgive you." Ellen was a little surprised. It came out of nowhere but it was true. She understood why things had gone the way they had and realized, in spite of those particular things, she would be just fine.

Katerina gave a slight nod. "Thank you." She didn't move.

Ellen remembered. "You said, 'some things'?"

"Yes, I did. You searched for a long time, all over, for their computing center and didn't find it."

A flash of inspiration hit her. "The boat. Oh shit."

"Yes, the boat. We have recently come to the conclusion that the source of their computing power is there. We think that it can control the neutronium plug. It is the single most dangerous thing on the planet right now. I need you to get on that ship and neutralize it without getting us all killed."

Ellen's insides crumpled. "I'm just a computer security gal."

"Exactly. You are singularly adept for the task. You are also one of the smartest people I know."

Her throat felt parched. She tried to swallow. She didn't like where this was heading. A whisper came out. "OK, I'll come after you take the ship."

Katerina shook her head. "We should be intercepting them as they reach their target. I think you realize how critical our timing is. I need you to be part of the assault. Which is why we are going to be very busy."

She gave Ellen a big smile.

***

Katerina was a stern teacher. The day would start in classroom, instructing Ellen how to build situational awareness and how to respond to different combat conditions. She drilled Ellen on what to expect, the cues to look for and what to focus on. Ellen flew through those lessons with no problems. Memorizing stuff was easy.

The afternoons were a different matter. Ellen had to wear one of Shtern's suits. It was hot, miserable work. The aerogel insulated the wearer very well. Even as the temperature slowly dipped, Ellen felt she was close to suffering heat stroke. The suit was hard to move in, hard to see out of, and hard to hear from.

She watched the Marines train with the equipment by Shtern, flying off the deck, going through their combat drills in the suits. The Marines remarked that the suits were remarkably good. They seemed so much more fluid in them, more capable. She counted herself lucky they were going with her.

Katerina offered encouragement. "You're doing great. Don't worry, I don't expect you to do any actual fighting. I need you to be able to handle a situation if it comes up, that's all. I just want to keep you safe so you can get that big brain of yours to their systems. You know how important it is."

The thing was, Ellen knew precisely how important it was. It threatened to paralyze her if she let her mind dwell on it. She buried it. She had outsmarted them before and she could do it again. Especially since she had to as there was no choice.

There was one thing in the drills that Ellen excelled at, much to her surprise. She was good at target practice. She could hit anything, stationary and moving, quite well. Katerina grinned like a demon and issued her a combat shotgun.

"I don't want it to be fair, if it comes down to it," she explained. "You just need to discourage whoever is front of you. Fast. You have more important things to do."

In the evenings, tired as she was, Ellen worked on putting together a different sort of arsenal. Katerina had made good with her earlier decree about her abilities after clearing it with the Captain. As the steamed south, Ellen consulted with a whole team of naval cyber experts. They hardened shipboard systems, worked on AI detection programs, wrote scripts and viruses on all sorts of platforms and media. They had an array of radio equipment developed and connection cables galore, an assortment of ways to get the fruit of their labor onto the enemy systems. She knew the file named for a dead car was important somehow and no human computer would stand in her way.

Into the lengthening nights, she worked until she collapsed from exhaustion.

***

The ready room didn't have any windows. Grey steel walls were adorned with memorabilia from previous tours of duty. A large, massive pedestal table dominated the room. Three people inhabited the room at the moment.

"So far, we haven't detected any signs that the hostiles are near us." The XO had a map of the ocean displayed on the screen that made up the table surface. Their track was a solid line on it. A dotted line went from the end of the solid one to a point marked in the expanse of blue. "No RADAR contacts, no satellite, no nothing. You'd think their wake would show up at least. If you hadn't shown me the pictures from before, I wouldn't have believed you."

Katerina stood on the other side of the table, nearer the door. Her face was stony. "They are a very dangerous adversary, with capabilities beyond anything we have. They can easily affect systems to hide their traces."

The XO looked skeptical. "If they are so powerful, what is the plan to even the playing field? How do we protect ourselves against them?"

Ellen cleared her throat. "Sir, if I may?" The XO looked at her. "They have a lot of computer resources, that's true. But your crew, with my advice, have been hardening systems all over the ship. I am a security expert and we've been implementing the best practices to safeguard the systems, isolating systems from the outside wherever possible. We even created machine learning systems to detect intrusions. We can cycle and restore systems to recover against them quickly."

Katerina spoke up. "Plus, they very much have a human component to accomplish things. We can handle that with the personnel and equipment we have."

"Until you can't. Very well, I will relay this to the Captain. The Captain expects results. We are almost at the point you provided when we set out. We have pushed the ship and crew hard to get us here. Without any positive contact, we will be forced to turn back soon. Dismissed."

Ellen and Katerina turned to leave.

"Oh, one last thing." The XO tapped on the table. A red line appeared across their projected path. "There are weather reports indicating a front up ahead. We'll be in for some rough seas."

***

Rough seas was an understatement as far as Ellen was concerned. Her training didn't let up despite how she felt.

"Katerina, I'm not feeling so good."

"Just open your mask, puke in the bag on your belt and keep going."

Ellen struggled through it. She thought that they couldn't possibly board the other ship in these conditions. One look at the Marines training alongside her disabused her of the notion. Sheer force of will kept her going, climbing, dodging, hanging on for dear life as the ship rocked and swayed. She followed Katerina's advice. Several times.

Mercifully, training was cut short that day. After cleaning up, Ellen lay in her bunk, queasiness afflicting her every breath. She still had to review the latest results of the security scans, to see if her measures had reduced the attack surface. Just as soon as she felt a little better.

There was a pounding on the door of the cabin she shared with Katerina, the one luxury afforded to her.

"Who is it?" She sounded weak to her own ears.

"Ma'am, Katerina sent me to fetch you. You're wanted on the bridge. There's been a development."

Ellen sprang out of her bunk. Following the crew member got her to the bridge of the destroyer. Twin wrap around desks held a sailor apiece. Rains lashed the large windows, wipers ineffectually clearing them. She recognized the Captain stoically standing at the rear of the room, surveying it.

Katerina and the XO were bent down over a station at the further of the consoles. They hovered over a sailor who was wearing a headset and staring at a screen. Ellen cautiously crossed the space to them.

"That might have been something." The XO rubbed his chin.

"Seaman, what is the signal doing?" Katerina peered at the screen.

"When I catch it, ma'am, it's seems to be warbling."

The XO straightened. "That's probably just storm interference."

Katerina stood to face him and shook her head. "It's in the X-band. It keeps coming back."

Ellen cleared her throat. Both of them looked at her. "If it's David, he's a radio astronomer. He would know the spectrum. He might try other frequencies."

Katerina stared off into the distance.

The XO frowned. "It's a big spectrum. Do you have any idea of where to begin looking for another signal?"

Ellen fought a surge of nausea. "What would be a special frequency for him?" She put her hand on table top to steady herself.

"1420 Mhz. It's the Hydrogen Line."

The XO and Ellen both looked at Katerina. She shrugged.

Ellen said, "Well, sir, can you scan that frequency?"

"Sir? I work for a living."

"Stand down, sailor." The XO glared at the operator.

"I'm sorry, sir."

XO said, "Better. Well, you heard the lady."

The seaman nodded and turned to his screen. Some deft keystrokes and a couple of clicks and his eyes went wide.

"Holy fucking shit!"

"Language."

"Sorry, sir. There's a spike. Huge one. That's a protected frequency. Nobody should be on it."

Despite her stomach, Ellen smiled.

"Found you."

***

They sailed closer to the freighter over the course of the night. In the morning, after the storm had passed, they came under attack. Systems started to go offline. The intruder detection systems Ellen and crew had installed and trained sounded multiple alarms. They battled back, rebooting systems, hardening them as vulnerabilities became evident. Ellen trained their system to recognize the new attacks. Slowly, they made progress and restored crucial systems. Soon, they were underway again, toward their target. Ellen supervised the efforts late into the night.

Katerina came for her. "Ellen, you need to rest, for tomorrow."

"I can't just go."

"You trained them. You have to trust them."

Ellen knew Katerina was right. Saying good night to the cyberteam, she left to get some sleep. In her bunk, listening to the soft snores of her roommate, Ellen wondered how could Katerina just sleep. She didn't think she could get any shuteye.

In the dark of the morning, Katerina roused her out of bed. "Come on, time to go."

They went to the hangar, where the squads of Marines gathered to be briefed on their mission. A grainy overhead picture of the target was projected on a screen the troops were facing. As soon as Katerina entered the door, an ensign handed her a folder. Katerina stopped and scanned the contents besides Ellen. Ellen wondered about the scowl that visited her companion's face before the folder was closed and handed back.

With determination in her step, Katerina left her by the door and went in front of the forty or so men gathered there.

"Good morning. Yesterday, we spotted the target that we were sent to intercept. We made radar contact and became subjected to a persistent cyber attack, affecting a broad range of systems onboard. Our weapon systems are currently offline."

A murmur went through the crowd. Katerina continued.

"Thanks to the prior measures and continuing efforts of our own security experts, we have regained control of navigation and electronic capabilities. They appear to be slowing down, no doubt to make their rendezvous and we will be upon them in a few short hours. Make no mistake, the enemy knows we are here."

One of the Marines raised their hand. "Ma'am, what about the rumors we've been hearing? About the really dangerous threat the target has."

Katerina looked right at the man.

"I don't know what rumors you have heard. I am not in a position to confirm or deny rumors about an existential threat posed by the target."

The room was filled with alarm and chatter. Katerina held her hand up and the space grew quiet.

"That ship contains a dangerous device is all I can say. It is our mission to deliver our computer expert," Katerina pointed at Ellen and all eyes turned to her, "to the device in order to neutralize it."

Ellen's knees felt like rubber.

Katerina and the Marines planned out their assault of the enemy ship. Ellen could barely hear them from the pounding in her ears. Dismissed, they went to get ready. Ellen donned the suit she had been training in for the last time.

What looked like a rusty freighter trawled the sea ahead of them, crossing their "T". General Quarters was sounded as they bore down on it anyway.

Ellen wasn't sure what it was anymore. She had to trust the cyberteam to keep the ship running while she got ready to do the unthinkable, stopping an alien computer that could destroy them. A cold realization came over her as she wondered if she would even recognize what she was looking for. But she took comfort in the fact her work on the hardening the systems was helping. Some principles still worked. She would figure it out. She had to. And the sea was relatively calm. Another thing to be thankful for.

Cold air poured over her, keeping her cool in the suit. She donned all the tools her team had prepared in twin belts that crossed her chest. Nervousness kept her alert. From her vantage on the deck she saw that the distance between them and the freighter was rapidly closing. Maybe too rapidly. Klaxons sounded as the destroyer struggled to turn. Men and women scrambled. Ellen thought they might collide and braced herself but the warship managed to turn and come alongside the other ship. The destroyer shuddered. The other ship rocked.

A sailor approached her and took her below to one of the launches. The hatch to the rear was up and the sea churned behind the ship. No sooner than she was seated on the bench that the launch was rolled off the back and they were after the freighter. The loud sound of air being battered into submission followed as the helicopter on the deck took to the sky from the aft of the destroyer.

Their boat sped toward the now receding hulk. The rusted hull reared high out of the water ahead of her, the sea starting to lose the smoothness behind her. The other launch was in the water with them alongside the enemy. Ellen gulped on seeing it.

A loud whine overhead drew her attention. A flight of marines flew with their jetpacks toward the freighter. The helicopter hovered over the freighter's deck. The sound of automatic fire reached her ears as the mounted .50cal swept across the exposed surface. Suddenly, the helicopter lurched and black smoke poured from the engine. It veered away.

One of the fliers flew backward in an arc that terminated in the water. More gunfire followed and an explosion.

A ladder came down. Two more followed. Their boat positioned itself under them. Yells and screams could be heard above the sound of the motor.

Katerina slapped her shoulder. "Button up."

Ellen closed the faceplate and looked at her friend. She had already closed her faceplate. Looking at Ellen, two thumbs up of encouragement were given and Katerina started up the boarding ladder.

Trembling uncontrollably, she checked the shotgun slung on her back and grabbed the first rung.

Adrenaline fueled her now. She went up the ladder at record speed and hauled herself over and onto the deck.

There were bodies clad in black lying in spreading pools of blood. Here and there were empty piles of equipment. Whiffs of ozone tinged the salt air. Belatedly, she recognized the gear belonging to the Marines that came onboard.

People were running on the deck. Men flew aloft. Something that looked like a machine gun with four barrels was sweeping the deck. Wherever it encountered a Marine, a spray of red across the deck would follow. One of the flying men dove at it and slammed into it. An explosion followed.

Ellen started to move away from the edge across the now slick deck. A man stopped to point a weapon at her. She remembered the shotgun and wrestled it off her back. The temperature in the suit was definitely going up.

BLAM! Even though she had fired many rounds in practice, the noise surprised her, rising above an increasingly loud high pitched sound. The man fell backward, onto his back. She wasn't sure what to do next. She went up to the man, to check.

Something tugged on her shoulder. She whirled around, shotgun at the ready.

"Whoa! It's me, Katerina!"

Ellen lowered her weapon.

Katerina pointed at where her ear would be, inside the helmet. "Do you hear that?"

Puzzled, Ellen asked, "What? Like a whine?"

"Like a turbine spinning up. Get to the bridge and stop this ship, by any means necessary. Then find the computers."

"Are you coming?"

"I have to finish up here. Go. Hurry."

Ellen gave her a thumbs up and started toward the superstructure. Ahead of her was a knot of mercenaries, blocking her way. She pumped a shell into her weapon.

An armored Marine appeared on either side of her.

"We're here to clear your way, ma'am."

Her escorts threw a grenade. The enemy took cover and returned fire.

"Go! Go!" Their assault rifles lay down a suppressing stream of bullets while their suits acquired a dull glow around the edges.

Ellen sprinted along the deck toward the tower. She felt her own suit growing warmer despite the cold.

Reaching the door, she opened it and readied her shotgun. Up the stairs she raced.

Nineteen

The Battle

David leaned against the closed cabin door. He heard the marching stride of the boots trail away. Forcing his heart to slow down, he looked around the room and made a quick decision.

He scrambled and gathered all the paper notes he had, everything detailing the Inkwell's scheme and his scribblings on the locations of the routers. He picked up the notes about his escape plan and stuffed them in his pockets. He didn't know what good they would do but at least he had had to try to get them out. Executing his scheme now was all that mattered. Grabbing the tablet on his bed, he hurried out of his cabin. It was only a matter of time before someone came for him.

According to the master plan, he had to get to the quartermaster first. Scurrying through the gangways, halting when he saw someone ahead of him, he arrived as the man was closing the door to the supply room.

"Wait! There's something I need to pick up."

The supply clerk stopped turning the key. "You have the receipt?"

David showed him the tablet's screen.

The man grunted. "Fine, hurry up. I gotta lock up and get to my station."

David went to the shelf specified. He heaved the trunk off the rack. Boom! It came down hard, hitting the shelves and knocking some other items off. Looking around, he was thankful there was no one in the room. He carelessly tossed the tablet on the now empty shelf space. No need to make tracking him easier. The case's wheels made a slight squeaking sound as they rolled toward the door. He grunted in effort as he lifted the packed boat over the door seal into the hallway.

The clerk raised an eyebrow when he saw what David had retrieved from the room.

David trundled the baggage down the corridor toward the fore of the ship. "It's for my experiments," David said over his shoulder.

Muttering something unintelligible, the quartermaster locked the door and hurried away.

There was only one place that David could think of that would be a safe location to stash the survival raft. Pretending there wasn't anything unusual about what he was doing, he pushed his load past crew and militia alike, pausing only to lift it though the compartment doors. A couple of times, his heart raced when one of the men-at-arms moved their weapon toward him but nobody stopped him. They were simply far too busy to deal with the unexpected change to routine that David represented.

He found the door to the hold. Looking around to make sure there wasn't a soul around, he opened it and went it.

It was deathly quiet, a complete change from before. David strained to hear something, anything. Not even the ship sounds dared to intrude. He shuddered, remembering the silencing field used on him before, except this didn't have the forced pressure of quiet that he was accustomed to. If anything, it felt more sophisticated, somehow more complete. The whole quiescent machine felt expectant to him, foreboding an ill future.

Steeling himself, he soundlessly pushed the case in front of him along the catwalk to the door in the hallway by his workshop. Leaving their means of escape just inside, he ran to his office and went straight to the array. Unfastening it from the workbench took all of a minute. He accidently knocked some components off in his haste but he picked them up and crammed them in his pocket for later. It took several trips but he transferred his project to the hold and deposited it next to the sealed boat.

Rushing out of the converted cargo space, he ran for the ladder to get to the main deck. Jack was coming down the steps.

Jack held a pistol in his hand. He levelled his weapon on David. "They're looking for you."

David gulped and wondered where Jack was going with his statement. "And?"

Jack hesitated and looked over his shoulder at the empty corridor behind him. "Come on, let's go get Pete."

***

In the increasing cold, a bitter wind cut through David's clothes. Jack marched him toward the aft of the ship. David held his hands on his head the whole time. The people in combat armor were busy making preparations on the deck, setting up barriers.

A man with a pip on his collar held up his hand and approached them. "Found him?"

"Yup," said Jack.

"Good. I need you to get to your station, just like we told you. Turn him over to me. I'll take him in."

David glanced around at the horizon. There was a ship heading straight for them. A short tripod had an array of four rods in a square mounted on it. A pair of handles allowed the operator to swivel the array around and point it. He recognized a large energy source attached to it. A man was swinging it around, sighting lines of fire.

Jack;s expression didn't change. "With all due respect, fuck off. I found him, I'm taking him in. Otherwise, you'll take the credit for it."

The other man's face turned beet red. His veins bulged on his neck. "Are you disobeying a direct order?"

Jack kept his voice even. "You don't command me. You're nothing but a glorified manager. Now, get out of my way so I can take him in."

"You're supposed to listen to me. Your old man told me to keep an eye on you. I'm going to tell him what you just did! Do you hear me?"

Jack shoved David in the small of the back with his free hand. David took the hint and started walking.

The enraged man yelled after them, "You're in deep shit!"

Jack calmly walked them away and went below.

An icy realization crept over David on the stairs. In a hushed voice over his shoulder, David said, "Jack, every time you said old man, I thought you referred to Rob, like a captain. You didn't mean that, did you?"

Several seconds passed before Jack spoke. "That guy has always been an asswipe. Never did like him."

"Jack?"

The two marched in silence in the corridor for a few more seconds. "Robert is my father," Jack finally responded.

David's step faltered and he stopped causing Jack to run into him. He turned around to look at Jack. "Do you think you could have told me that little detail before now?"

"Would you have helped me get off this ship if you knew?"

David thought carefully about what to say next. "Why?"

Jack didn't hesitate. "The man is evil. You know what he's planning. I don't want to go out on a stupid ship, slaving away like bugs for unseen masters. Besides, I think they are lying but he is willing to believe them. I'm not. I happen to like Earth just fine. It doesn't deserve to get carved up."

David nodded. "Do we know how we're getting Pete out?"

"There should only be one guard. I've got it taken care of. Now, let's go before someone else tries to stop us."

They got underway again. Passing other scurrying crew on the way to Pete's cell made David hopeful. They all seemed to be heading up, away from their target, leaving fewer people around.

Arriving, David heart sank. There were two guards posted at the door. They had a set of multifaceted goggles on, giving them an insectoid look. The guards pointed their double barrelled weapons at them.

A slight tilt of the head from the taller one acknowledged their presence. "What do you want?"

Jack ad libbed. "I'm here to transfer this prisoner to the cell."

"I wasn't informed."

"Things have been busy topside."

The tall guard stepped forward and pulled a small, handheld tablet from a thigh pocket. "I'm going to have to verify. Please step away from the prisoner." He looked down at the screen in his hand.

The shorter guard raised their weapon high and brought the butt crashing down on the first guard's head. The man went down without a sound.

"About fucking time you showed up!" The still standing guard pulled the goggles up from her face. Instant recognition hit David. It was the woman who had overheard him on the roof.

Jack gave a lopsided grin. "Sorry Lisa, I had to find him."

"God damned idiots!" She fumbled the downed man's belt and retrieved an old-fashioned brass key. "I can't turn the darkness off. Only he could. Grab the goggles off of him and get your friend."

David's mind was racing. "What's going on?"

Jack was pulling the goggles off the unconscious man. "Lisa is how I got word to Pete. She's coming with. She wants off this boat. She's my friend."

"A little less talk and a lot more action." Lisa finished unlocking the door. Pulling it open revealed blackness inside the door frame.

Jack handed David the eyewear. "Go get your friend. Hurry."

David nodded and slipped glasses on. He stepped in the room. Ghostly, silvery light outlined the edges of objects in the darkness. He scanned the room.

There, on the floor by the bed, against the wall was the sitting form of Pete. His knees were drawn up and David could make out that his arms were wrapped around his legs.

"Pete, it's me, David. Don't move. I'm coming to get you," he shouted into the forced quiet.

David reached his friend and bent down to help him. "Pete?" he yelled close to his friend's ear. There was no reaction, of course. He touched Pete's shoulder.

Pete lashed out, wildly waving his arms.

"Pete, it's me." David yelled in vain. Watching his friend, he grabbed the flailing arms, straining to hold them.

Pete's arms went limp. He slumped to the ground.

"Come on buddy, let's get out of here." Putting his arms around Pete, he gently lifted his friend to his feet.

Pete offered no resistance.

David guided him toward the door.

The light blossomed into miniature rainbow arcs through the goggles when stepped out of the darkness. Taking them off, he studied his friend.

Pete shielded his eyes and blinked rapidly. Tears formed in his eyes. "Dave! I'm so happy to see you." He tightly embraced David. Pulling away, he looked around. "Jack! It's good to see you, too." His eyes went to the woman. "Who's the lovely lady?"

Lisa smirked. "You have a way with words, don't you? I'm the one who got the messages to you earlier. We have to go. Now." She turned to face David. "You do have a way off this boat, right?"

David nodded. "I do. I've got an inflatable survival raft stashed. But we have to get something else first."

She made a face. "What?"

"We have to get the Inkwell. If we don't stop it, nothing else matters."

"Are you fucking stupid? Jack, you promised a way off this ship. I stuck my neck out for you. And now you spring this on me?" Lisa wildly waved her hand around.

David replied before Jack could say a word. "If you want to stay, fine, stay here. But we have to stop it. Otherwise, it'll take the planet apart using the thing in the hold."

The woman shuddered. She looked at Jack with her eyes wide open, pleading.

Jack's lips made a straight line across his face, his brow furrowed. "It's true."

The woman jaw dropped. "Fuck me." She shook her head. "Fine, let's go get killed. I hate to ask, but do you know how to stop it?"

David felt his ears grow hot. "I'm working on it."

The woman gave him a look that bordered on murder.

The corridor rocked violently to the side. David reached for the wall to steady himself. Pete fell and used David's hand to get up from the floor. The ship slowly settled down.

Jack looked at David and said, "We're running out of time. We need to get going."

David nodded.

Lisa was already moving down the passageway, toward the stairs. "Let's go, so we can get off this deathtrap."

***

They didn't encounter any personnel on their way to Rob's office. Empty ladderwells and deserted hallways was all they found. The diesel engines had fallen silent. A distinctive whining could be heard coming from the engine room instead. The ship started to vibrated as it knifed through the cold waters.

Pete huffed as he climbed the last set of stairs into the bridge. He cocked his head to listen. "That can't be a good sign."

David stood next to him, catching his breath, nodding.

The woman, Lisa, wandered over to the front window, overlooking the deck below. "I think you should see this."

Jack joined her and stared, his head twitching from place to place.

Alarmed, David went to see. To the port of the freighter was another ship, almost as long. But the newcomer looked sleek, deadly, all receding angles. Even the bow was angled back. Two turrets on the front of it were pointed at the ship he was on, but they hadn't opened fire.

Spray flew from its front. And yet, it was being left behind. There were a couple of launches in the water barely keeping up with the freighter. David could see men swarming up the side. In the air were a good number of what David assumed were marines, flying over and landing on the deck below. He could hear the rapid fire of automatic weapons. An explosion blossomed on the deck, by where the heavy weapon had been placed. One of the boarding men become a wisp of smoke.

As one, they turned away.

"Remember," Jack shook his finger at David, "We were helping you."

"Hey, anyone got any ideas on how we can get in?" Pete was at the doors to Rob's cabin, pulling on the comet door handles.

Jack thought about it for a second. "Get behind us. Lisa, aim at the top of the frame, where the doors meet."

Lisa pointed her weapon at the lintel of the doors David had gone through for dinner an eternity ago.

Under the onslaught of the twin barrels, a semi-circle about as big as a dinner plate just over where both doors met started to glow. First dull red, then orange, finally white. But the doors seemed unaffected.

"I'm running out of juice," said Lisa.

"Keep going. Look, it's starting to give."

David looked at the patch. Thin tendrils of black smoke were barely visible against the white-hot metal. The glowing area had buckled.

Jack held his hand up. Lisa released the trigger and examined the end of the barrels of her weapon. The tips glowed dull red.

She checked a readout on the gun. "I don't know if I have enough charge to fire it again."

Jack nodded. "David, Pete, grab that handle and pull!"

David and Pete made room for Jack. The three grunted and pulled hard. The door resisted, groaning under their effort. Suddenly, it gave way, spilling them on the ground.

Pete was up first. "Come on, we probably don't have a lot of time." He rushed through the open door. The three followed. Jack and Lisa had their weapons at ready.

Rob leaned casually on the front of his desk, his arms crossed in front of him. He looked relaxed and unafraid. "Well, well, look who showed up. And my own son, too. Traitor!"

David pointed an accusing finger at him. "Traitor? That's a funny word for you, of all people, to be using. You're the one selling us all out."

"Really? I'm just trying to survive the best I can. I bet you figured out what would happen if I don't update the Inkwell."

David shuddered.

Pete saw his reaction and said, "What is going to happen, Dave?"

"Oh ho, you didn't tell them? Go ahead. Tell them what happens if the transmitter in the center of the Earth gets turned off. I'll wait." An evil smile played across his face.

Rob occupied a strange sort of tunnel in David's vision. Everything in the room was ignored as David searched for any sign of weakness in him. "Can't we talk to them? Shouldn't it take years to get a response?"

Rob snorted. "Idiot. They'll know right away."

David felt the blood drain at the implication of what he heard.

"What is going to happen, Dave?" Pete repeated. Pete had turned and was now looking right at David.

David took a deep breath. "It will be like a six mile wide asteroid hitting the Earth."

Pete's mouth fell open.

"Wasn't, wasn't that what killed the dinosaurs?" a quavering voice said. David identified it as Lisa's voice. "So this is like that?"

David nodded his head.

"That's an important detail that you left out! Jack, did you know this?" Lisa stared at Jack.

"Look, we don't have a choice. We're doomed either way." David felt despair growing in him.

Rob laughed. "Well, I'll give you a choice then. All you have to do is keep me safe until this finishes the upgrade and I promise to take you with me, even in light of your indiscretion. Well?" He moved to the side, revealing the Inkwell behind him. Bands of light were moving through it from bottom to top in a fairly rapid pace. They glinted wildly in his glasses.

"You're a monster." Pete's voice was a low growl. He lowered his head and took a couple of small steps toward Rob. "You didn't tell anyone, you didn't give us a chance. Maybe we could have done something, all those years ago."

"There was never anything we could have done against them. You're even stupider than I thought. And that takes some doing. John, I can't believe you've thrown your lot in with these morons."

The bands were slowing down, evident even to casual inspection. A loud blast, close by, shook the air. David pointed at Rob. "He's stalling. I bet he knows how to stop it. We just need to convince him. Jack, Lisa?"

"Right, he can't stop all of us." Jack raised his weapon and Lisa started to move toward him.

Rob rolled his eyes. "You are boring me. Lights out."

The room plunged into complete darkness. David fumbled at his goggles.

The disembodied voice of Rob said, "Track them by the goggles and hold them."

An immense pressure settled all over David. He felt short of breath. The goggles hung in his hands, halfway to his face, frozen mid movement.

"I can't kill you all right away with that. Too many of you. But I can personally take care of you, nonetheless." The sound of something scraping against the desktop was heard.

Pete's straining, rasping voice called out, "You fucker. I'll kill you yet."

A pure, evil laugh resounded in the darkness. "Oh ho, you tried so hard, didn't you? I'll make sure you're first."

David tracked Rob's voice in the pitch black, moving toward Pete. "Don't worry Johnny. After I take care of all your friends, we can see about getting you a suitable girlfriend."

"Pete!" David managed to croak. He was having an issue drawing air in. Despite the lack of light, a different, purplish tinged darkness filled his vision.

Rob's voice rang out loud and clear, right by Pete. "Say good bye... what? Crush him, crush h.. hmpf!" A loud thud followed.

The pressure snapped off. David fell to his hands and knees. He pulled in a large breath, expanding his lungs freely once again. Scrambling, he put his googles on.

Looking around, he saw Jack and Lisa's limned forms, getting up from the ground. There were a series of slowly moving bands on what he figured was the desk. The Inkwell, upgrading, no doubt.

"Pete! Pete, where are you buddy?" David's voice carried his concern. He crawled toward where he remembered Pete being.

"Hang on." Jack's voice came from the taller of the spectral figures. "I know where to turn it off."

He watched Jack go to the desk and heard him rustle papers and move objects. All the while, David crawled forward until his hand bumped into something clothed. There was a tangle of lines on the carpet.

"Got it," came the exclamation from the desk. A loud click and suddenly, the lights came back on, dazzling David with psychedelic rainbows. He tore off the goggles. Two sets of legs were the source of the lines.

Pete's body lay on top of Rob, his hand over his attacker's mouth. The stiletto Rob used as a letter opener was in Pete's hand, buried up to the hilt in Rob's chest. One of Rob's hands was on the wrist that held the knife. The other, on Pete's shoulder. Blood spilled to the floor. Both their bodies were distorted, flattened. Rob's eyes were wide open, eyebrows arched, as though in surprise. Pete's features were relaxed, calm, his eyes half closed. A slight rising of Pete's back could be seen.

A growing ache filled David's chest and his vision blurred. Shortness of breath came on him again, but this time there was no pressure. "Pete, oh Pete." He rolled Pete off of Rob.

Pete struggled to look him in the eyes. "Dave, believe in... yourself ..." Pete became still.

"I have more bad news." Jack was staring at the Inkwell. "The stripes have almost stopped moving. This thing is finishing."

Grieving would have to wait. David hurried behind the desk and looked what was on it, papers, a couple of books, one of those tablets. A laptop was open on the desk!

"Drop your weapons and put your hands up," said a new voice, muffled by a mask.

David stopped and looked up. He saw a figure in what could almost pass for a knight in shining armor. Twin bandoliers with metal boxes crossed its chest and patches on the armor glowed red. An ugly, matte black weapon with two barrels in an over and under configuration was pointed at them. Correction, only one barrel. The other was a sealed pipe under the business end. The knight faced Jack and Lisa.

Jack and Lisa swiveled around, their weapons still in their hands.

"Wait! Don't shoot! They're with me!" David yelled as he put his hands up.

The knight turned to him. "David?"

Despite the muffled quality, David thought it sounded familiar. "Who?"

Jack grunted, Lisa pursed her lips but they both dropped their weapons and raised their hands. The figure by the door unlatched a catch on the side of the faceplate and swiveled it open. Golden, curly hair was plastered on Ellen's face.

"Ellen!" David squealed.

Ellen broke out into a huge smile. "Fuck, you're alive! We were so worried, after the drive was erased. Where's Pete?"

The corners of David's mouth immediately went slack. He looked toward the heap on the floor.

Ellen face transformed in an instant. She followed his gazed down. "No, no, no, no..." she said as she moved to the bodies and knelt down beside Pete.

"Real touching, but we still have a situation." Jack's voice had a hysterical edge to it. The lines in the Inkwell moved so slow that it seemed they might be going backward.

"Crap. Ellen, this is some sort of super computer." David pointed at the eleven sided crystal. "We have to stop it. Any ideas?"

Ellen stood and fished for something in one of the metal cases. "I have no idea how we could use it, but I brought this." She tossed something small at David.

He caught it and looked at what was in his hand. It was his old USB drive, the one that started everything. Puzzled, he said, "I thought they all got erased, by Rob. You lied to him?"

"I didn't know that Shtern had a copy. We put the original data back on it and made more copies. The additional data that he had found is in a file called betsy.bin".

David prayed to whatever cosmic forces there might be as he grabbed the attached mouse. The screen lit up. It wasn't locked. The desktop had a handful of icons on it. One was an eleven side polygon that was helpfully labelled "Inkwell". Selecting it brought up a dark grey window that was divided into a large upper pane and a smaller, lower one. The upper box blazed with words in white text saying "I am busy." The lower one had a blinking cursor, by a plus sign.

Lisa shouted, "The lines have stopped moving."

David typed, "I have something for you" and hit return.

No sooner did his words appear in the top part of the window than a new reply followed. "Make it quick. I am programming the constructor."

David clicked on the plus sign. A file selection dialog popped up. Hands shaking, he moved the cursor to betsy.bin and clicked on it.

A confirmation box showed up. The mouse pointer shook on the screen. He couldn't control his hand. David believed he knew what to do. He believed help was provided. No doubt clouded his mind. He stabbed the return key.

Twenty

The End is Nigh

The key clicked. The confirmation dialog went away. David held his breath. He looked over to the Inkwell. The bands of light in it had gone away and it looked like a giant, eleven-sided piece of dark, smoky quartz. His attention came back to the screen.

"Connection lost" was now displayed on the chat window.

His breath escaped him.

Ellen's voice broke the silence. "I found him. He's up by the bridge." The radio crackled saying they were on their way.

She came over and looked at the screen in front of him. "What's going on? What did you do?"

Everything seemed preternaturally clear and distinct to David. His chest expanded and he felt air being drawn into his lungs. He noticed the network of capillaries on Ellen's face, under a sheen of sweat. The gunfire outside had fallen quiet. Clumping sounds were approaching. His heart pounded.

"I'm not sure. I'm hoping that I just didn't kill us all. I uploaded the extra data that was in the signal." He drank in the screen, searching for any sign of reply from the Inkwell.

Ellen grunted. "Good. You worried about the neutronium?"

His head snapped over to her. "You knew?"

"Yeah, we figured it out. Nothing happened. We're OK. We figured the neutrons would come out close to light speed out of the ends of the rod if they detonated it."

"I thought they would boil out much slower and we'd have about five minutes for the shock waves to hit us."

She grimaced. "Well, that was something we considered too. We don't exactly have a lot of experience with neutronium based alien technology. I guess we have about five minutes to catch up."

"David!" a familiar voice shouted.

Tearing his gaze away from Ellen, he saw another armored figure standing in the doorway, removing her helmet.

Long, black hair cascaded out.

"Katerina!" He was up and out of the chair, racing to her.

They wrapped arms around each other. The armor was hard and sharp and still hot in places. It didn't matter to David. He pressed his lips against hers for a long time.

Coming up for air, he said, "I missed you so much."

"I missed you too. I was so worried. Where's Pete?"

David's elation evaporated. Reality came crashing back. "He, he didn't make it. He died killing Rob. He saved us all."

Katerina's face was drawn. She nodded and looked past him. She pulled back and held David's hand.

"Ahem, we're still not out of the woods," Jack said. "The first lady just said you might be right. We have five minutes. Four now, left for the world to end."

David nodded. Katerina looked somber. She embraced David again.

Looking over his shoulder, David saw Jack and Lisa holding each other. It sounded like Lisa might be softly crying. He also saw Ellen, standing by herself. Katerina followed his gaze and motioned Ellen over. Ellen sniffled and joined in a group hug. The three held tightly onto each other as the long minutes passed.

David was at peace in his soul. *This is not a bad way to go.*

The hug stretched out. David's arms grew uncomfortable but he refused to lessen his grip.

Ellen moved her arm to look at a piece of gear. "Time's up. And we're still here. We can let go now."

"I don't mind."

The three moved apart, still at arm's length of each other. Looking at the other two, David smiled at them. "We made it."

Katerina and Ellen smiled back and at each other.

A radio squawked for Katerina's attention. She keyed it. "Report."

A voice came clear out of the speaker. "The deck is clear. We are gathering the remaining crew from below. Ma'am, you have to see this. There's some sort of machine in the hold."

"Destroy it," David said without hesitation. "Put bombs on it and send it to the bottom."

Katerina looked at him.

He continued. "That thing is the reason they put the bomb in the Earth, to make sure that it got built. Nobody should have it. Not us, not anybody. It's too dangerous."

Katerina nodded. "Did you hear that, sergeant? Get some satchel charges on it right away. Evacuate the ship and scuttle it."

"Yes ma'am" was the efficient reply.

Turning to David, Katerina said, "Anything else?"

Looking at the Inkwell, David said, "One last detail."

***

Light from the table in front of David underlit faces in the Ready Room, giving an almost sinister appearance to the gathering. A graphic of the destroyer and the freighter was overlaid on the surface with the distance between them displayed. The XO's hands rested on the table, across from the three civilians. Only the XO spoke. "The Captain merely wants to know the reason for sinking the ship instead of bringing it into port. A prize would be suitable recompense for the damage sustained."

Behind him, half in the shadows, stood the Captain. Her arms were crossed and she looked sternly at the three across the table.

"I was granted full authority to issue that request." Katerina folded her own arms in turn.

"The Captain fully acknowledges your authority. But, in light of what some of the prisoners are saying about the apparatus in the hold, one would wonder if that is a correct course of action for the greater good. Also, clarification as to why the other piece of alien technology, the so-called Inkwell, was brought on board, if it is so dangerous." The XO looked back at the Captain who merely gave a small nod.

Katerina's eyes narrowed. "The reasons are highly classified and on a strict need to know basis. In the interest of performing the task at hand, I think it would be best if David told what he discovered in the course of being their prisoner."

David looked at her, a little surprised but he nodded and started.

"Last month was not the first time we were contacted by aliens. We were, in fact, invaded in 1908. The Inkwell, apart from being the delivery system for the highly dangerous bomb that was placed in the Earth's core, is a computing device far beyond anything we are capable of. The former owner of that ship, Rob, inherited the Inkwell from his father who in turn got it from his. They have used it to become rich and powerful with the goal of building the thing in the hold. He came here to finish the machine, with information delivered from the stars. Before he died, he hinted that the rod in the core has some way of instantly communicating with its masters."

David looked around. Everyone's eyes were rivetted on him. Swallowing, he went on.

"When it was completed, the ship was to be turned loose, to make more of itself."

"A Von Neuman machine." Ellen voice was hushed.

David nodded. "In a little over four years, there would be enough of them to dismantle the planet."

The Captain was pale. Speaking directly to them for the first time, her voice had a tremble to it. "Why? To what end?"

Shaking his head, David said, "I don't know the big reason for it. But one of the things that it would do is make more ships like the one that brought that abomination here. Presumably to do it to other civilizations."

Pausing for a second, because he realized he hadn't told anyone the last thing Rob had offered to him yet, he decided to come clean. "Rob was planning on catching a ride out on one of those ships. That was the deal he had. Him and his subjects got to escape. He offered me a ride if I helped him and told me I could bring companions, to keep the human race going. Breeding stock, as he called it." He looked at Katerina and Ellen.

Ellen looked on in stunned silence. Katerina was impassive and returned his gaze. "Our dear friend," David paused for a moment, forcing down a lump in his throat, "died stopping that madman from killing us. And our new friends from the stars sent us help, in the form of what we believe to be a computer virus, to stop the Inkwell and the bomb."

Mouth hanging open, the Captain brought her brows together. "How do we know we stopped it?"

David's response was flat and quick. "We are all still here."

A shuddered went through the Captain.

Ellen now spoke up. "We need to keep the Inkwell around. If it ever becomes active again, we need to know. And let's face it, we have no way of destroying it. It held a piece of a neutron star."

The Captain nodded. "I think I understand now. We'll have a detachment go over with demolition charges. And sink it for good measure. God help us if someone put it back together and started it up."

Sensing that they were finished, the three started to leave the room.

They were halted by the upheld hand of the Captain. "One second. I would appreciate if you three could join me on the bridge in an hour, to witness the destruction of the enemy vessel."

"It would be our pleasure," said Katerina.

The destroyer took up station about a mile away. Sending launches manned with demolitions, the crew swarmed over the ship. Over the course of the hour, the freighter was rocked by series of explosions, handiwork of the detachment of engineers. Thick, ugly, black smoke poured out of the hold hatches. Retrieving the small craft, the destroyer sounded its klaxons.

The three joined the Captain in the bridge. David was fascinated by the display of the gun barrels rising from their sleek housing. Both turrets pointed at the freighter.

"You may fire when ready," the Captain ordered.

The ensign nodded. "Aye, aye, ma'am." The twin railguns flashed. The cargo ship lurched under the impact but sat even keeled on the waves.

"What the? Damage assessment," barked the Captain.

"Sir, it appears that we did not penetrate the hull."

"Fire again and keep firing until that bastard sinks. Concentrate your fire."

"Aye, aye, sir."

The railguns fired round after round at a point just above the waterline. David could tell because the spot started glowing red under the impacts. Steam rose from the surface of the water around the area of impact. The firing went on, for long minutes. He wondered if they had enough rounds to sink the ship when the whole hull suddenly became small flakes and fell off the ship, leaving the bulkheads of the internal structure exposed. The skeleton of the ship quickly slipped beneath the waves.

The Captain stood silent, watching the spot boil on the surface where the ship went down. "I hope we did the right thing."

"Yes, ma'am, you did," said David.

***

David found Katerina at the port railing, watching the sun set as the destroyer steamed home. The orange disk of the sun was bisected by the horizon. The water had turned ruddy and golden sparkles played on the waves. Overhead, the clouds were pink, orange and red with a deepening purple filling the space between the brushstrokes of fire.

He joined her, at her side.

Without even turning her head, wind whipping her hair, Katerina said, "How did your talk with Ellen go?"

He gave a little sigh. "It went surprisingly well. We talked about expectations and boundaries, about how we were friends before. We talked about Pete a lot. I'm still invited to game nights. I don't know if I would go. It just wouldn't be the same."

Katerina nodded while the sun sank further.

"What's left to do?" David tried to keep his voice steady as he turned his head to see her. Katerina glowed in the magical light.

She didn't turn to face him. "I gave my report. We're burying Rob at sea tomorrow. At Jack's insistence, by the way. He said he didn't want his dad to be remembered in any way. He's a treasure trove of information and cooperating, so that's good. Pete will be given a hero's funeral."

David nodded his head. "We'll have to fly his mother out."

"Of course."

He sidled closer to her, almost touching her. "What about you? What are you doing?"

She turned to him in the deepening dark but still wouldn't look at his face. In a low voice, she said, "I think I'm going to retire. Maybe open a pottery studio, look at the stars."

Her eyes sought his out. They stared into each other's souls as the first stars appeared.

Putting his arms around her waist, he drew her closer. "Funny, I know a place. There's even a game night, I hear."

"I'd like that."

His lips met hers as the stars came out.

It was so right, David thought. He could hold her forever. It was perfect. Well, almost perfect. There was something sharp pressing against his thigh, something in his pocket.

Bothering him, he released her and pulled away, fumbling in his pocket. Katerina looked amused, a faint upturning of the corners of her lips gracing her face.

He pulled out the offending object. It was a square emitter, one of the ones he had used to make his prototype.

Epilogue

David's stiff fingers stumbled on his bow tie.

"Katerina!"

She glided into the room, dressed in a dark green velvet and satin gown. She saw him struggling with his neckwear and came over to him. "Coming, I'll get it for you, dear."

"Just want to look presentable."

Her fingers made short work of the knot.

"There you go."

"You look fantastic," David said.

Musical laughter came from her. David looked at her gray streaked hair, her beautiful grey green eyes with the happy lines and still thought himself lucky.

"When is Peter supposed to get here?" he asked.

"He should be arriving any minute now, with Ellen. We should wait in the foyer, so we can hurry. I don't want to be late tonight."

"Of course. Nobody will wait for us, tonight."

The doorbell rang and the couple moved to the front door. Peter, a man only a little younger than David had been on a fateful summer night so long ago, opened the door. An older woman in a turquoise gown with curly silvery hair followed him in.

"Mom, Dad, Aunt Ellen said she couldn't wait in the car and had to get out to see you."

"Of course, dear. Ellen, you look fabulous."

A long hug between dear friends followed. "So do you."

Katerina waved David over. "Doesn't David look nice?"

Ellen ran her eyes over him and gave a low whistle. "Yes, he does."

David smiled and gave her a hug. "It's so good to see you."

"The same. I've missed you guys so much. The project has been taking all of my time lately. But I'm done tonight. I am so glad you two decided to come."

Katerina beamed at her. "We wouldn't miss it for the world."

All four of them piled into the car. They all turned their chairs to face each other and chatted and re-told stories as the car drove. David smiled as he saw Peter's exasperated face as he heard the lifetime of stories again.

They arrived at a complex of low, interconnected, adobe style buildings with the one in the center reaching multiple stories into the sky. A small cloud of drones lifted to follow them from the car to where they entered the building.

Inside, a crowd of real, live reporters, with their own fleet of tiny camera drones vied for their attention. They paid them no mind as they crossed the lobby space to a set of double doors. Past the doors, a large room with a stage at one end held a large gathering of people. The raised platform had a single podium in front. A large display made up the wall behind it with a single glowing yellow line across it.

Ellen gave them a quick hug and left them in front of the stage with other VIPs while she went to the side and climbed up the steps to the stage and the waiting lectern.

Standing behind it, Ellen cleared her throat. Microphones picked it up and all present turned their attention toward her. Automated cameras trained themselves on her.

"Good evening all. Today marks the end of a journey that was begun over thirty years ago. We didn't all complete the adventure together. But those of us here remember those who helped make this possible. A little over seven years ago, the Peter S. Dainbridge Space Array replied with what is hoped to be the first of many communications with the nearer of the points provided to us by the benevolent message we received from the stars."

Ellen looked around the room before looking back down to the speech in front of her.

"Tonight marks the earliest opportunity in which we may receive a second message. We have many questions that we believe will be answered as we go into our future with the expectation of being welcomed as members of a broader community that lies beyond our planet."

"Behind me is a representation of what is being received, in real time, by our world wide array of radio telescopes. Refreshments will be served as we wait and hope. Thank you all for your continued interest."

With those words, Ellen left the stage and made her way down to David and Katerina.

"That was a lovely speech," Katerina said to her as she approached.

"I think Pete would have been proud," said David.

"I think he would be prouder of the job his namesake is doing. Your son has been fantastic."

David's heart of hearts was at peace on this night. Decisions and trust in friends from long ago would finally bear fruit.

"Look!" said Peter, pointing at the screen. "Something is coming in."

David looked. There was a small bump in the middle of the line. The line grew into a tall peak as the magnitude of the signal increased.

Afterword

Magnitude sprung from the very first story I ever submitted. It was short listed and the editor and I talked about what it would mean to the world if what I had described came to pass. The short story formed the basis for the Prologue to Magnitude, by the way.

The editor's comments on wanting to know the effects on our civilization had me wondering what would it be like to have some event that affected the whole globe and how I could visualize the wide ranging effects. As luck would have it (though like all these things, it would be bad luck), we had a global pandemic. I had to go back and revise what I wrote. What I had down on the page was nowhere as weird as what actually happened. In the world of Magnitude, the pandemic was a few years in the rearview, much like today. I have toyed with the idea of a prequel, detailing Katerina, Shtern and Cornelius' adventure during the time of the pandemic but I keep putting that off. To do it right, I would have to travel to exotic locales and that simply doesn't happen on writer's wages these days.

I have also thought of a sequel but I keep having other, more interesting ideas come up. Who knows? We may revisit this world somewhere down the line.

I have tried to keep the science in Magnitude as credible as possible. Many of the things I described exist in some form or fashion if not to the level shown, particularly for the alien technology. Indeed, as described in the book, that sort of stuff seems a few years away.

Not that I didn't take some liberties for the sake of the story. Yes, I know the sun isn't yellow and neutronium needs incredible gravitational pressure to keep in in sphere, never mind a cylinder. But I assure you, it's all a matter of good engineering. How else would you get faster than light communications?

As to how an EM bomb works, the devil is in the details. It's definitely harder than what got laid out in the book although if you've ever made a solenoid, you may have experienced the effect of a collapsing magnetic field if you weren't careful when you shut it off.

I hope that you enjoyed this little bit of reading. My next novel that should see the light of day is one that takes place after a climate disaster, leaving the planet in a post-apocalyptic setting where company towns scratch out a living and an insane warlord terrorizes the landscape leaving ruin wherever she goes.

About the author

Victor Jimenez is a mad scientist with a wide body of knowledge and an esoteric skill set. He is constantly trying to add to both of these, to annoy friends with the detail and efforts that he puts into projects. Living in a state that is described as a mini-Australia has endowed him with a wealth of stories and experiences. Extensive travel to far off, remote locations has filled in any gaps, giving him an appreciation for the diversity of his fellow humans. His wife encourages him to pursue his dream of being a writer. The sixty pound lapdog also gives her tacit approval as she loves to lay by him while he types.

www.ingramcontent.com/pod-product-compliance
Lightning Source LLC
Chambersburg PA
CBHW020630110726
47899CB00002B/716